Two Tan Lions

Alvin G. Brown

First published by Dog Ear Publishing
4010 W. 86th Street, Ste H
Indianapolis, IN 46268
www.dogearpublishing.net

dog ear
PUBLISHING

ISBN: 978-1-4575-2062-4

This book is printed on acid-free paper.

Printed in the United States of America

ACKNOWLEDGMENT

My thanks for this book goes, most of all, to the Holy Spirit (always "To God be the glory!")—and to the "lions" themselves. Then to a stream of kind, generous, and helpful folk over the years—most recently Robin (who actually rolled the wheels and took this book to print), Evelyn, Judy, Freddie, Marianne, and also the reference staff at Vogelson Regional Library, Camden County, New Jersey.

Also, I'm grateful for reams of reference works, including material gathered by the public libraries at Steubenville, Cadiz, and Elyria, Ohio. Among helpful publications were Cleveland Call/Post *and* Fleet Walker's Divided Heart *by David W. Zang.*

In putting this biographical novel together, I tried to grasp the documented truth whenever possible, but to use imagination whenever I felt it necessary. Indeed, life on earth, for each of us, is an amalgamation of feelings, facts, and fantasies.

Dedication

To Clara Gaynell Brown:
Long before your time on earth ended,
you lovingly provided me with this dreamer's desk . . .

Moses Fleetwood Walker
National Baseball Hall of Fame Library
Cooperstown, N.Y.

William Wesley Brown
Entrepreneur

1923

His hands misshapen, fingers crooked from fastballs more'n thirty years before, fumbled newspaper pages. The headline "*Teapot Dome*" was splashed across the front page. This latest scandal had President Warren G. Harding, a fellow Ohioan, in big trouble. But Moses Fleetwood Walker looked for yesterday's news about "Black Moses," as thousands called Marcus Garvey. Mention of Garvey was on page three of the Cleveland, Ohio, paper. What was Garvey to him? Only that Garvey, on this 22nd day of June, 1923, was a celebrated Negro and more a lion than even he himself had been. And Garvey was being persecuted now in ways that he himself had suffered. And there were some strained comparisons. Page three reported the trial of this dark-skinned man, who had his legions pronounce him "Provisional President, Empire of Africa." Moses Fleetwood Walker grunted. He was not a follower. His own skin being very light brown, he was not like the ebony folks whom "Black Moses" appealed to—neither he nor brilliant Negro leaders such as W.E.B. DuBois. But Garvey created businesses, and he, Walker, was a businessman.

"Convicted of mail fraud," the news page barked. The government said these letters Garvey was sending out, selling stocks in his Black Star Line ocean vessel, were fraudulent. Garvey and his company did not own the ship and were still struggling to buy it. Fleet—his family, friends, and fans had long ago nicknamed him "Fleet"— — let his gnarled hand slip from the page. He conjured up the year 1898, when he had been tossed into jail on conviction of mail theft. His thoughts roamed. In these wild, young 1900s, Garvey was drawing huzzahs as the first black mass leader. But *he*, Fleet Walker, was acclaimed in the 1880s as the *first colored Major League baseball player!* While Garvey, with his force of blacks hundreds of thousands strong, thundered about leading his people into a New Africa— — he, Fleet Walker, had published a manifesto calling for Negroes to unite and build their own new kingdom in Africa. While Garvey was tried for high crimes, he, Fleet Walker, had once been tried for murder!

Fleet grunted again. He was feeling poorly. Maybe his time on earth was growing short, but he was ready for more adventures as a theater owner in Cleveland.

This same day, William Wesley Brown (known as "W.W.") listened to one of his daughters read also about Marcus Garvey being jailed. W.W. and his large family lived a couple dozen miles just south of Cleveland in Elyria, Ohio. He stiffened his back and his face tightened. "Not straight, not straight 'nuff," he murmured, referring to Garvey's handling of big-time finances. Overhearing his murmur, Myrtle, whom he employed as bookkeeper, nodded silently as she strolled out of her father's office. W.W. hadn't paid much attention to the "Black Moses'" escapades. His own business and family matters kept him scheming and scrambling from dawn to dusk.

W.W.'s usually steady hand held his favorite drink. It was dark and mildly sweet, 100 - proof stirred into tea. Thoughts of Garvey's financial tribulations made him fret over his own business perils. He was now hiring men and making money, yet the prospects were shaky. Still fresh were his previous rises, then falls. And, though he wasn't involved in crooked dealings, the white hands threatening colored, prosecuting "Black Moses," too, worried him. He noticed the *toddy* glass beginning to tremble.

Another reason he had no time for Garvey's great movement (UNIA... . . . the Universal Negro Improvement Association) was, well, political. As he tried to tell his four hardheaded sons (one of them a Baptist preacher), "regardless of a man's skin color, being a successful manager means being also successful at day-to-day politics." Then, too, he had his nose to the wind: the allegiance of Negroes was shifting away from the Republicans to the Democrats, and Garvey didn't seem to care. His sons took their stubbornness from their mother. Becky raised her boys and eight daughters with an iron hand straight from the Bible — yet not letting them forget slavery and all the sellings of his people and the beatings and lynchings. But his workings were toward reconciliation. He would not let racism hinder him. Neither had the great Booker T. Washington, who had been the *sure* politician, not Garvey. W.W. sipped his *toddy*, his face creasing with the smile of regret. He looked at the clock; time to forget Garvey.

*   *   *   *   *   *   *   *   *   *   *

Now, this is the story of two men, like cousins, who sprang up as little lions about the same moment along the busy Ohio River—lions bounding in ways and times when their success was considered almost impossible. Nineteen twenty-three was just one season in their snarling romp. Seasons before, and after, were more hair-raising as they trampled the wilds. Fleet and W.W. lived a story well worth telling. This is it.

PART I

AUNT ANNA

A day before, stormy skies had sent torrents of water down the slopes. This day, though, the sun shone. Just outside Cadiz, Ohio, a certain highland melds into the Appalachian foothills. Aunt Anna—not my kin, yet everybody's "aunt"—lived on a slope there. It seemed she had been alive almost forever. Well, at least since her babyhood in the Civil War era. I had come to search her memories of W.W. Brown and Moses Fleetwood Walker, two local men of color whom history must not forget.

She was sitting on a wicker rocker, looking tired enough for a long, long rest. Around and above her were many old gimcracks and faded doilies. The cottage, also so old, was small but solid with heavy wood planking. On this first visit, Aunt Anna at the same moment welcomed me, as was the custom of Ohio's hill people, and glared at me with age-old suspicion.

"Aunt Anna, I truly respect your knowledge, your wisdom." Kneeling before her on the worn, carpeted, planked floor, I presented my request. "Git up!" she commanded. "Snatch that thar chair an' sit close so's I kin hear yeh." She was maybe the last of her kind, an original African American *griot*. "T'was a hard rain yestiddy." I nodded, wondering about her presence of mind. Though still independent, I'd heard that her neighbors up and down the slope looked in and tended to her needs.

But I needn't have worried that day. "Yessir," she finally spoke again, "I did surely know Mose...er, 'Fleet', as some say . . . an' Willie, too." Her thoughts and words were that of a schooled lady. In fact, Aunt Anna was proud of "completing senior high school back in horse an' buggy days."

She spoke again, while sipping from a teacup, her gnarled hands a bit unsteady. "Now what's your real purpose?" I explained that I wanted the *world* to know of what these two men accomplished. Her eyes began closing, but I believe I saw a smile quietly sneak across her face. Seconds slipped by, then Aunt Anna started a stream of memories. But some judgments also came with some of the memories.

PART II

WHEN THEY WERE CHILDREN

1858

$\mathcal{W}$ith his strong arms and skilled hands, Moses Walker was making barrels and buckets in a shed next to his home at Mt. Pleasant, Ohio. But while plying his augers, planes, and chisels, he was also scheming. He'd promised Caroline that something better than his being a cooper would not only come along—he'd go get it. Folks claimed him maybe the best cooper in Jefferson County, but Moses knew he could use his hands for greater good than shaping wet staves into grain barrels. Also, he needed more cash. Caroline had already delivered six surviving little ones, including their toddling twins, Moses Fleetwood and Lizzie. Moses had a white friend over in Steubenville who was doctoring, and who could teach him the medical trade. So many Negroes, fleeing slavery, were sneaking or being smuggled across the river from Virginny to this Quaker territory. They needed doctoring, and so did the free coloreds who could pay him cash. He was deciding to move his brood to the city. With all this war talk, and if western Virginny, along the Ohio River, was earnest about seceding, then Steubenville might grow bigger and busier as folks came over into Ohio for security . . .

1860

"Papa!" The little tyke came running up, grinning, proud of himself at being able to command his father's attention. Moses Fleetwood, all of three years old, grabbed a small stone and threw it to the road. Papa smiled. His son, imitating the older neighbor boys tossing baseballs, already showed interest in playing sports. Moses chuckled at his boy, but he was busy so he let "Fleetwood" dash away to play. Moses had completed his apprenticeship and was now a doctor.

1870

Moses Walker walked about with a smile. This man who was one of the first "colored" physicians in Ohio, was now a minister—with an A.M.E. congregation. His Fleetwood, at thirteen, was not just a quick student in Steubenville Colored School—he was fearlessly quick at the baseball game played by older boys. Moses was quietly proud.

Meanwhile, less than an hour's buggy distance over in neighboring Harrison County, George Brown finished his day's work and trudged up a slope to home. After washing, he staggered to the featherbed couch where he sagged, then dropped. A one-and-a-half shift down in the mine can tire a man to the bone. He needed the extra wages, and now he needed a doze. Here, five years after the war, coal mining was in full stride, and George could draw two dollars a day by working longer.

Besides Isabell—his loving "Bell," out of the Stephen and Elizabeth Lawrence family—at this moment were young Willie, little Alice, and baby Walter. Bell was feeling herself with another child, however. She was depending more and more on Willie to help her with things: Willie, named William Wesley, was smart and almost grown-up now that he was age ten. George said that Willie was the "studyin' kind." Willie did study, even while out doing farm work—he studied how people did their work and ways he might do them better or quicker. Neither George nor Bell had time for study.

While Bell was taking care of Walter and teaching Alice how to dress herself, or board-scrubbing everybody's clothes, or simmering beans with fatback, or mopping floors, her mind stirred with worries and wonders—from George's strained body to baby Walter's colic. Also, the new baby in her belly had her spirits going up and down. She was "off her feed." Bell liked to sing the new spirituals from the A.M.E. church down across the hill in Cadiz. She began humming "Ev'ry Time I Feel the Spirit." Her voice rose, her body shook with sudden joy as she pulled clothes from the big tin tub . . . until Willie walked in looking wide-eyed. "Aww, Willie, go see to li'l Walter." Tears wet her face.

Willie had seen his mother like this before. "Yesum." Slowly he whirled and strode past his sleeping father, wondering why his mother wept so often.

Shrugging out of his nap, George heard pans crashing, Alice giggling, Willie shushing baby Walter. Even as Bell determined to keep things quiet when he tried to rest, their home was always full of life.

PART III

TWO TAN LIONS

CHAPTER 1

$\mathcal{F}$or this moment Fleet climbed from his father's dream. He was, for sure, now an Oberlin College freshman—class of 1882—but he needed some fun. He welcomed the sound of hooves coming around the bend. With a canter William Wesley Brown rode his horse into Oberlin Village along the dusty road that was a short part of the "Old Oregon Trail." The two young fellows were meeting according to plan. Now Fleet noticed something unusual: the big sorrel was rearing, making a squeal, ears laid back flat. William Wesley, usually quite good with horses, worked to control the animal. "This one musta been mishandled as a foal," Brown said when he neared. Fleet nodded. William Wesley had hold of one of the new ones from the stable in Elyria where he served as hostler. He knew that an abused newborn foal could grow up "bad." So he took control.

Maybe, like the sorrel, Fleet was himself rebelling from control. First his father's strict discipline, gotten heavier when Moses Walker began pastoring. Next at Oberlin College, now stifling him with rules making him feel like a kid. He was age twenty-one—a man. He wanted some whiskey, he wanted to court student Arabella Taylor, and he wanted to play in baseball games not controlled by the college. "Hey!" Fleet shouted at William Wesley, who was sliding off the horse. William Wesley was only eighteen, but he was living loose like a man, living in Sam and his young aunt Julia Moore's house in Elyria nine miles and a good gallop away. He clucked. "I'm on time, like the Pony Express," then he snatched a bottle from the saddlebag. In a roadside thicket, obscured by the grazing sorrel, they drank whiskey together. "I can round up maybe fifteen fellows from Elyria for a game out here past the potato beds," William Wesley told Fleet. "Six will play fer your team, if you can gather two more, 'sides yourself."

William Wesley knew, and all of Oberlin Village knew, that Fleet Walker was an amazing baseball player. Fleet grinned. "Well, I got three boys waitin' already. We can field two good teams, if you'll pitch against me, and Skinny Walters pitches for my team." He figured William Wesley was only fair at throwing the ball—because he was more interested in, well, managing things. William Wesley took a swig of whiskey and nodded. "I'll be back in two hours with the fellas in a wagon, and an extra horse. An' after y'all and Skinny beat us, you promise tuh introduce me to an Oberlin gal? I got tuh return this crazy sorrel to the stable."

Grinning to himself, his heart hailed this young fellow—who'd spent babyhood down in the hill country during the "War between the States" like him—for William Wesley's own cunning mind. He's not about Elyria versus Oberlin in baseball, Fleet thought, but about wooing pretty girls. The girls of Oberlin were good-looking. Buttery skin, bright and charming, such as Arabella Taylor. Arabella . . . pretty "Bella." As William Wesley cantered the spirited sorrel away in puffs of dust, Fleet turned in the direction of the boarding house where Bella had recently arrived. He felt strong to see her before dark came, before she and other college girls probably would be cloistered for the evening. There was plenty of time to round up three players—anyway, it was just a pickup game among colored fellows, not a school event.

Summer 1881. Now, two years later, Bella bent her head and began sobbing. Words between them had been harsh. But he'd never heard her cry before. Evening bright began to fade over Plum Creek, nature's warning for all proper young ladies to get home. And as they sat there on the creek's wild-grass banks, their spirits sank as the sun dwindled down. "Now, why're you weepin', girl?" Fleet asked, though he thought he knew. For some time she had refused her hand in marriage, because—because she was too young and had dreams to bloom . . . because of his liking another college gal named Ednah . . . because she didn't trust his heart . . . because the hurrahs over his baseball exploits might have gone to his head . . . because her parents, visiting Bella from Xenia, Ohio, and trusting her suiter to be a polished, scholarly undergraduate, were alarmed by his roughneck sports sideline . . . because he didn't fit?

Between sobs she moaned, "Getting late, I'd better go to my house."

Gently, he draped his arm over her shoulder. "Bella, honey, you mean the most to me. But I got to report to Cleveland. You know this team's owner, the White Sewing Machine Company, is giving me money. It's a golden opportunity—in more ways than one!"

The taste of success was now in his brain—even more than Bella. It was one of those moments when the mind parades, in one second, big things one has done or felt recently. These crisscrossed his mind:

Six weeks ago Oberlin's varsity played Michigan University's team.

Harlan Burket pitched and I was the catcher and Harlan drove batters crazy with his curve, which none had witnessed before. The ball began straight, then veered away and the batters missed most every time. The Michigan manager noticed how smoothly I caught the pitches. The manager told a Michigan official, who called me over after that game. Harlan's curve worked great, but I hit some long balls. Michigan talked to me about switching to their school. Because of my technique, nobody noticed how banged-up my hands got. Michigan made a good offer for me to study law there. They also talked Arthur Packard and my brother Weldy to transfer, too.

Fleet was excited about playing for Cleveland and going up to college in Michigan next. He should feel sorry about leaving Oberlin. After all, this was where his Papa had moved his family when the Methodists called him to pastor at Second M.E. Church in '77. Oberlin had welcomed them with love. His Papa was highly respected here—especially because they had learned that, in addition to being a Reverend, Dr. Moses was also the only colored physician anybody had ever heard of. Papa had to leave in '78 to pastor in Indiana; by that time Fleet had passed the exams to enter Oberlin College, where his younger brother now was a student. He should feel sentimental about leaving; however, he was restless. Before practicing law—he knew he had a flair for logical arguments—he wanted to make a name for himself in baseball. He glanced at his hands. They were sore, but they would callous alright. With his bare hands he could handle those wicked fastballs better than all other players, and he could throw and hit with the best. He looked at Bella. Lately she had become whiny, so he really should let her go. Someday he'd return and take Ednah as his wife. "Okay, girl, let's go now."

Arabella was slow in rising from the creek's grassy bank. Her lovely dark eyes, like black onyx, were washed by tears. "Fleetwood, we have to get married . . ."

"What? What'd you just say?"

She repeated her words, but with more force this time. "We have to marry!"

No fast or crooked ball had come at him harder. Instantly a dryness formed in his throat, causing him to swallow. My God, he thought, this is a ploy to keep me from leaving for Cleveland. "Look, I've made up my mind to go play baseball. Anyhow, you ruled out marrying me months ago, so I'm moving on."

"Do you love me?" she asked, staring up at him. Confused, frustrated, he nodded his head. It was true—she was part of his heart. "Well, Moses Fleetwood Walker, I may be carrying your child. I've had signs lately." Now he was thunderstruck! "Carrying my child?" Never in those few daring moments that they'd found enough privacy had he thought of this. Their actual couplings, twice, were so quick, and this was so soon!

"How do you know, Bella?" he asked, then fast realized she was too modest about her body to describe . . . Oh Lord, he was glad that Papa Moses, preacher and doctor, was not here. And Mama Caroline, she'd be distressed over them. And, Lord, what about Bella's folk? He felt the sun dropping over them in more ways than one. Nearly in a stagger, he clutched her, grateful that Bella was strong enough to brake his lean.

Their minds in a stir, their tongues halted, they trod to her boardinghouse. "Bella, I'll figure something out." She peered into his eyes. "I can't go through this alone, Fleetwood. I can't . . ."

But his figuring came second. First he boarded the Lake Shore and Southern Michigan Railway train in Elyria and rode to Cleveland so he could play baseball. He guessed only a handful of colored fellows had ever been allowed on White Sewing Machine's squad, so he was excited by this privilege. The LS&SM car clanked and shuddered madly, oddly reminding him of savage pitches he would have to catch against the big boys. Between these thoughts, though, Bella kept breaking into his mind. How could she be with child? How could she do this to him now? Outside the windows, country towns staggered past. Raindrops baffled his view of mule teams and red barns and rows of yellow corn—not allowing the distractions his now racking mind sought. Bella . . . Weldy . . .

At Oberlin Papa and Mama had left him in charge of Weldy, three years his junior, when the family moved to Indiana in '78. Weldy was now following in his tracks, not only on the Oberlin squad, but also in other ways. Some ways he knew were wrong. He had to steer Weldy right or he'd pay for not. There was his strict Papa to answer to and, more scary, God. His grades at Oberlin College had dropped, partly due to being a beau, an admirer of Bella and other girls. And Ednah . . . lovely Ednah Jane Mason, who graduated from Oberlin High and now was an honored student at the college.

He needed to see that Weldy, who was going with him to Michigan to study and play ball, did not fail or get himself in trouble.

While these thoughts were churning, Fleet heard a foghorn. The train was rolling into Cleveland. In addition to his new worries, Fleet had no idea of what terrible things awaited him.

CHAPTER 2

1881. As the train carrying Fleet Walker pulled into Cleveland station, left twenty-eight miles behind was a rural settlement called Carlisle. It hung onto Elyria town's south end like a caboose. Carlisle land seemed quiet and peaceful. But then sounded three thunderous cracks. Gunshots! And then two deputies of Lorain County Sheriff H. E. Corning could be seen riding quarter horses with their rifles raised. They rode swiftly past fields of rye and alongside a corduroy road into town.

"Willie Wesley, you'd best get outta town now — in a hurry!" Uncle Samuel Moore was angry and jittery. Aunt Julia had worried over her nephew for months. She'd stopped trusting him with her son, Caleb, who was nearly the same age, because Willie was far more worldly. "I ain't gonna let them white fellows malign me no more," Willie snapped. "They surely already done enough, ridding me from the building trades."

Samuel didn't tolerate backtalk, even by a twenty-year-old, but he realized Willie had a point. His nephew had learned masonry, carpentry, and plastering when helping to build the county courthouse, which had been finished in Elyria last year. Willie was good at this. He wanted to employ himself, yet the Knights of Labor — in fact, all the white unions kept him out of this. "But you can't whip up on these men. You might be strong wit' yer fists, but they'll gang up an' kill you!" Samuel had seen a lynching down South, so he was fearful that the whites would come harm his family. "Are they lookin' fer you?" Still heaving and keeping his eye on the window and listening for hoofbeats, Willie said, "Aw-w, nossir, I don't figure so. They called me 'boy' - and them's fightin' words . . ."

"Well, Willie Wesley, you best be leavin' here."

On the southbound train to Cadiz, William Wesley Brown didn't fret. Like his father, George, he was not a worrier. "Blows of life may cause you tuh stumble," Papa had told him, "but jus' git up an' giddyup."

For some horses he used spurs, but he needed no spurring himself — he had "giddyup." He thought of his few years in Elyria: girls sashshaying up Middle Avenue together to the ice cream parlor; going sparking with three of them, but not quite in a courting manner; riding some gals on a fine palomino who had a straw-colored mane; toiling on the new county courthouse, sawing and fitting boards and watching sandstone blocks being unloaded, trimmed, and set. There was wasted time, he noticed— men who loafed because of materials not delivered timely. Plenty of wasted money, too, on account of poor arrangement of supplies or poor management. He could manage things better, if only he could get a job where he ran things. Yessir, that was the skeleton key for him, yes!

But first he would reunite with the girl he'd met several years ago when her parents brought their family up to Cadiz's colored Methodist church. She was Rebecca Thomas— — strong, perky, and skin like black satin. William Wesley was recalling Mr. Nel Thomas and wife, Harriet, hidebound Christians who had pride in their pure African bloodline. They looked with some suspicion on brown-skinned fellows such as him; even more so on all those high-toned mulattos down in Flushing town.

The train jerked to a slowdown, a bundle of newspapers was tossed off and a mailbag snatched from a hook, then the steam locomotive's wheels rolled faster and his car jerked forward again. He decided he didn't really like riding these smoky, sooty railways. Annoyed, he drew the freshly ironed handkerchief from his waistcoat pocket and brushed off some soot that his spats and polished shoes had collected, guessing dusty railway cars would be an adversary for the rest of his life.

Soon Harrison County and the town of Cadiz, where his folks still are, would appear. Tomorrow he'd take a buggy over to visit the Thomas family, who'd moved up from Flushing to Cadiz. Rebecca had birthed a son since he'd seen her last. He and she had a lot of catching up to do.

Across from Cadiz station, a familiar face, Ted, waited in his hack buggy for any fares. "While you be up North, I got a good-lookin' young gal fer you. Name's Anna. Lives over on the slopes. Ever met her?"

"Reckon so, Mister Ted. But I already know a girl in Belmont I intend to look up. Much obliged anyway."

Ted showed a letdown on his face. "How was yer work in . . .?"

"Town's Elyria, Ted. Near Lake Erie."

As Ted's horse-drawn cab lurched toward his family home, William Wesley described his hostler work and the pickup baseball games that Fleet Walker's team usually won, and the building of the Lorain County Courthouse.

"It's grander than Cadiz's courthouse," he said, telling of the sandstone slabs toted from local quarries and set, the flat imitation columns that ran up along the outside walls, a great dome sitting on a stone drum, the wide staircase with fancy banisters. Ted, being a part-time carpenter who at times worked on houses of moneyed white folks, was impressed.

"But seems to me there needed to be more managing of the work."

"Well, even as a li'l fella, you was always lookin' tuh manage things."

Ted halted his draft horse at the Brown house's curb and was handed a quarter for the ride. Seeing how well his fare was dressed — pressed suit, starched collar, and spats — Ted figured on a dime tip. He got just an extra nickel, a firm handshake, and a smile. "That'ar young buck's got a frugal streak the measure of a Scotchman," he said to himself.

Mama Isabell, with baby Ginney in her arms, little Henry and Anna underfoot, followed four other children out to greet William Wesley. His next-in-line sister, seventeen-year-old Alice Jane, was away doing day work. To Isabell, he was a proud sight for sore eyes. To his younger brothers and sisters, who hadn't seen him for at least a year, "Willie" was a hero. To his father, George, and some other men in town, out laboring in the fields this day, he would likely be too close to the "prodigal son's" wanderings from Luke 15 in the Holy Bible. "Willie" gave his family a joyful shout!

Isabell had always depended on her firstborn to help with the young'uns and the other household burdens. When Willie was reaching his manhood, she began to call upon his quick understanding of problems she faced. Yet on this afternoon, his mind often seemed elsewhere as she was unburdening herself. "Oooh, Lord, Willie, what be on thet keen mind a yourn?"

His mother's almost plaintive question — and this sudden switch in her train of thought — jarred him. "Sorry, Ma. I heard what you were sayin', but just was thinkin' 'bout my future, here or someplace else."

"Your future, huh? Well, you always been swift with schemin', but I hope you'll let the Holy Ghost hold the reins. He'll take care of the future. Right now yer Pappy be workin' hisself to the bone, so we kin use yer help here, fer sure."

"Yes, ma'am." His family's need, and his mother's will, was so strong . . .

Yet Rebecca Ann Thomas had a powerful pull, too. Late afternoon William Wesley borrowed a good neighbor's fine Crozier & Son carriage and hitched up (with Mama's permission) Pappy's big old Standard bred, "Jack." Then he drove away, after saying, "I'm heading over yonder. Tell Pappy I be back near sundown to speak with him." Isabell, instinctively, knew her son's intentions. She had mixed feelings about the Thomas girl. Still, Willie needed a mate strong enough to put some brakes on him—and from what she'd heard, Rebecca was a strong lass. Isabell shook her head, waving her forefinger as a reminder to return the carriage to the neighbor not too late.

He figured the carriage, a small maroon and black two-seat phaeton, would impress Rebecca. Jack was used to pulling this phaeton, and he remembered that Willy was a sure, gentle driver. Jack also knew the hilly roads. So Willy said, "Jack, let's go to the slopes — hey, boy?" Jack took the cue. Soon Jack had warmed up and changed from a walk to a trot.

Across from where town's edge curved, William Wesley saw a flock of sheep on the hillside. Flocks were many throughout Harrison County, as wool was a big business. He wondered whether there might be some moneymaking for him in that line. "Naw, these sheep farmers and wool-sellers be as *tight* an' as *white* as their wool crop when dyed," he muttered. Or maybe running a vegetable farm on the rich land at the hill bottoms? He recalled how sheep dung washed down the hillsides, creating the most fertile soil for growing corn, hay, and the best grass for milk cows. He had ideas. Jack rounded the bend. "Whoa!"

He had halted Jack because, from a short distance, he saw a young, dark-skinned fellow talking to Rebecca outside the Thomas home. After a minute he nudged Jack forward at a slow walk. Now he could see that the young lady was not Rebecca, but Martha, her twin sister, who was talking with Joseph Smith. His next, joyful breath came with the smile of a relieved suitor!

"Mighty good t'see you again, Martha! Afternoon, Joe." He tipped his straw hat to bosomy, cheerful Martha.

"Hey there, Willie. Heard you been livin' with Mr. 'n' Mrs. Moore, up by the Great Lake."

"Yessir," Joe added. "We heared you hep build the courthouse up there, well as hostlerin'."

"Yessir, I done that, an' some other things, too." They chuckled. "Now, is Becky around?"

Joe and Martha grinned. "Becky," she called into the house. "Come on out with the baby! Willie Wesley's here!"

A long minute passed, then Rebecca Thomas emerged, holding her year-old boy. Rail-straight, buxom, and ebony-skinned, Becky hesitantly spoke. "Hello, Willie." Willie, already having climbed out of the carriage, walked over to embrace her. She let him hold the child.

"Handsome li'l tyke. Don't recollect hearing his name."

"William." It was an awkward moment for both of them.

"Just got into town. I came with Jack an' that there carriage, hopin' we could go fer a drive — that is, after greeting your folks. Will you grant me this, Becky?"

Becky paused, staring directly into his eyes. "Glory be, we need tuh do that, Willie." She noticed the maroon-and-black phaeton. "Looks like Mr. Sternheiser's buggy." He nodded his head.

Becky's mother, Harriet, opened the door. Her father, Nelson Thomas, stood inside frowning.

CHAPTER 3

$\mathcal{F}$leet Walker was causing "O-o-ohs" and "Whews" among his White Sewing Machine teammates this summer of 1881. But not all of them. Four or five had a thing about teaming with a *nigger,* so bitterness put a damper on their praises. In this sense, he learned that Cleveland was a long way from the seeming color blindness of Oberlin. He even studied the team advertisement card — a die-cut image of a maple leaf fading from forest green to red to yellow, with "The White King" emblazoned on its face. Though the team's owner was Thomas White, this maple leaf and this resentment of certain teammates kept reminding Fleet that he was a "black" player on a "white" team, and now less than twenty seasons since so many of his people had been plantation slaves.

"Pay little heed to thuh jackasses," the team manager told him. Fleet stood above the "jackasses" in his mind and in his play. Tall, lean, strong and nimble, Fleet had admirers in these mostly white crowds watching the games. Some women whispered of him as the "bronze Adonis." To their brothers or husbands, he was the "jiggerboo peculiarity." His job was catcher, the best catcher the "Whites" had. The next game was Louisville in Kentucky against the Eclipse Club, his first game south of the Ohio River.

It was a hot August morning. The fellows, having arrived by train in Louisville at Hotel Saint Cloud, went for breakfast. The waiter captain welcomed the team. But before they sat down he pointed at Fleet. "I'm sorry ta have ta tell you—the colored boy, we caint sit him. We'll give him his meal ta eat outside. This be thuh rule!" A couple players and the manager began protesting, but an angry Fleet shushed them. "I ain't hungry, fellows. I'll see you at the game." He was baffled and furious, but knew better than to cause a scene. This was Rebel country.

Fleet was sitting on a bench, wearing a coat and vest, when his team bounded onto the field in uniforms. Facing the blazing sun he could barely make out the two men approaching. They were his team's managers, wanting to ready him for the game. But not only was he not ready, his mind was heavily burdened. And he had lost his will to play.

Like the great prophet for whom he and his papa were named, Moses Fleetwood Walker suddenly felt himself a stranger in a foreign land.

"You're our catcher today. You got to put on yer playin' clothes!"

Loud voices interrupted the managers. "Hey, gentlemen, we need tuh talk some wit' you!" The Eclipse officials were saying, "The mulatto is rejected as a player. Our team's agin' 'em!"

Fleet looked up at the sun and shrugged. He felt his self-pride melting, even while his wrath burned hot as the sun. Used to be that being called "mulatto" raised him above the average Negro. His high-toned skin, his mixed blood, his almost-straight hair were envied by the more "African" folk because his complexion was close enough to "white" to gain him favors. Now in Kentucky, though, he was a *nigger*! If he could, he'd take the next train north. He just let the sun beat down.

He heard his managers argue. "Without Walker our team is crippled." The Louisville managers shot back, "Unless ya'll relinquish we won't play you, an' ya'll have ta forfeit this he'yuh game!" So they yielded.

Besides a baseball, the substitute player named West caught hell. His bare hands got nicked and blistery. Cleveland pitcher Jones was hurling scorching balls. In the second inning West's hands were so bruised, so bloody, that he raised his hand and staggered off the field. Seeing the situation, the Louisville crowd, having come for a good, rivalrous game, took to their feet. "Bring on the *nigger!*", they yelled, "Play the darky!"

Oh, his eyes, dulled this moment by his mangled mind, took in the rising crowd. Much more his ears were stung by the screams. "Put the colored boy in!" Fleet's fists clenched, his chest heaved, and his blood surged. These Kentuckians were calling for him! Just as his self-pride returned, so did his preacher Papa's warning from Proverbs:, "Pride goeth before destruction, and a haughty spirit before a fall." He heard the man approaching, an official of the Louisville Eclipse, who touched his shoulder, beckoning him. Should he please these hounds? Well, if he did not, the game would be forfeited, his team would not be paid—or even worse. But he was his own man, and he'd been persecuted. The official pleaded, the crowd kept hollering like fiends in a frenzy. He stood up, making his way toward the diamond, still debating inside himself. As he passed in front of the grandstand, the crowd burst into thunderous cheers, "Walker! Walker! Walker!"

Fleet still felt the devil upon him. After struggling with himself, or with Satan, he finally shucked off his coat and vest. He decided to test the field, to practice some catches, to give the bases a once-over. His team waited, stunned, swallowed up by the noise, and surely being made subservient to the Eclipse officials.

Hushed became the crowd as Fleet worked out. They had never seen anything like the way Fleetwood Walker scooped up fastballs and curve balls with his bare hands. They'd never before seen such a stance, his easy and square crouch, his power in rifling the ball to second base. "He's a marvel!" someone shouted. An Eclipse player, fidgeting anxiously for the game to resume, shot back, "He's a jiggaboo!" Two other Eclipse players, named Reccius and Pfeffer, then headed for the clubhouse and more began refusing to play. But the crowd cheered for Walker. On the field things got so ugly that Fleet was forced to walk away. So a less able Clevelander had to be the catcher. As White Sewing Machine tried to compete, the Louisville fans hissed over their own team's shameful behavior. And they were not pleased with their team's "victory." While returning to Ohio, Fleet shed the first tears of his career.

Neither fury nor tribulation are demons clinging to him. His Papa Moses had told him early on to "not let the sun go down upon your wrath." Again, about those who persecute his people, Papa related also to the Scriptures: "Let no man trouble you, for you already bear on your body the marks of Jesus." As train wheels rolled them into northern Ohio, Fleet sat separate from his teammates and peered out at the moonlight. He admitted his own quick temper. He lauded himself for not letting his fury make conditions worse. Papa was right, because he was going to show the bigots up. In the darkness, and now with the humming of wheels rolling smoothly, he managed a private smile.

Once back in Cleveland, he put his baseball skills, mostly his precise catching and throwing, on full display. "You amazed these people," Bella said to him with a grin, "and you amaze me in other ways." She and a couple of friends had just seen one of his Cleveland games, after which Fleet returned to Oberlin with them. Alone together now, he braced himself for a discussion regarding marriage plans. Bella looked as slender as ever, showing no outward signs of her pregnancy. He dared not broach the baby subject lest she break into sobs again.

"You know, Fleetwood, I must begin to serve notices. So when have you arranged for my departure?" She was speaking of their getaway to

Michigan for his entering the university at Ann Arbor. When autumn leaves began to fall, they feared her belly would be noticeable. They wanted to avoid this embarrassment. And she hoped he would do right by wedding her. Thus, Arabella was preparing to leave Oberlin College.

"Bella, since I'm staying with my brother in his room overnight, and since he's going to be traveling with us, I'll discuss calendar dates with Weldy, then maybe we can all agree on the time."

"All right." Bella paused, rubbing one of her dainty hands with the palm of the other, reminding herself of how unpredictable he could be sometimes. He saw, by the gaslight, worry in her eyes. "Fleetwood?"

Instantly he knew what her question, in the form of his name, was. "Bella, I promise we'll get married. As soon as we light in Michigan. We just have to settle somewhere — me an' Weldy at the university, you with your kinfolk. Soon as we can get situated."

Truth was, Fleet was unsure exactly of his next moves. He had a few more summer games with the White team to complete and earn some cash. Meanwhile both Bella and Weldy had, blamelessly, become two millstones hanging on him. And transferring from Oberlin College to the University of Michigan turned out to be not so simple. Something about his application bothered President Angell of Michigan, who was writing to Oberlin President Fairchild questioning Fleet's grades. Fleet knew he hadn't lied about his grades, but maybe he'd embellished them? At any rate, this issue, of which he had only third-hand knowledge, weighed on his mind. And then there were his feelings for Ednah. Of course, he didn't mention Ednah, or his plan to visit her this evening . . .

". . . writing to Uncle and Aunt in Michigan," Bella was saying to him. "Hillsdale . . . maybe getting into Hillsdale College. And then, truly, I've got to solace Ma and Pa 'bout my leaving Oberlin College . . . becoming your wife. But first . . . oh Lord . . . the most critical matter of being with child? So, I'm . . ."

"Uh-huh." Ednah Jane Mason, the twenty-year-old beauty, was full on his mind. Ednah already has the walk and talk of a professional lady who intrigues all men. Him especially. Skin of soft-spun gold. Hazel eyes that reach out and grab. Clinging lips. Sophisticated manners. If only . . .

"Do you really love me, Moses Fleetwood?"

"Huh? I surely do, gal. I'll help you get things straight here in town and in Xenia and in Michigan, Hillsdale, with your kin." He took her in his arms, kissing her gently. "I'll see you 'fore I go at noon tomorrow."

Loosed in his five-minute jog to the Masons' house were a half hour's worth of questions. In the evening dew he felt the crush of damp grass 'neath his plimsoll sneakers and wondered whether he was trampling on Bella, too? She was going to make him a good wife, but would he make a good husband? Why was he wanting to see, maybe spark with Ednah, when pretty Bella needed his loving? Rounding a corner in the twilight, he heard a skitter, then a brief caterwauling amid some bushes. And somehow this loud meow of an angry or frightened cat caused Fleet to think of the baby in Bella's belly, and of Bella herself. How must he plan for the little one's coming? Would he, or Bella, be able to rear a child? What did he have to say to Ednah this minute?

He passed some neighbor folks chatting on her street as he neared the Masons' house. There she was! Sitting in a rocker on the front porch, just as she'd hinted she might be doing on summer evenings, in case he chose to stop by. That is, whenever some other chap was not keeping her company—and if she wasn't attending a church or town or family activity. Ednah had her jet-black hair up in ringlets, and she was wearing a simple white dress with a belted waist. She looked, as always, elegant! "Well, I do say, it's Fleetwood Walker, the magnificent baseball player—come to pay me a visit?"

Though Ednah chuckled kiddingly, he couldn't help but sense a trace of sarcasm in her tease. He bounded onto the porch. "Good to see you, too, Ednah."

The street gas lamp on a pole next to her house was not yet lit, but t'was light enough to admire his handsome face and tall, lean, athletic frame. "I heard you played a great game in Cleveland today," Ednah said. He grinned. "And afterward, here in Oberlin, have you spent time with Arabella?" Her question caught Fleet off guard. "Uh, well, yes, we had a friendly palaver . . ." Was she guessing? He felt she knew.

CHAPTER 4

Down in Cadiz, in the year 1882, William Wesley lived with Rebecca Thomas. They were happy enough, yet he was frustrated. To provide for Becky and little Willie, he worked fields and farms, but this didn't satisfy him. Up in the dark of rising mornings, head bent under the sun or out in the wintry blasts, fatigue and sleep coming too soon. He fed his new family, but he wanted another way. His body had been made strong on the farm, in the field, yet the Lord had also given him a keen mind and he needed to use it more. William Wesley had planned not to follow in his father's manner of toiling. Of course, Pappy had done alright, considering that few men in slavery times had either the skills or education to be anything other than laborers.

William Wesley was studying Harrison County, looking hard at all the Cadiz businesses or occupations—both among whites and coloreds. Almost every Negro man he knew suggested he become a miner, since coal was a big industry locally. Maybe they be right, he thought.

He circled the hills and the hollows at sunrise—with the swelling light changing colors and tones several times within a blink of his eyes. The subtle swiftness of the changing sky amazed him! He made note of this; its meaning was to become part of his nature forever afterward. He gazed at rolling green mounds, these woody footings girdling the yonder Appalachian Mountains, where flocks of sheep grazed. He'd already decided the wool business was surely closed to coloreds. To the west rose Boyle's Hill astride running waters divided so one stream flowed to the Tuscarawas River and the other to the Ohio. He saw bountiful farmland sloping from the ridges to the hollows. The many grazing, honey-brown cows of the Jersey breed gave milk so rich that it sometimes needn't even be churned to get butter. He turned his nag, an old workhorse, toward the hill upon which Cadiz town sits like a coarse crown. These farms, he figured, are prosperous and troubled at the same time. Prices were strong—butter at twenty-three cents a pound, a dozen eggs at twenty-two cents, a peck of potatoes at thirty cents, and so forth—but land was mighty expensive to keep up. And taxes high. Besides this, all the new-fangled machinery, such as steam-driven harrows and harvesters that farmers felt it necessary to purchase, cost a pretty penny, too.

Riding his nag past the large Maffitt farm, William Wesley observed that field hands like himself were becoming fewer. Only a handful of planters could pay the $1.25 daily wages. He knew he couldn't afford to buy or lease a farm anyhow. But he surveyed the land, counting barns and silos and cornfields and beasts—and pieces of big machinery. He believed that someday the Lord would lead him to an endeavor which he had the ability to manage. He believed it.

By autumn, when going to and coming from harvest fields, he noticed that his "Becky" seemed to be a bit out of sorts. She was rising slower before dawn to fetch water from the well, and to put breakfast on the stove. Often she would touch her belly and grimace, so he could tell she was suffering from dyspepsia. In the evenings sometimes he'd catch her retching. Becky was robust, stronger than her twin sister, nearly strong as young Anna from across the slope. Why did she retch? The answer soon spilled from her on a November morning when the moon was still bright and little Willie was waking. "Lord willing, we are goin' to have another child." Becky's deep eyes sparkled with flame.

"Truly?" he said. "Well, I been wonderin'. That why you been taking thuh horehound herb?"

Becky grinned at his alertness. "Yea, and why I been usin' a comfrey root poultice on my bosom when yer not around."

"Ah, Becky, the Lord is blessing us. We're growin' a family now." He spoke gently, comforting her, but his mind was racing and without glee.

"You willing to pray with me? I believe it's time," Becky gushed.

Much to his silent discontent, Becky was always insisting they pray. "Uh, yeh, I be obliged. You kin lead." As if on cue, their little Willie apparently went back to sleep in the other room.

They held hands and got down on their knees. He prepared for five minutes, maybe ten, of her beseeching. "Our Father," she began in her alto voice, smooth and thick as gravy, "hear this prayer of our'n . . ."

While Becky's voice poured out, he let his private thoughts play. He was not ready yet for another baby in the house, although they expected to have a large family. Somewhere in Genesis God does say, "Be fruitful and multiply." He guessed that he'd follow his Pappy in siring many young ones. But he'd wanted this to come later. Later, after he started one kind of business or another. He'd heard it preached that "God helps them who help themselves," and that was his want — to help his family.

Now Becky was working too hard, hauling water from their well and stocking kindling to cook meals on the woodstove and gathering fruit, pumpkins, walnuts, plants for canning, and doing the wash, cleaning house, ironing, feeding their yard animals, 'sides mothering little Willie. All across the slopes and in every hollow "down at the heels," wives slaved from dawn to dusk, and into the night. At bedtime she would be sewing, quilting, patching his britches . . .

". . . and the vittles from the merciful bounty of Thy body, Lord," Becky was praying . . .

Yes, vittles. She grew many things and wrenched them out of the dirt herself. He thought of her good cooking, despite working her fingers to the bone keeping house for him. "An', my Lord," he uttered to himself, "her dishes be so tasty." Before morning light Becky could whip up the best biscuits he'd ever tasted in this hill country known for its luscious meals— even better biscuits than those famous ones made by young Anna across the slope. Becky used the pure leaf lard her Mama Harriet rendered right after the butchering from hogs raised on pine roots and fattened on sweet potatoes. And Mama Harriet always stirred the melting fat with a bough from a sweet-bay tree, fragrantly flavoring this lard. He often watched Becky shorten flour with the rich lard, shape, then bake her biscuits in their three-legged spider skillet. Folks like to drop in at mealtimes to sample Becky's biscuits and gravy and smoked ham and baconed collards. Well, it's not from her cooking he wanted to spare Becky, but from all the hard day or evening muscle work which a successful young husband would hire a servant gal to do. . .

"Lord, you been givin' us so much . . ." Becky continued, her eyes shut, shifting her bended knees and straightening her aching back for half a minute. "A fine man tuh provide . . ."

As she unfolded her hands to limber up her stiff fingers, he saw this, then inspected his own hands. They are rough from field work, from felling trees, from carpentry, from handling horses, from other toil. He was trying to provide, but he needed to do it better and in smarter ways.

"Now, Lord, you're givin' us another blessin' . . . a new baby for to love an' rear in our little family . . ."

The baby? This is going to burden Becky more, like so many young mothers in Cadiz Township are being overstrained by childbearing, he told himself, gone old or broken 'fore their time. Also he, struggling for cash, was already giving help to his younger sisters and brothers. This is the first-born's responsibility—meaning now he's got two families to worry about. In his calculating mind he pictured the new one, his own flesh and blood, squirming inside Becky's belly. The baby was either fighting to be born or not to be born.

Then something overtook William Wesley. He edged closer to Becky and joined her in finishing this prayer. She squeezed his hand.

CHAPTER 5

$\mathcal{B}$ecky being with child was a concern for William Wesley down in Cadiz. Also, earlier—during the first month of 1882—Bella's pregnancy had become a mystery and a concern for Fleet up in Michigan. They'd expected the baby to come in January. Something was wrong. Fleet made Bella see a doctor. Though she had few certain outward signs of it, she insisted that there was a baby inside her. Bella testified about "the curse" being absent for nine months, about her fuller breasts, about her belly feeling heavier and even some quickening inside. But her older kinfolk women let Fleet know they were suspicious of her condition, that she might be tumorous. After examination by several obstetricians, the diagnosis sent Fleet and Bella into a tailspin.

"It's called *pseudocyesis*," the physician patiently explained. "What?" Fleet gasped, let go of Bella's hand, and sat bolt upright. "Soo-do-si-ee-sis," Dr. Menke groaned. "False pregnancy. Miss Arabella, you won't be delivering a baby!" In part, this confirmed her kinfolk's suspicions.

Fleet had suspicions, too. He wondered if Bella had faked her condition to get him away from Oberlin and into marriage. The physician, however, assured him that, though he couldn't find a big tumor, Bella's physical symptoms were real enough to mimic pregnancy—a true condition that sometimes did happen. The doctor told them about the famous case of a queen of England, Mary Tudor, called "Bloody Mary" three hundred years ago, who had two false pregnancies. Nobody was sure why.

"Mercy, what shall I do now, Doctor?" Bella's question was between a whimper and a plea. Mentally she was touching her belly, her swollen breasts. In shock . . . deep, instant grief overcame her. She was losing her child! Her stomach became upset. Fleet glared at her in confusion.

Dr. Menke eyed them both. "The symptoms will pass. I suggest you get back to normal living." But Bella's anguish would not be eased.

After they left the doctor's office, Fleet began to comprehend the real nature of Bella's grief. That evening he caressed her and comforted her. A tinge of anger remained, but he hid it. After all, she had given herself to him. She had left Oberlin College and faced her parents—they were abashed!—down in Xenia, Ohio, to be with him and have his child.

Her head on his lap, he gently brushed her jet-black hair while he mulled things over. If he were unsympathetic, that might be wicked. He recalled his father, not as the doctor but as Reverend Walker, delivering a sermon from the book of Daniel, saying, " . . . none of the wicked shall understand, but the wise shall understand." So he tried to understand. He hoped that Moses and Caroline Walker, now back in Steubenville, understood, too.

Still, Bella and Weldy were hampering his plans. This Hillsdale town was quite a ways south of Ann Arbor. So he was taking the train to visit Bella too often for concentrating on class assignments. He wanted to nail down his law studies at the University of Michigan. The courses were demanding for any ordinary student, but he was not ordinary. He was on the school team that practiced baseball nearly every day. On days of Ann Arbor snow and ice they tossed the ball around, dashed the distance between bases, and built up their stamina inside the gymnasium. Usually, after classes, they spent cold, darkening days out doing demon drills. Swinging their heavy ashwood truncheons, batters scattered foul balls, some whacking his shoulders and feet. He'd begun using a fitted wire mask to spare his face. Pitchers scorched his bare hands with fastballs, so he'd started wearing leather gloves with the fingertips cut out so he could still catch, grip, and throw handily. He was the best college catcher, which was why Michigan had recruited him. Baseball first, then lawyering were his goals. Taking care of Bella and overseeing Weldy were getting in his way. At the moment he felt like a harnessed lion!

"Fleetwood," she murmured, "I'm grateful. Your soothing me shows how much you understand . . . how much you love me. Reckon I had my doubts 'til now. I will truly have your child someday, my love! Are you taking the 5:15 train this evening back to Ann Arbor?"

"I have to get back . . . for classes and also for team practice tomorrow outdoors, if the weather holds." He was glad that she'd stopped crying. But her words about truly having a child, which would lead again to talk of marriage, only tightened the harness. What should he do about her?

Bella pulled herself together, sitting up on the couch. Her aunt and several older women cousins stayed in the front room chatting. "Don't you worry about me. I'll be alright. How are you, Fleetwood? I think this is a tragedy for you, too! You've been in deep thought, yes?"

"Right, Bella." He hugged her. It's good she hadn't read his mind.

"Well, when you come back to me—hopefully within the fortnight—we'll fix our occasion, won't we?" Teardrops drying on her cheek made her pretty face glisten. Her brown eyes suddenly sparkled. Fleet felt her spirit surging. He could almost hear the wedding bells playing in Bella's thoughts. She looked so delicate, so deserving. Yet it was Ednah in Oberlin who was really enchanting him. "Yes, girl . . ."

Not two weeks but a month passed before he rolled back to Hillsdale. With new hope, due to the promised skill of Fleet Walker now behind the plate, Michigan started its 1882 season early. Along with splendid catching, Fleet wielded a ready bat. Michigan's team won six games in a row. Baseball fanatics (they shortened "fanatics" to "fans") and local sports writers around Ann Arbor were calling Fleet a "wonder."

Bella called him a "wonder," too, on an April evening when he stole away to visit her again. Green grasses were shooting up, trees were budding, Michigan breezes were pregnant with spring. Fleet was joyful because he and Arthur Packard, two former Oberlin mates, were going to pitch and catch against their former team in a week. It gave him a chance to see Ednah, who bounded into his day and night dreams. But this soft, warm evening he handed Bella a bunch of lilacs whose lavender blooms smelled sweetly. To his delight Bella burst into giggles. "Fleetwood, I surely needed to be with you! And I shan't weep . . . I shall smile, wrapped in your strong but gentle arms." She placed the flowers into a vase, then hurried back into his embrace. He needed this, too.

Bella had made a shepherd's pie for their supper, and for dessert she served him a flaky sweet apple dumpling, with heavy cream, that her aunt had boiled. So they sat on the porch—eating, sipping a fruit punch that Fleet sneakily laced with gin, laughing, and talking. Bella never mentioned their wedding plans, and this very pleasantly surprised him. When the spring darkness gathered about them, when folks had retired for the night, Bella led him into her bedroom. And she latched the door.

Fleet Walker and Art Packard made eyes open wide in Oberlin the next week. As a pitcher-catcher battery, the two amazed a thumping crowd. Ednah Jane Mason, though, was not in the crowd. Fleet would have been puzzled, except that he was aware of her disposition. Ednah was not one to be part of any rowdy crowd. She would be studying or writing song lyrics for young composers at the conservatory or other genteel things. He had to go find her.

They strolled down Main Street in the early evening. Townspeople hailed him or stopped to chat. Others pointed to him, saying, "That's our boy, Fleetwood . . . he's playing for Michigan now!" At Plum Creek, the echoes of him there with Bella rang in his mind, and he steered Ednah away to the east side of town. "I suppose you played excellently today," Ednah said. He nodded his head, grinning. "Uh, how's Arabella these days?"

How foolish of him, a law student, not to have anticipated Ednah's question! His rejoinder, though, was quick. "Oh, she's well, I suppose. I visited Arabella and her kinfolk one day last week. 'Twas a brief visit. The town where they live is maybe seventy miles from where I do."

Strolling together, Ednah felt his long arms brush against her body, and his nearness felt good. He was quite an admired fellow, very light-complexioned, with wavy hair like hers, tall and muscular, amusing at times and witty. She and Fleet could be a match—if only . . . She gazed up at him. Her question crackled. "Word is, Arabella left for Michigan about the same time as you because she was with child. Is that true?"

Lying "confuses one's social mechanics and abrades the soul," his father had often warned. Fleet wanted to be truthful. He also wanted to veil what was going on between him and Bella. "She was never pregnant, just living with some of her people," Fleet replied, feeling relief that he had told the truth—well, at least part of the truth.

"Is the old saying that 'where there's smoke, there's fire' true, Mister Walker?" Ednah asked this of him with a wise smile.

He grasped her hand. "Not always." He chuckled. "You know, too many Negroes have been hung from a tree due to false rumoring. So don't be quick to hang me, girl." She matched his chuckle, but Ednah was neither convinced nor placated. When they reached her street, she curtsied gracefully and bid him good-bye for now. He knew she meant it. He watched her sashay toward her house—so lovely, yet a dream walking away. Fleet wondered if it was possible another fellow had stepped in front of him in her life. He stood there at the corner eyeing her house for a long time. Then he jogged off to find Weldy, whom he figured would have half a bottle of whiskey hidden somewhere. His body was tired and his hands hurt from baseball, and his mind was on fire from his encounter with Ednah. He needed something wet to wash away his miseries. He could get drunk tonight!

"Weldy," he mumbled to his younger brother. "You wanna play ball wit' me?" Weldy touched Fleet's sagging shoulders and reminded him that they'd both be playing for Michigan next year, 1883. Was the liquor dimming his mind?

"Naw . . . uh, naw, brudder . . . I mean this here summer . . . for money!"

Weldy didn't know what Fleet was talking about. He shrugged and let his big brother fall asleep. Weldy knew Fleet most desperately wanted to be with Ednah Jane Mason this evening, instead of him.

Returning to Michigan, Fleet went on to finish the college baseball season like a giant. Between games, though, he found time to visit Bella again. Even as they sat close enough to caress each other on the porch, enjoying soft June breezes and the sweet scent of hyacinth, Bella seemed nervous. After a while Fleet said, "Are you alright, Bella? You strike me as fit to be tied!" He took her hand and gave her a perplexed smile. He couldn't have expected what was coming.

Her kinfolk and everyone else on the street were inside having supper. But he and Bella had foregone the meal because they had walked to and devoured the ice cream parlor's confectioneries. So, with nobody out watching them, she took this opportunity to climb onto his lap. Before now Bella had always been ladylike, but he welcomed her behaving like a brazen hussy. Her lips pressed on his as if they were stuck in a fever. He got anxious and urgent.

"You dare to question my fever, Fleetwood? Well, sir, this evening I am surely carrying your child! The Lord has finally opened my womb as He once did for Rachel of the Bible. Doctor Menke has agreed that all signs prove my true pregnancy this time! I know it happened that night in April when I made for you that shepherd's pie."

Nervously she looked at him. He studied her for what seemed to her a full minute. This news put his mind into a tizzy! He felt the harness tighten further. "Whew!" Fleet uttered this, letting her shift off his lap.

An early summer breeze whipped strands of silky hair across her face, and she brushed them away from her eyes. Her eyes, he noticed, were big and beautiful. In fact, she is pretty, his mind told him. Also, quite shapely still. But now she's assuring him that he's going to be a father. Something in her eyes and voice made him believe. "Yeah, I remember that night. We were like rabbits, weren't we, gal?" At this he forced a chuckle, though his thoughts were scrambled.

"Uh, Fleetwood, you were a tomcat . . . a lion!" Her embarrassed laugh was rapid. She was awaiting a response to her news.

"Well, Bella, I promised we'd be married. 'Tis time—for certain now. Let's set the day! When do you figure our baby'll be born? Oh, by the by, a white manager from Pennsylvania wants to hire me for his team called the 'Neshannocks' this summer, so we'd best get hitched directly."

Bella gasped and had to catch her breath. She'd wanted him to be enthralled by her news. She'd wanted him to make a joyful noise unto the Lord, and unto her. Fleetwood was dynamic, she realized. So much dynamic that this moment he was all spurred to "get hitched" . . . due to obligation? Where was his sentiment—for her, for their child? Was he willing to have a wedding, as Down South folks say, "Dry Long So?"

"Baseball in Pennsylvania?" she asked.

"Uh-huh. Town name of New Castle. But it won't hamper any plans for marriage, if you're willing. We could wed next week, next month?"

"But, Fleetwood, you'll be traveling—playing games in Pennsylvania or Lord knows where! This'll not be the manner of marriage I reckoned on. And me heavy with your child . . . where will I be?"

Bella stared at him. She shook her head. And troubling spirits shot up within her, tightening her chest, aching her heart, clenching her throat, squeezing her stomach. But Fleet calmed her. The Neshannocks of New Castle offered him enough money to give Bella, him, and the child a good start—and it would only be for about two months. He pledged to be steadily by her side long in advance of the baby's arrival, which she figured would be before Christmas.

On a good day three weeks later she, resembling a Spanish princess, was helped by Fleet into a hired George IV phaeton. A half-dozen girls and a young man stood by the elegant carriage, singing "To where your heart will feel no pain, and where the fields are fresh and green . . ." The popular song was "I'll Take You Home Again, Kathleen." Two dapper horses pulled their carriage over mostly macadam roads the twenty miles from Hillsdale to near Hudson. There by Hudson village a local favorite marrying man wed them. He in tie-and-tails, she in frothy white gown, Fleet spread her veil, bent over, and kissed her. Bella broke into a smile.

Fleet's sudden, swift move to make them husband and wife did gratify Bella. But the next tick-tocking of time unsettled her. In seven days he was ready to follow his newest dream. His carpetbag packed, Fleet fingered a horsehide baseball and tried to make plain to Bella his goal. "I been blest," he told her, "to maybe be the best baseball catcher in all America."

He showed her his bruised and calloused hands. "These represent my lighted candle. Scriptures say not to hide it under a bushel but to let it shine! I must play baseball while I can. I've been given this talent, Bella, and must use it—as a step toward gaining success for me, for you, and for our family." Fleet was telling her this, but even he did not know what it really meant. They were about to find out.

CHAPTER 6

*W*illiam Wesley stumbled out of the bedroom. He needed his toddy. In fact, some friends and kinfolk had given him "Tod" as a nickname. So "Tod" Brown fetched a bucket of cool water from the cistern, toted it inside, then half-filled a teakettle, which he placed on the kitchen stove heated by wood chunks. Then he put a lump of sugar into a warm glass and added boiling water, stirred in Old Guckenheimer's bourbon, laid in a slice of lemon, and sprinkled on a bit of Becky's home-grated nutmeg. Now this was his hot toddy for cool mornings!

Long before gray light began creeping over the hills, he took a neighbor grangers cows to pasture, shoveled manure from milking barns, and fed the animals for sick and needy folks on nearby farms. He did this early while the dew dried enough to begin his own work in the fields. Some folks paid him; others couldn't. Becky and Willie and their new baby, Charlie, were still asleep. In this hour when the pearly moon drifted slowly east above the treetops outside his window, "Tod" sipped and pondered.

First about Pappy George. He and his father had had words. He was an adventurer . . . ambitious. "Footloose" was what Pappy had called him. And a "prodigal." Since he was a boy—when he helped his ma, Bell, tend to the house and the young'uns—his feet were always moving. Ma and Pappy got tired of wondering where he was. He was exploring the town and peeking into stores, apothecaries, and shops, but came home timely to finish his chores. Occasionally Pappy found him at a livery currying the horses or in a worn-out field pitching baseball to other idling boys. But that's not what Pappy means now by "footloose"—no, he's talking about "Tod," or "Willie," as he still insisted on calling him, traveling to Elyria, where his mouth nearly got him killed, and now his present itch to ramble to other towns. Pappy didn't seem to realize he wanted more opportunities to make money than he'd found in Cadiz. He had looked around over in Steubenville, hard by big Ohio River. Also, he'd studied jobs a little ways south in Mt. Pleasant. Whereas Pappy accepted an old man's own lot as a toiler in the coal mines, Pappy's eldest son had greater things in mind.

For one thing, there's the new business of coke cooking. When he was up in Elyria working a hostler job in '79, a manager at Edison & Tilden iron furnace a few miles over in Lorain rented draft horses from the livery. After delivering these horses, he heard talk of coal cooked into coke. Well, this coke supposedly was the best fuel for making steel. Might coke be cooked from the plentiful coal here in his hill country? And another thing on his mind was timber. The coal mines were buying lots of hardwood timber. Could he make money delivering cut tree trunks for the coal mine pillars and posts?

Now as to being what George called a "prodigal," a dark smile crept onto his face, the sort of smile that says, "I just got caught sneakin' an undue piece of cake." Pappy once saw him coming out of a roadhouse with some ladies (but not Becky) and some fellows. George and Isabell desired their sons to be straight and sober. He knew he didn't always fit this mold, so Pappy had dashed hopes for him. He liked good liquor and pretty skirts . . . no doubt. He determined to straighten things out with his Pappy. But for now he was intent on enjoying his toddy 'fore Becky and the young'uns stirred, and before going to the fields. Dark would be merging into light, with the slow quickness that always amazed him, in a few minutes. A rooster would be calling *cock-a-doodle-doo* before long . . .

CHAPTER 7

New Castle, the little city north and west of steel-making Pittsburgh, was a baseball town. Some wealthy men had put together a team by 1882 and named it after a big old creek where Indians had fished long time ago. The Indians called the running water Neshannock. The "Nocks" team, though, needed a spark to make its season successful. So in came Fleet Walker, with brother Weldy along with him. Folks in New Castle and the "Nocks" players were excited about Fleet. His catching brought cheers. Weldy played a few games in the outfield, against teams in western Pennsylvania and Ohio.

Before the Nocks' final game in September, Fleet also got Weldy transferred from Oberlin to Michigan. Weldy was anxious to be a doctor like their father. He signed up for studies called homeopathics—a practice of medicine some folks labeled spooky or silly or useless. But Fleet figured that his brother, in such serious study, would be occupied so much that Weldy would be out of his hair.

His Bella was happy to see him jogging up to her door. He snatched her off her feet. "'Sakes alive!" she squealed. "You're squeezing me so hard even the baby is boggled!" Fleet laughed, set her down, and felt her belly. "Dang," he said with a smile. "Girl, you beginning to bulge. Must be a boy!"

"No, Fleetwood, I think it's a girl." She chortled.

"You're now a 'seer,' huh? Sometimes you women have strange ways of divining the truth!" He laughed again, yet she noticed a frown begin.

"Does it matter?"

"Uh, naw." But Bella could tell he fancied a son.

His courses at the university, literary and legal, kept his mind too busy to worry whether Bella was heavy with a boy or a girl. A professor told the law class that students were expected to serve as apprentices between

36

their studies. Fleet thought of the white friends his father had made as the one colored doctor in Steubenville, maybe in all of Ohio. He decided to make contact with two Steubenville attorneys named A.C. Lewis and John McClave, Esquire. He figured they'd already heard of his baseball triumphs.

Oberlin College had lit up his mind. He'd studied Greek and Roman mythology. There were moments when his hands became the hands of Zeus armed with the thunderbolt that splits skies—and he would rifle a ball to the infield, stopping a speedster from stealing second base. Or he had the rings and robe of Pygmalion, who made a stone statue of a beautiful woman and turned her marble into living, loving human flesh—perhaps as he could transform the lovely but sometimes cold Ednah. Now Michigan University was opening his mind to the power of lawyering. Until this day his suffering and oppressed people were dependent on the beneficence of white lawyers to seek some justice. But he'd heard of Macon B. Allen and J.J. Wright, the first colored lawyer and judge, and he determined to follow in their footsteps—just like Weldy hoped to follow Moses Walker in medicine.

In the Michigan autumn, as cool winds from Lake Erie whipped and whistled, as trees dropped their brown leaves, Fleet remembered what brown-skinned people faced. Michigan was not quite as racially inviting as Oberlin, but it was a far cry from places south. He saw the weary brows of those who came out of slavery. He glimpsed the struggle in their wizened eyes, their gnarled hands. He could nearly fathom their souls praising the new light of free mornings in Steubenville and Oberlin—even here in Michigan. They're not his kin, but are his black "uncles" and "aunts." He himself had witnessed Jim Crow. And it kept stirring up an anger within him—like the fury he feels whenever white baseball fanatics shout *nigger* and *mulatto* - either to humiliate or to cheer him.

He didn't claim to be a true *mulatto*. His skin was so light, lighter than Weldy's, and his hair so wavy, white folks naturally called him that. He didn't object, shamefully realizing the benefits of having fair skin and wavy hair. Shamefully, because often *mulatto* signified a higher class and allowed him to avoid some of the ridicule darker-colored folks had to endure. He knew this was not prideful of the African in him. But he was becoming more and more disquieted, inwardly, due to the shifty bigotry visited on all colored folks, including him.

On a November afternoon Fleet stared through the window. Outside the boardinghouse gold, copper, and maroon leaves were snatched up from ground heaps and blown by a humming wind. Restless, dried-out, brown blades wandered wildly above the earth. The wind, he opined, can sing songs with messages to the soul. "You ever think of the difference 'tween the 'sot free' an' the 'bona fide free' Negroes?" he asked Weldy, who was across the room trying to study.

"Uh? Oh, you mean those colored emancipated by Ol' Abe, the 'sot free' they call themselves, and folks like us Walkers who left slavery 'fore most people. Well, brother, f'sure there's a cleft 'tween the two. I guess some of us been lordin' it over t'others . . ."

"'Specially we 'high-yaller' ones, hey?"

"Yeah, bro." Weldy chuckled. "Such like your Bella—and Edna Jane, too. Those members of the 'blue veiner club,' those whose little veins show up kind of indigo on the underside of their near-white wrists. We don't like to admit this, f'sure. Them bein' sarcastic, the black folks call this the 'blue vain club' so I heard."

"Well, I'm sick of prejudice and Jim Crow, and sick of 'blue vein' stuff, too. Weldy, these past years since Reconstruction have seen our people get more and more crushed by the coils of that great serpent—racism. I'm thinking of writing a 'manifesto' calling for action."

Weldy pushed his textbook aside. "Elder brother, what sort of action would this be?"

Fleet was pondering. Windows rattled, leaves swirled outside, a wood beam in the room creaked as the brothers faced each other. There was blood dripping off trees this year they both knew—not here in Michigan yet as far north as the Mason-Dixon Line, whose crown stones had been a boundary separating slavery states and so-called free states. Blood dripping from Negro men, even pregnant women, being hacked and lynched. Several dozens of killings this year. Also the "soul blood" of seven million colored folk draining out of their spirits all across the land. His brother's compulsion roused Weldy's own feelings about these racial troubles that had worsened since Reconstruction.

"Endeavors to halt this bloodletting," Fleet answered. "We coloreds ought to assemble our own mass organization, Weldy, to finance all the necessary litigations to . . . to hold on to the *Act* of a few years ago."

"The Civil Rights Act of 1875, huh, Fleet?"

"Yea, the *Act*. You 'member when we in were in Steubenville when Papa had a special meeting and colored cheers rose to the rafters of our church . . . 'cause we, finally, had a law recognizing our human rights. Not only is the *Act* turning out to be a tiger with no teeth, wise-ass lawyers are making a mockery of its wording to keep us powerless."

"Mockery, you say?"

"For certain, Weldy. The *Act*, it says any 'state' is prohibited from racial discrimination. Lawyers agin' it now argue that Jim Crow does not represent the 'state,' since those committing it are 'private' persons. This be making the *Act* as hollow as the voice of a parrot speaking!"

Weldy's eyes opened wide. "You're gon'ta make a good lawyer! When do you plan tuh come up with your 'manifesto,' brother?"

"Oh, that's just one of many points I'll offer. I'm hell-bent to develop a thesis, and this shall take time. I want to sound a loud trumpet! The gist of this 'manifesto' will be that America better get on with true liberty for our people—or . . ."

"Or what?"

"Or me and you will personally lead our folks, the millions who be willing, to Africa. Even 'blue veiners' have Africa as their Motherland."

"I read that our diplomat over in Liberia . . . uh . . ."

"Name is Henry Highland Garnet. He died some months ago. He's the one whose words got me thinking—not as much on Liberia, which, you 'member, was created for people of slavery over here in America, but of forming a New Republic in Africa."

"Fleet, as ever I be treadin' with you." Fleet grinned. Day after day, year after year, Weldy was his disciple. Then his grin vanished. Being his disciple, Weldy could also be his pest. "You figure 'blue veiners' will go 'long with us? Ednah and your Bella, too?"

"I fret about our 'high yaller' folk, brother. Some be too comfortable now, in league with the whites and all. I can't tell about Ednah, but Bella would go with us. Bella has to, she's my wife and soon she'll be birthing my son."

Mention of Bella's condition drove his thoughts in another direction. "Say, by dawn I must absent myself from school, sally forth to Hillsdale to see my wife. I've got to make sure she's fit for the deliverance."

As Fleet sallied forth by train on a bright and chilly morning, he day-dreamed about the son Bella would give him. Fully warming up to her pregnancy had not been quick or easy, but today he had ideas. The boy would not be reared in the same way as he was. His Papa, Reverend-Doctor Moses, did not ignore his children, but he was always busy with his professions. He, Fleet, was going to give his boy closer attention. Of course, he would have to quit playing baseball after college and focus on law practice.

By the time his son was in high school, perhaps playing professional ball would be possible for . . . Well, he'd have to come up with a strong name for his son first. It's a father's privilege.

Meanwhile, Bella was dusting gimcracks in her aunt's house and trying to capture a special name she would give her and Fleetwood's daughter. Given what she'd already gone through, her daughter would be so special! She would be a princess or a saint! Back at Oberlin College, Bella, like Fleet, had been introduced to classic fables and legends. And she recollected the story of Saint George and the princess. Suddenly she had the name!

Fleet found her in good humor. With a smile, he told her she was prettier than ever. "Ah, husband, you say the same thing—skinny me last year and pudgy me this year—I don't know if you're truthful, but I'm tickled anyhow." Her belly so heavy, looking as if she'd give birth any moment, she staggered up to kiss him lavishly. After their bounteous afternoon dinner, Bella lay sidewise on a couch. "We're both glad you discovered a path back to us. Did you see how your baby bounced its bottom just now?" she asked, patting her tummy.

He felt Bella's belly. "That his head bobbing?"

"No, silly, it's the butt. Her head's way down here. For God's sake, we don't want a breech birth." Bella giggled. "It's a girl, I still believe."

Traveling back to Ann Arbor on an evening turned wintry, Fleet tried to will himself a son. He usually was able to command or wrest a desired outcome from Fate. However, it hadn't worked with Ednah Jane. He thought about praying, but instead he allowed the train's rhythmic rumbling to rock him to sleep.

Two weeks afterward a telegram summoned him back to Hillsdale. He held Bella's hand in the warmth of her bedroom as December snows danced outside. Bella had a troublesome delivery. The experienced midwife would not explain, only shook her head. Bella was happy that their daughter was perfectly formed and pretty. A smiling Bella said, "Her name is Cleodolinda."

"Cleodolinda?"

Yes, and Bella reminded him of the fair little princess whose father, a North African king, allowed her to be sacrificed to the dragon, only to save all other children. Then Saint George the Christian Knight entered to slay the dragon and save the princess. "A-a-ah, my princess—Cleodolinda—you be so precious!" Fleet uttered to his grimacing new daughter. Bella, hearing this, grinned above her pain and was satisfied. The Lord had answered her prayers!

By the next spring, the year 1883, Fleet buckled down to his law course and also started another season with the University of Michigan's baseball Wolverines. Weldy joined the team, though struggling with the homeopathic courses. For a short period Fleet went to Stuebenville to be mentored by white attorneys Lewis and McClave. And, during these few weeks, he managed to dine with the girl named Anna from over in Cadiz. As everyone—particularly young bucks—realized, there was a mystic air about Anna. After he told her of Bella and Cleodolinda, she let him know about the family doings of his once Elyria pickup baseball games buddy, Willie Brown, now settled back in Cadiz. "Perhaps 'settled' is not the best word." She laughed. "Neither of y'all are the roostin' types—seems to me. Both y'all are like, well, prowling lions."

Anna did not add this, but as summer unleashed itself, his newest prowl would be in a great, boiling jungle!

CHAPTER 8

Cadiz, Ohio. William Wesley Brown tilted his head and searched the sky near dawn. As always, he beheld the so rapid, but subtle, changes. Eastward a beam of silvery light suddenly appeared in the dark heavens and he smiled. He would not see this little bit of daylight again until the morrow, so he relished it. Meanwhile, Becky was frying salt pork and eggs for his breakfast. He would eat this in a hurry, because he dare not be late for work. "Lord, girl," he said to her, "this biscuit is most delectable!"

Becky responded, "You tell me that ev'ry mornin'. But be they as scrumptious as young Anna's over on the slope?"

He wasn't quite sure how to answer, so he tried his cunning. "About the same scrumptious I'd figure—'cept she's got folks on that 'ere slope braggin', whilst you discourage any boasting. From Jeremiah you keep telling me that a man should only boast 'bout the Lord. Ain't that so?"

"Yea, that be so." Yet out of the corner of her eye, Becky's sly glance, and her scornful smile, was saying, I'm on to you, husband.

The large, open wagon pulled by a horse team arrived at the end of his street, so he dashed out carrying the lunch sack Becky packed. About a dozen neighbor fellows, white and colored, worked at the local coal mine and rode the wagon. "Hey, W.W.!" they grunted sleepily. He was called either W.W. or Tod these days. "W.W." had a more formal and dignified sound than "Willie," so he began using this mostly. And it better suited his future business plans.

Finally, his father and other older men had coaxed him into the mines. This, however, was not just to appease his elders. No, he would use this experience to benefit his future endeavors. W.W., you see, had studied people and situations in Harrison County. He knew his own people well. He was friendly with both poor and well-off white folks, too. He'd troubled his head about why there were such differences in their living conditions. He fretted about the better or lesser status of folks with "high yaller," "brown," and "black" complexions. Some, like Reverend-Doctor Moses Walker in Steubenville, also the razor-sharp young preacher, Reverend Reverdy Ransom from down in Flushing where Becky was born, were the educated elite. Hundreds of men in this hill country, however, were sons of slaves who'd made their way across borders into Ohio, with no means, to be welcomed by the Quakers. And these fellows felt blessed just to toil in the fields aboveground or in the mines below. Only a dozen, plus six barbers he knew, had rising trades.

W.W. thought about this. While peering out from the wagon, he saw sheep beginning to be loosed from sheds so they could graze on the hills and thought about this, too. From one generation to the next, rams and ewes and lambs forever had the same pattern. If men always followed the same pattern of their pappies and grandpappies, their conditions would hardly change. They'd be repeating, on and on. He would not imitate his Pappy's pattern. He would glean from the mine what he needed, then move on.

"Hey, Tod," one of the miners uttered. "What be on yer mind this mornin'?" It was rare for W.W. to be so quiet; usually his sly joking or teasing stirred the sleepy fellows awake.

"Movin' on," he replied with a grin. "Just movin' on."

The wagon rolled up to the mine, with its big, tall breaker looking like a monstrous black insect—a gigantic praying mantis. Time for toil!

The shift crew scrabbled down into the black depths. The darkness wasn't why W.W. had avoided the mines 'til now. In fact, he'd often sought the nights aboveground to enjoy his moonlight rambles—either with his lady among silent buckeye trees or with jubilant dudes in noisy, gas-lit roadhouses. For some reason he liked to prowl at night, as do tomcats and lions. It wasn't the bending and stooping, either. He was strong and nimble from shoeing horses. And it wasn't even the big, brown rats that scurried across the mine floor gobbling oats spilled from feedsacks of mules that lived and worked in the tunnels. Miners appreciated the rats: They could sense when the roof of the tunnel was starting to shift, and when the rats ran out, the miners would run, too, because a tunnel was about to collapse! W.W. let the rats sit on his lap, waiting for morsels from his lunch pail . . . Squeak, squeak, squeak.

No, the problem was being one of a pack taking orders from a boss who didn't know how to handle his workers right. W.W. didn't much like

43

being subservient. It reminded him of Jim Crow. Also, it was the dangers underground. For example, the "damps." These were the gases called "fire damp" and "white damp" and "black damp"—which could easily explode or choke a man to death down there. Becky, as did all wives and mothers of miners, feared to see the "Black Maria" come rolling toward the pits. That horse-drawn wagon, used as an ambulance or a hearse, signaled a mine accident—sometimes a disaster. And W.W. loathed the dust, dirt, and grime of mine work—more even than he hated soot on railroad cars. He'd much rather be a fashionable jack-a-dandy than a dirt-covered drudge anyway. Young Anna over on the slope said he had the makings of a "gentleman." He thought so, too.

Yet neither the pit boss nor his fellow miners considered him a slouch. W.W. always was at work on time, and he handled the pick and shovel with the best of them. But he always was thinking of moving on, even though his Pappy grumbled that "Willie" was a "dreamer."

With the flickering of his headlamp, and listening for seeping water that warned of danger, he crawled another yard or so. He prodded the coal seam with his pick, gauging his next cut, but his mind was on his father. George Brown, he figured, was a notable sort of man. One of those who'd climbed out of the dark mysteries of Maryland in slavery days to build a strong family in Ohio. Somehow, though, his pride of Pappy had been shoved aside by their differences.

But the more he toiled, down where the sun never shines, the more his mind was illuminated. And he was more and more convinced that he and Pappy needed to talk. It was just not fit for father and son to always be at odds. They need to plumb their differences. And to reconcile . . .

CHAPTER 9

*M*uch like W.W. Brown, Fleet Walker was always eyeing, or sniffing out, future prospects. As Anna of Cadiz called it, these young fellows she knew were, indeed, "prowling lions." Fleet considered a law practice and being a writer or being an inventor or being a businessman—even being a baseball player for steady money.

"Lord knows that as your school ball playing ends this season, this baby and I shall delight in you spendin' more time with us." Bella had Cleodolinda lying with her on a couch suckling her teat. "We shall be proud of having a father and husband as an attorney—yes, indeed!"

Fleet nodded, offering an uncertain smile. The Wolverine 1883 season was half over. His catcher's hands, these battered and reddened sinews gotten strained now across finger bones that had suffered a dozen or so little fractures, were aching already. He had to apply tincture of benzoin, which trainers called "friar's balsam," to toughen his hands. Nevertheless, he hoped to play ball just long enough for his catching and batting and throwing skills to attract him to important people. He figured this would give him a running start on whatever his profession was to be—lawyering or whatever.

Baseball suited him now. He said he was a better catcher than any other player in baseball, amateur or professional. But, skillful as their black players are, the colored teams which are barnstorming across the country just don't serve his purpose. They're not respected by whites, and they don't make much money. Big league players and teams are respected and pay big money, but doors are shut to players of his race. "I'm surely gonna take good care of you and 'Linda,' for certain." He bent over to kiss both his wife and daughter. His thoughts were on what else he would do.

Fleet wondered what he could offer the world. He retraced his college studies: Latin, Greek, German, French, logic, mathematics, civil engineering, chemistry, botany, astronomy, zoology, philosophy, and rhetoric. At this same moment, unbeknownst to him, baseball was calling his name.

William Voltz was well-known as the sports editor for the *Cleveland Plain Dealer* when some businessmen from Toledo, a city a little more than 100 miles west of Cleveland, met with him. In a railway terminal's fine dining salon, one chirped, "Bill, our city is baseball territory, an' we're gonna make Toledo sparkle on the Midwestern map. On paper we put together a new team, this a jin-oo-wine professional team." He shoved a packet of these papers into Voltz's hands. "You thuh best baseball mind we know, so we need your leadership fer the team . . ."

Over an early dinner and liquor, Bill Voltz took the job of assembling the Toledo Blue Stockings in the Northwestern League. "But there's a proviso," Bill insisted. "I want Harley Burket, that curveball pitcher who's been playin' with the New Castle 'Nocks'." This was approved. "And there's another proviso. Burket played with a colored boy name of Walker both at Oberlin College and the 'Nocks'—"

"You mean that colored catcher, that mulatto feller folks been talkin' 'bout?" one businessman asked with a look of disgust.

"Yeah, Moses Fleetwood Walker. I got tuh have him, too. Burket tol' me that's a helluva ballplayer—he kin catch a bullet on a windy day! Smart feller. Got a good character." The men argued about a black on the same field with whites. A dangerous trial. "Well, if I'm buildin' a first-rate team, I'm doing it with Walker!" Finally the men agreed and put the onus on Voltz. "I'll get contracts drawn up," Bill said.

Fleet's jaw dropped. On a late spring day in Ann Arbor this man, Mr. Voltz, was offering him a job with a new Toledo professional baseball team—not a semi-pro troupe like the 'Nocks,' but higher quality. He knew of Bud Fowler, George Stovey, and several other colored chaps who hustled around to play for white teams that were a step below the big leagues. Toledo was now in the Northwestern League.

Bill Voltz was persuasive. "Day before yesterday I signed Harley Burket to a contract. He's been wantin' you an' him ta form a battery agin', for bein' the best pitcher-catcher duo in this here league." Fleet liked this thought—Walker and Burket once more. "Pay's good, too," Voltz added. "And Toledo's just fifty-some miles from your college here at Ann Arbor." He considered asking Bella, but signed anyhow.

Bella wasn't pleased. "You're so . . . uh . . . impetuous . . . so headstrong!"

46

"I'm a baseball player, Bella. 'Tis a God-given gift, meant to be used profitably—or it will be taken from me. Papa Moses once made me read The Parable of the Talents. Gospel of Matthew. You know, I can make some big money in baseball."

But Bella was equally astute. "I've, too, studied that parable. Whilst you are spouting Scriptures, husband, would you explain what it means where Proverbs, I think Proverbs 15, says, 'A *greedy* man brings trouble to his family'?" Fleet could not answer this.

With hands roughened by baseball, he gently swayed baby Cleodolinda right to left, left to right. Their baby's eyes followed her father's and she bubbled joyfully. Bella and Fleet inwardly agreed that his catcher's skill, almost as flawless as a bobcat's swift pounce on a wild rabbit, was a gift from God. And Fleet inwardly understood that forsaking his family for the chase of money could cause Bella tribulation. Demons were always trying to corrupt this gift. He'd wrestled with these devils for five years, since baseball enticed him to turn away from Rev. Dr. Moses Walker at Oberlin, and enticed Weldy to follow his lead.

Weldy welcomed Fleet's intentions. In fact, Weldy wondered if Mr. Voltz would sign him, too.

Three days later, on May 5 in Toledo, Fleet pulled on a gray flannel uniform and high, blue stockings. He felt proud. He didn't expect any other colored players to be selected, but thought of Weldy joining him since his brother was like his shadow. He helped Harley and a couple other pitchers warm up, while the team from Bay City, Michigan, came romping into League Park. Though he had a pair of lambskin gloves (the glove finger ends were cut off to allow his hands their needed freedom) with palm padding, he decided not to use these. Well, all baseball players loathed wearing gloves—gloves weren't "manly." Attracting particular attention as the team's only Negro, he sure wasn't about to be called a "sissy." He, Moses Fleetwood Walker, was ever *machismo*, tougher than most men. But he had sense enough to wear a catcher's mask, a wire cage modified from a fencing mask. If professional teams didn't know his toughness already, they soon would learn.

Other than Harley, his white teammates seemed to be ignoring him. "Don'tcha fret 'bout it," Harley said. "They'll warm up t'ya once they watch you carry this squad on yer brown back." Charlie Morton, the team manager, whispered the same thing. This was nothing new, of course, because he'd faced it before—but Toledo was professional!

On this sunny Saturday afternoon, Fleet glanced at the grandstand. A swelling noise began to jar his ears. The screaming and stomping was like a circus crowd. He heard a man shout, "Over there . . . over there's Walker, the colored boy!!!" Fleet's nerves felt on fire. He'd never played before a crowd like this. This was how it was for professionals?

For a swift minute Fleet imagined something. Two thousand years back. A Roman amphitheater. He, a black gladiator, emerging from slavery. Most gladiators had a thick piece of armor and were called "light shields." A few others had thin armor, or were fighting naked—these were the proud ones—called "heavy shields." Today he, with only a wire mask as armor, was a "heavy shield . . ." He had signed up for this extravaganza! His bladder and bowels were loosening, so he tightened up.

When the phrase "Play ball!" was trumpeted, he crouched ten feet behind home plate. Rules were that pitchers delivered their torrid throws from just fifty feet away. Therefore, catchers took a distance back of the batter's box to better keep those balls from mangling their hands—except when a runner was on base. Soon as this game began and the pitcher started his hurling, Fleet stopped worrying. No time for musing now, only the hurry to give signals to the pitcher and catch the damn ball! He had been doing this for years, but now at League Park this game was pure professional! Fleet settled in and tried not to shame himself.

The Toledo Blue Stockings were not hindered by this "colored boy." Fleet had eight putouts, committed only one throwing error, and had only one ball escape his catch. And at bat he hit a double and scored a run. After this opening game, Manager Charlie Morton grinned and slapped Harley Burket's shoulder while gushing, "You hit the nail on the head. Walker's some kind of wizard!" Two games afterward a foul ball tore into Fleet's face, twisted his wire mask, and put a knot over his right eye. He stumbled and fell, but scrambled back up and refused to leave the catcher's box.

His Bella, though admiring her husband, was concerned. "I guess, Fleetwood, these professional players might be glad to hurt you—see you ruin your body." Bella scrunched her lips, closed her eyes, nodded her head. "I expect not seein' you for days at a time, but when you do come home to us, I hate to see you staggering in half-crippled."

He sighed. "Bella, this is prime baseball! Once in a while, all players get nicked—particularly catchers. I don't b'lieve they're tryin' to get me injured . . . necessarily."

Fleet was correct about a catcher's risk, more correct than he let on to Bella. He knew that one of a catcher's claims to greatness was his ability to handle fastballs barehanded and in pain with hands swollen. In fact, the swelling actually served as a cushion! A couple of weeks later one madly whistling, crookedly traveling ball busted his thumb. No way he could properly catch or play a game. But he pulled on his fingerless lambskin gloves and tried. Besides proving his toughness, Fleet knew he wouldn't be paid for any games he missed. The Toledo team was so limited by their catcher's disability they lost three games in a row. Still, with Fleet Walker catching sixty games and batting .251, his own Blue Stockings won the Northwestern League Championship. For a moment he was the team's top lion, its bravest warrior, and he was feeling high.

This moment didn't last long. In Chicago there was a baseball fellow of some notoriety. Adrian Anson, a large man, played first base and also managed the major league Chicago White Stockings. This team and others of the National League arranged to play exhibition games against minor league teams, such as Toledo. "Cap" Anson said, about a scheduled game with Toledo, that his Chicago team would not play ball with "no damned nigger!" Word of this reached Charlie Morton.

The two men angrily approached each other an hour before game time. A crowd was filling the stands, and baseball fever was high. This game between the minor league champion Toledos and the major league Chicago White Stockings had raised much excitement. Morton held his ground, reminding Anson that, without Walker playing, the game would be forfeit and Chicago would lose their guaranteed share of some heavy gate receipts. Finally, "Cap" Anson said his boys would take the field.

What Anson didn't know was that Morton had planned to rest Fleet for this game, on account of his badly bruised hands. But in response to Anson's ugliness and his raising the issue, Charlie Morton had his catcher play right field.

Fleet, in this event as in most others, half-buried his inner thoughts. When sunshine honeycombed the ballpark, his eyes checked for any seductive shadows. When zephyrs swept about, littering the field with Three King cigaret or Tutti-Frutti chewing gum wrappers, he calculated the effect of those breezes on a ball traveling through the air. Whistles, screams, and fans knocking on wooden bleacher seats were his afternoon concertos. But it was baseball in Kentucky's Louisville and Virginia's Richmond, where naked racism came puking out like searing lava, that caused his half-buried thoughts to rise—even in the middle of a game.

As he moved among Caucasians, his near-pale skin and wavy hair often gave him a *pass* that darker-complexioned Negroes could only envy.

Of course, his education and manner of speaking also helped his passage. Yet he was still colored, still a Negro—sometimes this meant being looked upon as a *nigger*. It seemed he was hearing the epithet, as a professional athlete, now every time he pulled on his blue stockings and gray flannel uniform. Maybe it was just that a fire in his soul was tuning his ears more. He seemed to be overhearing *nigger* when white players talked loose among themselves. None dared to use this word to his face. There was a burning in his eyes they could see and feel. While some fellows were as muscular and strong as him, only few possessed his catlike quickness—the tightly coiled, steel-spring promise of a raging lion. Even more than his physical prowess, it was his mental fierceness they feared. Their senses told them that this man's mind was even more dangerous than his body! Bigots stayed out of his face.

So the team paraded its Northwestern League Championship in the autumn of 1883. Fleet and Bella were invited to fancy dinners and events in some towns where the Toledo Blue Stockings played. And he had the chance to visit Oberlin, where Ednah Jane was finishing college. Two or three times Ednah even came to Toledo, on the "q-t."

Bella was beginning to accept the fruits professional baseball and her husband's celebrity were yielding. Her health, she knew, was a little doubtful, however. The next year, Fleet's career soared. Based upon the Blue Stockings' success in '83, Toledo felt that the team was "too good" for its minor league. The nation's highest baseball echelon was the National League. By spring of '84, however, some wealthy men had put together the "American Association" as a rival to the National League. Toledo purchased a franchise in this new organization.

He began this season, with the sun dappling and forsythia blooming yellow in Toledo, jolted by two big pieces of news: Bella was "with child" again, and he, Moses Fleetwood Walker, was the first of his race to play in baseball's major leagues! He was stepping high, and he'd need every bit of his $2,000 salary now that his family was growing.

Although Bella worried about his not being graduated from Oberlin College or University of Michigan, she had to admit that the money was good for his half year of work. Ordinary laborers were only being paid around ten dollars a week. Too, she was proud of her husband's gaining fame. Her pregnancy was going okay, yet her body felt strange.

Bella remembered that almost ever since she started having her monthly "curse" at age thirteen, there were crazy episodes. Once in a while during a year she flowed so great it scared her. Then there was the baby who was only a ghost. Then she had Cleodolinda. Then more crazy bleeding. Now that her doctor confirmed her pregnancy, the bleeding mostly had ceased—yet she felt a queerness down below. The doctor said these queer feelings were not unnatural. He seemed more concerned about her deep struggle with Fleetwood's baseball absences.

Fleet was not pleased that Harley Burket was cut from the team, due to not being "good enuf" for the big leagues. In fact, only several men were carried over to '84. However, after the first few games, Manager Charlie Morton brought Weldy on board to play outfield, giving Fleet someone with whom to share his racial predicament.

From Brooklyn, New York, across and as far south as St. Louis, Missouri, the team battled American Association ball clubs. They also engaged some National League teams in exhibitions. Almost everywhere crowds whistled, stomped, then fell into silence, then clapped at this tan Adonis. They marveled at how this Walker snatched blurred balls out of the air, how he rifled balls to fellows fielding bases, how princely he swung his sometimes explosive bat. Surging alongside the field and clamoring in the grandstand, there was one thing they could not see. They couldn't see the awful swelling of his hands, the splotchy purple bruises or the bloody mess of his palms (especially the left palm). They weren't close enough to tell how his thumbs and fingers were being busted crooked. And, of course, the damage to his elbows or shoulder went unseen.

They just witnessed Fleet's poise, speed, power, and graceful play, which was more thrilling than of most Caucasian players. But Fleet was also having unseen troubles, making his efforts more taxing than they should be. There was the racism, as well as his family vexations.

One early August day 'tween games, with the summer sky appearing like shiny saffron, he'd jokingly called Bella a "prude." They were in a green glade, unpacking a wicker basket for a picnic. He thought Bella most attractive with her puffed-out belly, her skin buttery and her coal-black hair glinting in the sun. When he'd tried to draw her closer for a kiss, she leaned away—a motion that reminded him of Ednah Jane's sometimes moody ways. "Oh, now you consider me prudish? You see all the people around us?"

"But we're married, darlin'." He chuckled. "Ain't it proper fer a man to buss his wife out amongst people, and if you don't think so—ain't that being prudish?" Bella answered with the look of both a grin and a scowl in the same instant, which seemed strange to him.

"I don't know. Why not ask the ladies over there who keep looking our way?"

"Those ol' biddies?" He reached for little Cleodolinda, who was scampering toward the picnicking women. "What can they say?" He chuckled again.

"Well, they could wonder if this be the same *gentleman* who kissed another gal near-bouts, on the sly." With this, Bella snickered.

Her snicker suddenly tore his funning mood to shreds. Ednah Jane skidded across his mind. "Meanin' what? What're you saying, girl?"

One thing led to another. Feeling rancor, they finally gathered up the picnic array, then strolled Cleodolinda to the small carriage Fleet had rented. He spoke only to the horse he was driving. This represented just one of the thorns piercing his mind—his trouble with pregnant Bella.

Bella regretted what had happened. She wasn't sure why she had soured that picnic afternoon. What was wrong with her? She only understood that she was feeling uneasy, uncertain about the coming baby— about everything.

As Fleet, wearing his blue shirt, white trousers, and blue stockings, trotted into the diamond, a couple fellows welcomed him back. During the soured picnic day, he had been off the team. The week before, he had broken a rib—an injury he hid from Bella, figuring she already was fretting too much. The agony was still on him, so Manager Charlie Morton had him play outfield, but his fielding and throwing was only so-so.

Days later a messenger on horseback arrived at League Park, breaking his gallop and shouting Fleet's name. "Moses F. Walker, yer wife's delivering a child!" Fleet didn't have time to change out of his uniform. He found Bella lying on bed in a peculiar position. A woman, who happened to be the messenger's wife, was comforting Bella. He jerked his head 'round. Bella's cousin was wrapping a baby in clean cotton towels. He turned back to Bella. "That's yer son over there." The messenger's wife pointed with elation. Then he heard Bella's tiny voice: "We are blest, Thomas is fine . . . I'm alright." The baby was squealing. Fleet breathed with relief. "Thomas Fleetwood Walker," Bella's cousin announced. "He's a most big 'un—must weigh eight or nine pounds, at least!" He stepped toward his new son, and the baby emitted a cry. "I b'lieve he sees this tall figure dressed up in a baseball suit an' has got scared." The cousin chuckled.

Soon as he got sure baby Thomas was square into life and that Bella was comfortably situated, Fleet returned to the Blue Stockings. He told Charlie Morton he was ready to catch again. He couldn't let on that his ribs were still not healed. Hands sore, he played two games against the Columbus, then was off to Kentucky to tangle with the Louisville club.

Down in "Cain'tuck" against the Louisville Colonels, and down in Missouri against the St. Louis Browns, and down against the Richmond Virginias, all the hissing and "nigger" shouts began to pique Fleet more than ever. His play got fierce. His angry throwing pained his ribs. His furious batting and running taxed his body. Though he'd begun using fingerless gloves, his frenzied catching almost crippled his hands.

Fleet tried hard to disguise the distress in his body and mind. For his few friendly teammates, he played such tunes as "Grandfather's Clock" and "My Darling Clementine" on the piano when fellows relaxed on the road. Even with sore hands, and although only an amateur, Fleet's piano-playing could charm folks.

This all came to a close in October. The Toledo Blue Stockings didn't have a particularly successful major league season. They won forty-six games, lost fifty-eight, and finished with a .442 winning percentage. So the Blue Stockings slipped back down to the Minor International League—and among the team members let go that October of 1884 was Moses Fleetwood Walker. His battery partner, pitcher Tony Mullane, for whom Fleet regularly caught, later confessed this: "He was the best catcher I ever worked with, but I disliked a Negro and whenever I had to pitch to him I used any pitch I wanted without looking at his signals."

Bella welcomed him home. "Husband," she blurted out, "I sure feel so blest having you here now in this cold season tending to Cleodolinda an' Thomas—an' me!" She didn't mention that he was without wages from baseball and he'd not qualified for a law career. While it was a good feeling to have Bella and the babies beside him now, he also was feeling stymied—at odds with himself. He went out and got a job as clerk for the Toledo Post Office. Time would come when this innocent job decision would lead to the call of Satan.

CHAPTER 10

*H*ere a few miles from Cadiz, it was the year of our Lord 1888 already. W.W. had a two-hundred-acre farm he was managing. The white owner let him employ a colored fellow and a white boy to do most of the grub work, while W.W. took care of all the farming details. Mrs. Shuster trusted and liked him, though Reverend Shuster, a Methodist circuit rider, kept an eye cocked on him. Pappy George was suspicious when Willie walked away from coal mining, figuring his "dreamer" son, roaming around on horseback, a pistol in the tack, might yet get into some kind of trouble.

W.W. and his Pappy had halfway reconciled, at least when he worked steady down in the mine. He was learning more about Pappy's life before setting foot in Ohio just before the war. Drug it out of Pappy.

"Mine Number Five be buildin' a 'stension," Pappy had told him yesterday.

"You say, sir? Well, Pappy, they be needin' fixins, I s'pect. Like timber posts."

"Fer sure, Willie, an' bringin' up new good loblolly costs 'em aplenty."

For several years now W.W. had dreamed of furnishing timber posts someday. When working in mines himself he'd seen props hauled in—close to the seams, for framing the chambers. The timber was yellow wood from southern pine. Pappy told of these fast-growing, tall trees that rose in Maryland's low wetlands, which folks called "loblolly" areas. These loblolly timbers were sturdy and desirable, but hauling them north was expensive for mine owners. And northern timbers, fit for gangway use, were scarcer than hen's teeth. Now, this day, W.W. trotted Tom, his big roan, to Mine Number Five. As farm manager he could roam about Cadiz.

Machinations of his mind came easier on horseback. While he was scheming, Tom carefully made his way upstream and overland, bearing him to where Mine Number Five sat wide in rocky country. He halted Tom at the Superintendent's office and went looking for Deacon. Deacon did paperwork for the boss. During run-ins with mine management, when he was leading the miners protesting work conditions, Deacon had kept him from being fired. In a private moment Deacon had once told him that his Pappy seemed much like Deacon's own father, who'd worked a mine in a country named Wales, over in Britain. He felt he could now talk to this Welshman who had no ax to grind with him. Deacon was shuffling papers and chewing on a cigar butt in a back room of the cabin. "Well, I'll be," Deacon said, startled. "Young Tod Brown—come back here with us?"

"Naw, Mr. Deacon." W.W. grinned. "Just to ask a question."

"Well, sit yerself down, then. Pull up that'ar chair."

They trusted each other. Deacon assured him that an extension was planned. Number Five was doing real well. And, yes, they'd be needing timber posts. Local lumber, the kind that wouldn't rot, would certainly be prized, but there wasn't any such around. "Wish there were. You could earn a good wage haulin' Ohio timber for some local contactor. As it is, we'll be shippin' in southern pine, 'course, at a fancy price."

After chatting awhile with Deacon, he rode over to the slope where Anna was. Not just to catch up on news from all the letters Anna exchanged—including the goings-on of Fleetwood Walker—but, mainly, to talk timber. Years ago Anna's father was the butler for a big landholder who died and left him title to a grove atop the hillside slope where Anna lived. Anna's pappy died and the grove still sat idle.

He figured Anna would be home this day. She occasionally went to social or church affairs in Cadiz or Steubenville, but when she did most folk knew of these in advance. Tom trotted his master knowingly and happily 'round the slope to where the jolly woman often came out and greeted him with peppermint bits. Anna heard the hoofbeats, looked out an open window, and fetched a handful of peppermint nuggets. Anna, short of stature and shapely plump, had a face as beckoning as a bowl of new butter, framed by curly dark hair. W.W. slid off Tom's back as she scampered outside. Tom's big head turned her way. "Howdy, Willie. Got peppermints here for Tom . . ."

"Hallelujah. Now what sweets you been savin' fer me, gal?"

"Aw-w-w, you're as much a rascal as ever. That why you're here? Tuh beg my sweets?" She gave him a naughty grin, then pushed the peppermint to Tom's mouth on her flatly opened hand.

"Just lookin' to talk with you. I be behavin' m'self today."

"Well, that's rare." They strode inside her little house, chuckling.

Anna kept a nice, neat house, even with its big-built Caledonian wood-burning stove with an oven large enough for the bake stuffs she sold, and the back room where she laundered clothes for a fee. W.W. could tell from fifty yards away when Anna was at work in her house. The good aroma! She baked cakes, pies, or cookies for sale while also doing her loads of wash. Her two wood tubs had a fastened whisk, almost like a big egg-beater, so she cranked this and didn't have to bend or work so hard. Today she was not baking or washing, just ironing. She could sit and chat as the iron base was heating, before attaching the handle and smoothly, swiftly pressing garments. He leaned over, bussed her cheek. "What seriousness be on your mind, Willie?"

He pulled over a straight-backed chair and sat facing her, his straw hat on the floor. "That patch of woodland above this here slope . . . is it still your'n?"

"Yessireebob, my name's now on the plat deed. Why? What you schemin' t'day, Willie?" She rested the iron base back on the heat.

"Mine Number Five is in need of timber, and I'm thinking on sup-plying some timber for framing the chambers." Every Cadiz woman knew about chambers where miners toiled deep beneath the ground. "Oak, swamp white oak, would make decent timber, but I—"

"But you own no such timber."

W.W. grinned. Anna's thoughts could strike like lightning, he was well aware. "No, but you do, sugar." Her patch was a woody knoll up where the ground dipped, catching water from a small hillside stream. "Maybe I can buy a bunch of oaks from you, must be at least a half hun-dred—or more." While roaming he'd once counted fifty-four tall trees.

"Maybe, 'cept those oaks, in rainy weather, hold water that otherwise be flooding this slope."

"I'd be most considerate of this, removing only them what can be spared. Right now there's an overabundance. Don't you think?"

He seemed so humble and thoughtful. Though her face didn't change, Anna was grinning inside. She had seen Willie, a few years her senior, in many circumstances since she was a tot. And she knew him sev-eral ways. He could be mean, savage as a beast; he also could be charming. This day he was the considerate Willie, or "W.W.," which he preferred to be called, or "Tod," which his pals liked to use. But to her he'd always be "Willie." She was quiet for a moment, letting his patience get tested. She knew how fidgety he could be. A pause would settle him and cause him to be more sensible.

"I suppose, Willie, t'wouldn't hurt to thin out that oak stand. Fact, it could help the health of those oaks remainin'. Now, what's it worth to you?" Willie, she knew, would take the trees for nothing if she let him.

But he was ready. "Ah, I figure to pay some in produce, an' the rest in commission. We kin work out a percentage. Well, I be takin' this as business, you know." He winked at her.

"For certain I'm takin' this as business—nothin' else!" Then Anna snickered as she picked up the heated iron. "Iffen you plan any trickery, better keep in mind I'm quite skilled with this here red-hot sad iron." This iron, called "sad" because it was heavy, could be a feared weapon.

Some kind of heat always traveled between them anyway—in waves that crackled. In a way they were two of a kind. He was drawn to her spunk and wit and business sense. She was attracted to his dreams and ambition and gumption. Anna resumed ironing on the padded wooden board balanced on a table and chair back. They exchanged glances.

Shafts of late summer sunshine dazzled through a window, blanching parts of her furniture. He noticed swift, subtle changes in the light, just as he'd detect shades of the morning sky. The brightness was upon half her face and form, bringing out her beauty. Made him think of flowers hereabout such as the Carolina rose. She also saw him sitting half into the light. His broad shoulders, rugged hands crossed over his knee, a good man's strong, hard form. Their moods were changing subtly, too—in a natural, rousing way.

"Need a tea or coffee?" Anna asked, she and he realizing their pickle.

"No, Tom an' I best be goin' back to the farm. Gotta turn in produce receipts to Reverend Shuster's missus 'fore the reverend gets home."

As Tom trotted him along the slope, W.W. spotted a familiar horse and wagon moving slowly past him across the road. "Gol'durn it!" The driver was Joe, the husband of Becky's twin sister. He waved at his brother-in-law and kept going. This was the second or third time he'd encountered Joe when leaving Anna's. He prodded Tom into a gallop, leaving puffs of dust between himself and Joe.

Moments after reaching the farm, he tendered produce receipts to Reverend Shuster's wife. He'd hoped to get there before the sun started to settle, but he was late. Sitting at her husband's desk, Emma Shuster was going over the receipts. One fell to the floor and skittered under the desk, so W.W. got down on one knee to fetch it. That instant the door he'd left ajar creaked open. "What there!" Reverend Shuster's bass voice boomed. Emma had lifted her skirt hem and spread her legs to allow W.W. the room to reach the paper that was beyond his grasp. Emma swung her head and W.W. quickly struggled to his feet. "This be what I feared!" Shuster barked.

"No . . . No, husband!" Emma smoothed out her dress. "Willie was just reclaiming a slip I dropped to the floor."

"What slip? Don't see any paper in his hand!"

W.W. shook his head. "It be still under the desk—couldn't reach it."

Reverend Shuster wheeled 'round, stomped into another room, and slammed the door behind him. "I need t'have a word with the Rev—" W.W. said.

"Just leave, for now, Willie!" Emma spouted excitedly, her voice full of tremble and her hands shaking. The stories rushed through her head and veins like wildfire. Stories of heinous crimes, horrors inflicted on colored men and white women like she because of hateful accusations. Her sister, Mildred, from Tennessee, had mailed her newspaper articles from the Memphis Ledger. These told of an esteemed physician in '86 who tracked down his own wife who'd run off with her colored carriage driver, but couldn't find the Negro. His wife's shameful peccadillo, and the vanished coachman, so inflamed the town that the doctor, his wife, and their children had to leave Memphis for an unknown destination. This and similar tales had caused Reverend Shuster to exclaim that "such filthy acts by creatures of Satan need be avenged at the point of a gun." And, for some reason, he kept a loaded pistol in the house.

"Just leave us," she mumbled to W.W. "I'll straighten things out 'fore tomorrow. But, for now, the Reverend's feelin' wrathy—so you just go along home."

Without being directed by W.W., Tom sauntered slowly toward home. He felt his master's moods, whether joyful or fretful or angry or sad, by the way W.W. sat him and held the reins. W.W. was brooding. What happened at the farmhouse was cuckoo, yet such craziness could get him jailed—or somebody killed. He believed Shuster had, besides a double-barreled shotgun, a pistol. W.W.'s own tack bag carried his pistol. This minute he thought of a letter Anna had lately received from Fleetwood Walker's Oberlin kin. According to Anna today, the letter enclosed an article from one of Lorain County's papers—something about an Elyria colored man facing prison on account of a white woman accusing him of rape. The woman's husband, a minister, was away on a trip when she later claimed she was assaulted. But the colored man, whose reputation in Elyria was sound, said loudly that the woman had enticed him into their criminal conduct.

W.W. took a chaw of tobacco. The ruminating of his mouth, chewing and spitting, made the ruminating of his mind easier. Reverend Shuster spent his days away ministering to souls, that was why he needed Willie to manage his farm. On the one hand the preacher was fair and courteous. On the other hand, he didn't trust much. He had enough trust to have him, W.W., manage the farm and the hands—likely because he hadn't found any white fellow sharp enough. But he didn't trust him with Missus Emma, and he didn't trust his own wife. "Missus Emma is a fine-lookin' woman!" he uttered out loud. But she, probably nearing thirty years of age, seemed to be barren, not havin' any children yet. Her being lonely during the day might be partly why the reverend had little trust in her. He could be a man who didn't even trust himself down deep—or even trust the God he preached about . . .

Approaching a fork in the road, W.W. jolted out of his ruminations. Before shifting his body and brushing Tom's neck with the rein, he saw Tom had already chosen the longer road to home. Somehow Tom knew his master was still daydreaming and in no hurry. "Good boy, Tom!" he uttered. His gelding was real smart, and W.W. had trained him well.

Reverend Shuster's suspicious nature reminded him of Pappy's wariness, albeit not the same. Seemed to him that white men, even preachers, were always suspicious of any goings-on between their women and colored men. They'd created the idea of lusty black savages, and it was this very idea that was haunting them now. It was mostly why so many Negroes were being hung from trees or lynched in other ways. Pappy's wariness, though, was of the white man's own brutal or serpent-sly actions. And Pappy was fearful that his sons, particularly his Willie, would do something brash to end up being a victim of the white man's wickedness—and his wrath.

The long route was hilly here and there. As Tom approached a rise, W.W. leaned forward in the saddle to shift his weight off Tom's hindquarters to make his ascent easier. The sky was deepening into early evening, and once again, he noticed how subtle the light of the heavens changed. Under a bright-silver glow, he could shut his eyes, open them right away, and see a deep silver glimmer changing quicker than a blink.

His thoughts already had flitted to timbering. This hour his scheme to harvest Anna's swamp white oak trees was more pressing. Who knew what fix he'd be in tomorrow morning? Reverend Shuster might still be in a wrath, and decide to sack him . . . Well, for two years the minister had

had a first-rate manager, so he'd be foolish to let him go over a damned jealous notion. And the reverend shouldn't be troubling his missus, either. She was a clean wife—never enticing him in any way. Anyhow, the time for hitching himself to his own business was *now*. He had a wife and little ones to provide for. Of their five sons now, Willie was eight, Charlie was five, Clarence was three, Ottie was two, and Clinton had just been born in July. The boys would become strong and handy workers for him in a few years, but right now they had to be fed and clothed and schooled. He needed more money. His family also needed a bigger house.

Tom, rounding a bend to where the Brown house stood on a flat belly of bushy land, began picking up his gait. The horse was eager for some feed and water and rest in his own paddock. Into the opening, just past several apple trees, W.W. saw little Charlie and Clarence romping about in the front yard. The boys ran to greet their pappy and Tom. After hugging them and taking care of Tom, he strode to the house. "Uncle Joe was here today!" Charlie called out, as if it was his manly duty to report whoever had visited. Charlie's pappy shook his head, then frowned.

Becky was at the kitchen woodstove, humming. "Afternoon, darlin'—"

"Evening!" Becky interrupted to reply, then resumed her humming. It was not a good sign. Furthermore, her deep melodic voice was singing "Do, Lord, Remember Me." He knew this: Colored folks, especially the God-fearing ones like his Becky, in their private moments chose spirituals to sing or hum that fit their mood. He knew the words to what she was sounding: "When I'm in trouble, Lord, remember me . . ." Her mood was between discontent and sorrow, he figured. She was greasing warm bread, smearing the loaves with lard after pulling them from the oven. Smelled good. All Becky's cooking was delicious both to the nostrils and the tongue. "Woman, I'm mighty hungry for a chunk of that warm bread," he said smilingly.

Becky stopped humming. Her strong, stocky body stood rod-straight. Her face, with her jaw jutting, was doleful as gloomy evening. Her eyes were troubled. "Didn't Anna give you some?"

Obviously, Joe, Becky's brother-in-law, had placed him at Anna's today. "Naw, she ain't served me nothing." He looked into Becky's eyes boldly, because he was telling the truth. "I'll make plain why I stopped at Anna's today and what we hashed over." Becky wiped her hands, sliced off a hunk of bread, which she handed to him. She sat down, placed an elbow on the table, rested her cheek in her palm, and uttered a long sigh. "Aye"—her voice sounded tired—"tell it to me."

As he talked, their eight-year-old Willie, trained well by Becky, guided his three younger brothers to the big porcelain basin with hot water he'd fixed for them to wash up for supper. Becky wasn't sure whether she was so tired from all her worries and consternation and pique, or just plain bodily tired from her day's labor. Her son Willie's deed, without being directed, made her feel better for this minute.

Her husband was talking about Mine Number Five and a need of timber, setting the stage for why he went seeing Anna today. Anna was not the only comely girl who claimed a friendship with him—just the most potent. By this, and other instigations, he kept her on the edge of a honed razor. The ideas he conjured up—most often castles in the air—turned her balance upside down. He was a good enough husband and a fairly good father, but he was likely riding his own trail. Her motherhood seemed to please him, yet he was often not home. And sometimes when he was home, he was not home. The boys seemed to be her full responsibility, not his. She felt overburdened. She felt unsettled about some of his goings-on, including his visits with Anna. And her body was still mending from birthing baby Clinton six weeks ago, so neither her body nor mind felt like carrying out all her wifely duties yet . . .

"Anna agreed for me to harvest plenty of her timber at a percentage—and this will allow me to get into a new business," he said. W.W. had hesitated to explain why a new business was so important today, but he decided to reveal what happened at the Shuster home. Best tell her now rather than later. "Then I rode to Shuster's farm to deliver receipts . . ."

Becky felt she could accept his visit with Anna. At least Anna was colored, not a white girl who could make matters even more tricky. She knew how to contend with another colored woman.

W.W. was continuing his account. "Finding me crouching there on the floor, Reverend Shuster burst into the door with some crazy notions about his missus and me . . ."

Becky's jaw dropped. Her eyes burgeoned, then closed. Words without sound sizzled through her mind: Lord ha' mercy . . . a white lady in the picture . . . now her husband—a preacher at that—with the jealous hell within him boiling his blood! Oh my Lord! Her heart, already as heavy as a smithy's anvil, was sinking fast. For some reason, she could not cry. Then, like the rebound of a seesaw, her soul sprang up. Was Willie being truthful about what took place ahead of Reverend Shuster's entrance? She knew her husband well enough; he was too smart to tell her a bald-faced lie—'specially concerning white folk. "Time to pray and eat!" she barked, seeing her

61

sons holding forth their just-washed hands. "Then I must busy my tired self tonight an' bake a fresh pie for someone hither."

W.W. sat stunned. Becky'd take a lot of time painstakingly making her pies. Was she even listening to his account? Why would she put herself through such baking, deep after supper? "Hither . . . for who, Becky?"

"For Reverend an' Missus Shuster." She would add a twist more nutmeg, she told herself. Maybe her pastry was not grander than Anna's, but some fancily sliced apples, a bit more nutmeg—and, oh, a few more chunks of butter beneath the top crust would make hers special.

This confused W.W., but he said nothing—just sat his family at the table, while Becky served them supper. After supper Becky turned the boys over to her husband so she could get busy in the kitchen. Soon an aroma of apples and spices filled the room. She searched and found her fanciest pie dish, made of heavy redware with a flowery design. She also took out an ordinary dish for the family. When pastry and filling were in place, and the pie was baking, Becky thrust her hand in the oven. She counted the seconds until she had to withdraw her hand—twelve seconds, enough heat for a pie every bit as good as Anna's! And fancy enough for the Shusters.

W.W. slept fitfully, all kinds of thoughts swamping his mind, not the least being his job, and a confrontation with Reverend Shuster by the first sunshine. Before dawn he was up hitching his horse cart to Tom. In case Shuster was still in a fit of rage, causing him to quit or be sacked, he'd need to collect his tools and work clothes stored in Shuster's main barn. Furthermore, he needed a flat surface on which to tote the large pie Becky had baked. He didn't know why Becky had done such a thing under these circumstances, but he'd promised to deliver what she baked.

He took his kerchief and wiped out the compartment beneath the bench seat of his two-wheeler. In it he gently placed the big pie, which was wrapped in waxed paper and tied into a small croker sack. Since even white preachers in their madness sometimes shot or lynched colored men, he snatched his Scofield .44 revolver from the saddlebag and shoved it also into the compartment. After all, Shuster might be aiming at him. His .44 would match whatever a crazy, vengeful husband might be leveling.

Riding the cart, he looked for wayside things he usually missed on horseback. The mud gullies were drier and the hills not as lustrous. Passing by cornfields he could see the ears were now silked, tasseled, heavy, and about ready for harvest. The many flocks of sheep grazing yonder hills would soon get fat as ewes fed on cornstalks after the gleaning. But even quicker than the changing tints of the morning sky, his mind was on Becky and the apple pie carried beneath his seat. Again he wondered why she'd spent precious time on a gift for the Shusters. She had no liking of white folks. She'd seen too clearly what the slavers had done to her kinfolk down below the Ohio, down in Virginny, and she trusted no paleface. Fact was, Becky cared only for Negro folk, being partial to those whose faces were as black as hers. She was most proud of her unmixed African blood. Being religious, she talked of her people as Black Hebrews marching to Canaan. Why should she be having him give what she'd baked to these white Shusters now? What might she have buried inside this pie in the redware dish? My Lord, could she have laced this pie he was toting with pizen?

Tom, who made this trip daily, felt the leather lines wielded by W.W., but did not need to be directed. The horse pulled the cart steadfastly, although for an instant W.W.'s hold on the lines jerked. No, Becky would not harm the Shusters. She was a Christian woman. Also, she knew better. And she knew that he, unlike her, saw opportunity in all folks he met—not color. He sought accessibility to all people.

A hundred yards from the farm, Tom began pulling the cart a little faster, as if he smelled fresh, clear water in the trough by a hitching post next to the Shusters' house. W.W. let his gelding jog, though he wasn't finished mulling over how he would meet Reverend Shuster. They neared the house. Shuster was standing out on the porch gulping from a coffee tankard. Seeing the horse and cart approaching, the preacher turned around and went into his house. On previous mornings the preacher would have waved a greeting.

Either Shuster or his wife had already filled the trough with cool well water. After letting Tom drink, W.W. pulled the croker sack from the cart. He fingered his Scofield, then decided to leave the gun where it was. Carefully he carried the croker to the Shusters' front door.

He was reading signs: the fact that Reverend Shuster didn't wave to him might be a bad tip, or maybe his attention was simply dulled because his mind was crowded; someone had filled the trough where Tom—not Shuster's own horse that used a stall-trough in the rear—was a good tip; and he didn't know what to make of Shuster leaving the front door half-open. Emma called, "Come right on in, W.W.!" The lilt in her voice was a good sign.

"Mornin', Missus. How be you?" When Emma declared she was in fine fettle this morning, and sounded as though she meant it, he felt halfway relieved. Though not smiling, she seemed settled—but where was the reverend?

"'Sakes alive!" she uttered excitedly. "What d'ya have in that croker bag you're carrying so gentle-like?"

He placed the sack on her table, then slid out the apple pie wrapped in wax paper. "My thoughtful wife felt like sharing her baking with y'all," he said, giving the sense that it was just one of Becky's good-natured gifts.

Emma's eyes widened as she carefully peeled back the waxed paper, examined the pie, and gushed, "Lovely, fancy . . . and how scrumptious it smells!" Traces of dark apple filling oozed out of the pie and got on her fingers. Embracing the heavy dish with both hands, she hurried toward a back room—yammering, "Ooo, Reverend, see what wonder W.W. brought us from his Becky!" W.W. stood uneasily, anxious to face Shuster. For two or three minutes he heard them mumbling.

Reverend Shuster came out, following Emma holding the pie. His head hung low, then he raised his face to meet W.W.'s eyes. Slowly he extended his right hand. "Well . . . uh . . . I've done asked the Lord for forgiveness. I'm asking you now to forgive me, too." His basso voice quavered. His eyes were weepy. W.W. grasped the preacher's hand. "I did give in to the Devil," Reverend Shuster moaned. "Satan reaches ever'body sometimes . . . an' he overtook me yestiddy . . . makin' me disrespect Mrs. Shuster . . . an' about to bear false witness toward you . . ."

"My husband searched and found the paper where it skedaddled," Emma butted in. She moved to take his hand, too, but hers was syrupy.

"Says in Deuteronomy—nineteen, I think—that a false accusation must be purged, so I'm ridding this evil before you and Emma right here. This dessert made an' sent by Missus Brown caps this moment off."

W.W. nodded in acceptance. A white man professing his guilt to a colored is rare, he was thinking. Shuster is honest about his sin—a good man! What would I have done without Becky's timely smarts?

They conversed for a half hour. Shuster was regretting that the coming winter would mean less need for farming services, but W.W.'s mind was on felling trees on Anna's patch, then taking timber to Mine Number Five.

CHAPTER 11

*I*n a little church on the road to Steubenville, Anna from the Cadiz slope sat smiling. This special service was remembering "Honest Abe's" birthday. On the program was printed Abraham Lincoln, God's Instrument. In Commemoration. February 1891. Anna and a few others smiled because this was also the seventy-fourth birthday of the colored leader, live Frederick Douglass, whom they celebrated in their hearts even more than the dead, white Lincoln. Anna also smiled proudly because she and Fleetwood were sitting together. She'd heard he was in Steubenville visiting his kinfolk and she'd figured he would be here. After the service, after he'd shaken hands with a gaggle of admirers, they had a few moments in the fellowship room to talk. He said, "Gal, me with Bella and our three children—the youngest, George, is four years now—might be moving back to Steubenville, if the Post Office Department allows me a transfer I've put in for." Anna knew Fleet's Pappy, Rev. Dr. Moses, had left his wife and was living now in Detroit. So in Steubenville there would no longer be any fussing between him and his Pappy. He asked about Willie Wesley. Anna told him Willie Brown had his own business now, a busy operation furnishing timber to a mine. "Willie's truly on the rise!"

Soon as she said this, Anna wished she hadn't. She feared she had just clanged an unwelcome bell. And how do you un-ring a bell once it's been rung? While Fleetwood was interrupted by an old couple who knew him as Steubenville's famous baseball player, Anna searched his face. His eyes and slower, uneasy motions told her that his spirits were not as keen as when he had been riding the sun as an athlete. She should've answered his question about Willie in a different manner. Not that Fleet and Willie were jealous of any success the other had. She knew they were much too sure of their own masteries. No, Fleetwood surely was wrestling now with some of his own disappointments. Anna's soul saw some trouble ahead of him, too.

Fleet had to catch a train. He gave Anna a farewell hug. "Bless you, an' watch yerself!" she called out to him.

On the night coach back to New York, he tried to read the book *Life and Times* by Frederick Douglass, which his mother had pushed into his hand as he left Steubenville. The coach's overhead oil lamps were not very bright, so he placed the book aside after a bit and studied the passenger car's ornate wood paneling. Drawing from his Oberlin College classes in mechanics and geometry, he admired the hand-carved wainscoting and painted geometric designs. Handsome decor! No wonder coach fare was so costly, he told himself. Seemed only like yesterday when the price of tickets or most other stuff did not matter. Well, he'd made big money playing ball. Those days were over now.

The coach lighting was not steady. Oil lamps did give an even glow when train wheels rolled on even rails, but their dimness changed to bright flares and then flits of dark when the track's path curved or when the track beds were not level. Fleet, in the low light, examined the colored lines and geometric designs and edges of the gold leaf. He liked precise designs. In fact, he looked for balance and accuracy in all things—even in the ways of people. He didn't like sloppiness of ideas, either, which caused some quarrels with his father. Although Moses Walker was a physician who made his diagnoses and dispensed medicines carefully, he was also a preacher, Fleet told himself, whose ideas were not always rational. *Faith*, Moses would argue with his son, was stronger than *reason*. Fleet couldn't accept this, particularly when his father argued that what seemed irrational could over the long run be most right. "After all," his father had said, "to those who founded this nation, slavery was perfectly reasonable. 'Twas faith in God that set us free." Fleet had not tried explaining to his father that it was for political reasons that Negroes were emancipated by federal law in '65— twenty-six years ago now—not because of religion. And he didn't fire back that Negroes still were not free!

Reverend-Doctor Moses would've just started lecturing him—and accusing the law studies at Michigan University of teaching him "Satan's logic." He hadn't wanted any more lectures from this preacher-doctor who had left his family and moved to Detroit, Michigan.

Well, maybe he was being too harsh with his father. In the smoky lamplight he could almost make out the shaky figure of the man. Or was it the figure of himself? At this moment it was he who was being irrational! Fleet began to analyze his own predicament. The truth was, the path he'd set for himself had itself gone crooked. Lack of logical progress in his life bothered him. What Anna had told him about Willie Wesley Brown's progress in business interested him. Willie now supplying timber posts to the mines? It was himself, not Willie, who had studied at Oberlin College and at Ann Arbor. It was himself, not Willie, who had become the best catcher, a top professional, in baseball! So, why was Fleet Walker clerking for the post office and drawing such a measly paycheck these days? He fished out his small flask, sipped brandy while trying to logically figure the answer.

Soon the brandy swept his mind to Anna. Why did she tell him to "watch himself"? Anna's injunction puzzled him. Anna was even more flighty than his father, but he knew that she was wise. Old folks 'round Cadiz claimed she had the "gift"—born with a caul, that veil over her face. They said the girl had the "mysteries." Townspeople seemed to always be wary of Anna, though she was liked by everyone. Was she warning him of something? He didn't cotton to superstition—or did he?

As the hackney horse trampled light snow on the taxi ride from the Syracuse train station, Fleet resolved to concentrate on the mechanics he'd studied at Oberlin. He had a flair for mechanics—maybe this was more his calling than lawyering. He decided to check on the status of his first invention, an improved artillery shell. Until now shells for the army and navy, using dynamite to propel the cartridge, had been failures. His invention was for an outer casing design that would prevent a fired shell from blowing apart before reaching its target. Lawyers, sponsors of the Syracuse Stars baseball team he last played for two years ago, were handling his patent application for two-thirds' interest in his clever invention. Even at one-third interest, he was hoping to earn a fortune.

He climbed out of the hack, stomped a little snow off his boots, and opened the door of his home on Green Street. It was early, cockcrow time with just shards of milky-orange light breaking through darkness, so Cleodolinda, Tom, and George were still in bed. Bella kissed him and drew back. "My Lord, you been drinking all night?"

Bella did not mind an occasional, social drink, but she objected to his taking shot after shot of liquor. She understood her husband's frame of mind—at times his fits of melancholy—that instigated his drinking. It was only a half-dozen years ago that he'd soared to the heights of fame in baseball. Newsprint frequently connected his name to greatness. Even when the racist fans or newsmen mocked him, they did it because he was a better player than most white players. Fleetwood Walker, then, was a celebrity! But the sport had whipped and racked his body. Some of his fingers were crooked, his bones and joints jangled by wrenching pain. His once keen skills had dulled. When he wasn't able to make enough games, his last team, the Syracuse Stars, had to let him go. His spirits had splintered. Although his job with the post office was steady, now he was forced to live lower on the hog. His drinking worried her.

On Thursday, the ninth of April, Fleet was still waiting for a decision on his request for postal reassignment to Steubenville. He continued doing railway postal clerking in Syracuse. After trying to find a man to whom he needed to deliver a postal message, and on his way home, he decided to stop for a beer or two—the saloon being only several blocks away from his Green Street house. He needed an hour or so still away from Bella and the children—to have camaraderie and to enjoy some hard spirits without Bella's disapproving glances and, maybe, to talk some baseball with fellows who appreciated his service to the game.

Less than a half-dozen were in the saloon, this being before evening quaffers trooped in. All the faces were white, but he did recognize Eli, to whose house he'd delivered packages, and Eli's wife, Eva. "Ho, 'tis Walker!" Eli looked up and called out in his drunken way. Eve patted Eli's hand and barked to the bartender, "Give him a drink on Eli's tab. This here gentleman is the best ballplayer Syracuse ever had." The other patrons gathered around, eager to hear stories from Fleet.

A stiff breeze was rising, and the sun had begun to set when Eli and Eva left the saloon with Fleet. Eva was trying to keep her husband from stumbling. "Should I walk your way?" Fleet asked. She looked into his face, wanting his company, but knew he should be going the opposite way. "Thank ye, Mr. Walker, good of ya. However, we'll go it alone." She said this, lurching toward him, and raised her head and kissed him on the cheek before steering Eli away.

Four white fellows were loitering and guffawing at the corner of Orange and Monroe. They saw a white woman holding a white man's arm while planting a kiss on a colored fellow's jaw. As Fleet strolled toward the corner, the four hurried toward him. "Hey, nigger!" one snarled. "Whatcha doin' in *our* neighborhood?" Fleet kept walking. The four were all ruffians and younger than Fleet. One, known as "Curly," crowded Fleet. Curly bellowed, "'Sides bein' stupid, nigger boy, you hard hearing too?"

"Back up, you bastard," Fleet growled. "Get away from me!" Curly rushed up against him.

In a mad twinkle, all of Fleet's frustrations and all the "nigger" ballpark shouts and all the busted fingers and broken ribs and teams letting him go because of his injuries and more than a thousand past insults—all of these, and now this Curly's threat, crashed down upon his soul. His white teammates, who had feared the violence of his mind even more than his quick fists some years ago, had feared correctly. The serpent struck!

Bella didn't see her husband that night. Not until the next morning after an excited police detective rode to 339 Green Street with the news and a dashed-off message from Fleet. And not until after two news reporters rapped on her door, one ready to give her a carriage ride to the police lockup.

But Patrick "Curly" Murray's wife, Kittie, the evening before had hastened to a cousin's home, where Curly had been carried by his gang, to attend to her husband. Kittie found Curly awake but in terrible pain, puking blood. A doctor was trying to staunch the bleeding from Curly's belly. He sent for another physician. Then a sheriff's deputy, a prosecutor, a priest - and another doctor arrived, who dosed Curly with morphine.

About the same time this night, Fleet opened his eyes from a restless sleep. His head was throbbing. Because of beer from the saloon? No, he remembered—he'd been knocked in the head outside on the street. In a room near this tiny jail pen he heard voices, then noticed several policemen buzzing. They were talking about him. In a moment in which he pieced jagged bits of memory together, Fleet realized why he was all crumpled in a stationhouse and not at home with his family. A thought leaped off a shelf in his aching brain—it was Anna's warning: "Watch yerself!" Was this day, this night, what she had pictured? He felt his trouser pockets. Of course he'd stopped carrying his revolver three years ago when fined for "threatening to shoot" a menacing man after a game in Toronto. Now his pocket knife must have been confiscated by the police! As he braced himself and sat up, Police Captain Quigley noticed and strode over. "What kind of chap was that I cut?" Fleet asked. Captain Quigley said that Curly Murray was a pretty good fellow. Fleet shook his head. "Well, he made a bad break when he came for me . . ."

"Uh-huh. But he could die tonight, an' you'd be facing a first-degree murder charge!" Quigly said this and strode away.

Fleet, writhing through a night of worry and woe, kept thinking of Anna. "Watch yerself!" she was pleading. Instead of wide and pretty, her face was ghostlike. Or like he imagined an *oracle's* face would be. He asked her to explain, but her answer continued to be, "Watch yerself!" He tried to erase Anna's image. He tried to be logical, rational. He tried to make sense of his predicament. He was between wakefulness and a dream. Then at sunrise a jailer notified him that "Curly died during the night."

Patrick "Curly" Murray was lying on a couch in his cousin's house at 614 East Adams Street. Doctors and the coroner could tell that a knife blade had plunged into his left abdomen, pentrating his entrails. He died about 3 a.m.

Fleet was jolted upright. The jailer handed him a lined sheet of paper and a pencil. Fleet thanked him, then began a hasty but long note to Bella. He begged for a police officer to deliver his message to Arabella.

Fleet, of course, had a strong legal sense. That morning he sent for a locally prominent white attorney, Harrison Hoyt, who arrived at the lockup with his assistant, M.Z. Haven, to defend this famous former ballplayer for Syracuse. Fleet told Hoyt of the days he spent learning lawyering from Addison C. Lewis and John McClave down in Steubenville, Ohio. Hoyt agreed to also contact A.C. Lewis for him.

Bella hurried into the police station with the change of clothes Fleet had requested in his message. Her lovely dark eyes more liquid than ever, Bella was nearly the image of a half-frightened beige doe. Led into a small room where her husband had a bit of temporary liberty, she slipped into his arms. "Oh Fleetwood . . . Fleetwood," Bella moaned. She knew of his deep, hidden rage—yet she also knew that he did not intentionally kill the fellow called "Curly". Fleet caressed her face and asked about the children. "Only Cleodolinda, with her sharp, nine-year-old mind," Bella answered faintly, "has any inkling that something's wrong. She's such an alert little lady . . ."

She could only stay with him in that little room, crowded with an old beat-up desk, mops, and pails, for ten minutes. Ten minutes much like a thunderstorm inside a brick and iron cubbyhole. Ten minutes realizing that some walls of their lives were now crumbling. The loud chatter outside this dim and drab room was nothing compared to the silent thunder crashing down upon their souls. Fleet, facing a charge of murder, would not be coming home. His job, the means of supporting his family, was in jeopardy. In fact, his own life was in peril. Bella's future as wife and mother was looking dark, too. She grasped his hand, and his face grew steely—as though firm against the gods, or maybe refusing to break in front of her. Bella dabbed at her own wet eyes. They set themselves for a terrible ordeal. They even prayed together.

"I got some smart lawyers," he whispered to Bella, "and most white folks in Syracuse know an' like me. Lord knows, I'll escape this thing."

"How long till you'll be coming home—a free man—Fleetwood?"

He caressed her forearm. "Maybe six weeks or so. I'll be staying in the penitentiary. They'll bring this charge before a Grand Jury, and if I'm indicted there'll be a trial." Bella began to whimper. "Honey, think your mother can come stay with you?" Bella nodded and clutched him as the jailer motioned that it was time for her to leave.

Cool springtime was approaching early summer when the trial began on June 1, 1891. Fleet was charged with second-degree murder, and Judge Kennedy officiated. Fleet was handsomely dressed, tall, slim, and composed. Bella, plump-faced, wide-eyed, and Spanish-looking (the *Syracuse Courier the* next day described her as "looking more like a dark brunette than a colored woman"), sat holding his hand. Among the other cast of characters were the prosecuting and defense attorneys and witnesses. The spectators, well-behaved and mostly Caucasian, seemed surprisingly sympathetic to the colored ex-ballplayer.

Within four hours a jury of twelve white men was selected. When Assistant District Attorney Shove opened the prosecution's case, he laid out the dead man's blood-soaked garments. For this one moment both Fleet and Bella wept quietly, then watched the prosecution's case unfold. The next morning Bella arrived at court with their second child, seven-year-old Thomas. The boy presented his prisoner father a wrapped bunch of wildflowers. As Fleet grasped Thomas with one arm and the flowers with the other, sounds of praise softly wafted among observers. It was a day for the defense: Fleet and Bella steeled themselves as they had done ever since Fleet had been jailed in April.

So often our dealings with people, whom we don't expect to meet again, turn out to be especially meaningful years afterward. This was what Fleet recognized as A.C. Lewis, his one-time mentor from Steubenville, came to masterfully advise his other defense attorneys. Attorney Hoyt shed some important light on Curly Murray, who was known to have a mean character and had served time at Auburn Prison. Regarding the prosecutor Shove, Hoyt announced, "I have heard that the good die young, and if that be so, the assistant district attorney has earned the longest life that I know of." Attorney Hoyt also called the witnesses for the prosecution "snakes, lizards, pickpockets, and burglars." And Hoyt, in his summation for the defense, criticized the display of Curly Murray's bloody clothes saying, "It was unworthy of the prosecution . . . when the only object in doing so was to steel the jury against all sympathy for the defendant." Hoyt eloquently touched the jurors like summer sunbeams.

A.C. Lewis made Bella a special onlooker in the courtroom. He'd put Fleet's family into seats—making Bella; her mother, who was in from Xenia, Ohio; and the children, Cleodolinda, Tom, and George, feel as if they were in a steam calliope, inside a carousel going 'round and 'round at a circus.

Bella clasped little George, who was five years old, while her thoughts gyrated from heaven to hell and chaotic, confounding places in between. Before her mother arrived, Bella felt as if she was losing her mind. So many problems suddenly being Mama and Papa! Her vigor was fading, too—something she hadn't told Fleet, even when he was still free. Then there was the awful *shame*. Until Fleet came along and there was that ghost of a baby, she'd never felt shame personally. She'd been reared in a proper family that avoided any disgrace. Even though she believed Fleet had acted in self-defense, his jailing was humiliating. He shouldn't have been drinking that sad afternoon. Well, her mother was both practical and loving—this eased her burden now. Mother Taylor sat near her, holding Linda and Tom close. They felt part of a circus.

The crowded courtroom added to the Walker family's sense of spectacle. This Wednesday, the third and final day, seemed to go on forever. Though his family members sometimes closed their eyes or nodded—except when Fleet himself testified—he never sagged, never tired of studying the participants. When District Attorney Hancock hell-fired the jurors, calling for a second-degree murder conviction of one Moses Fleetwood Walker, Bella trembled and shed many tears.

Cleodolinda moved into her father's lap. "Papa, I heard someone say it's a right smart chance these men will find you guilty. What do you figure your chances are, Papa?"

He held Linda tightly, but stared forward, not at her. "About fifty-fifty."

"Well, Papa, I been prayin'. God knows yer not guilty. *He's* goin' to lay *the truth* on those men's minds. Just you watch!" Fleet's eyes filled up. He tightened his embrace, looked his daughter square in the face, and thanked her.

About 5 p.m. the trial ended. Judge Kennedy sent the jurors to deliberate behind closed doors. It had been a long, wrought-up day, but neither Fleet's family nor most of the crowd dared to leave the court building. One of Bella's neighbors brought her family a basket of fried chicken, hoecake, and ears of corn. Bella, on pins and needles and busy praying, could not eat. Her mother, Mrs. Taylor, whom a reporter for the *Syracuse Courier* was already describing as a "middle-aged colored lady with gray hair and a handsome, intelligent face," took the children for several walks just outside the courtroom.

Just before 8 p.m. recess ended. In her seat Bella, eyes shut, was muttering to herself. The crowded room was hushed—folks were in full suspense. The twelve men took their seats, ready for revelation.

Jury foreman James Hill stood to answer Judge Kennedy's question. In the span between Kennedy's voice and Hill's, time itself skewed into another dimension. Bella had no breath. Her eyes burned. The words, "I pray this in Jesus' name," hung on her lips. The jury loomed monstrously, Foreman Hill grew ten feet tall, and everything around them was vacant to Fleet . . .

Fleet's jaws clenched. He thought of his buck knife, its five-inch blade that he used to cut the cord on postal parcels, smeared with Curly's blood and guts. He kept hearing the jarring words coming off of Prosecutor Hancock's lips.

Then humanity's unmoving time moved forward again. "We find the defendant not guilty," answered Foreman Hill.

Instantly the Syracuse courtroom filled with whistling and cheers and stomps. At first Bella was confused. Quickly she realized what was happening. She reached to touch her husband, who was gripping Linda and biting his lips. "Papa," 'Linda called out, "God has made it okay, is that so?" Fleet shook his head, eyes full of tears. "'Tis so, child . . . Thank the Lord." He tilted himself to buss Bella. "Tol' you so!" their Cleodolinda squealed. Squealing was also all around them. Not only the tiny group of Negroes able to be there this day, but the majority of whites, too, wriggled in applause!

The courtroom exploded so that the revelry was much like that at a baseball game. Trying to regain some decorum, the judge thumped his gavel so hard on the desk that the hammer's head flew off. When the clamor simmered down, Foreman Hill asked the court if it would entertain a request the jury had to make. "Of course," Judge Kennedy replied. "What is it?"

Foreman Hill answered slowly and clearly, "Your Honor, the jury desires to ask the court to give Mr. Walker some advice that will guide him in the future and help him be as good a citizen as he was before this trial became necessary." Judge Kennedy agreed. While he gently lectured Moses Fleetwood Walker, the words of young Anna-from-the-slopes came back to

Fleet, "Watch yerself." Fleet bowed to the judge, then sat back down beside Bella. Bella was weeping, but this time from joy.

In this joyous hour, when white and colored praised the verdict, Fleet put off any bitter brooding about white racism or Jim Crow or even lynchings. Holding young George, he watched Attorney A.C. Lewis walk Bella over to Judge Kennedy, where she was wholeheartedly greeted. He and Bella then thanked the jurors, shaking their hands—one after one.

The glowing crowd, growing boisterous, almost swallowed them up. So Attorneys Hoyt and Haven found a way to sneak the family—Fleet, Bella, Mother Taylor, and the three children—to a rear Clinton Street door from where the Walkers walked home alone. Fleet felt chains breaking away from him for the first time in two months. If he hadn't felt restrained by the children and Mother Taylor, he and Bella would've skipped home together!

"Fleetwood," Lawyer A.C. Lewis said to him before leaving the court building, "soon as I hasten back to Ohio, I'll put in a good word for you with the U.S. Postal Department. You need a change of place anyhow." This was just what Fleet wanted to hear.

Two weeks later Fleet was preparing his family's move from Syracuse to Steubenville when a telegram arrived. His father, Reverend-Doctor Moses W. Walker, separated from Fleet's mother, had died in Detroit. Fleet's life track now took another turn.

CHAPTER 12

$\mathcal{W}$.W. Brown set his right booted foot in the stirrups and nodded his head as Tom took him into the fading, morning blackness. When he'd heard that Fleet Walker and his young family were coming back to Steubenville, he figured on inviting them—just over some hills and hollows—to the Brown household in Cadiz. But Anna mentioned Rev. Dr. Moses Walker's death in Detroit, so W.W. decided to wait.

Though still a restless fellow, W.W. (or "Tod," or "Willie") had gotten less anxious now in his thirties. His business of hewing and shaping trees from Anna's thicket, and hauling these to Mine Number Five, was going well. He was making some big cash, some of which he tried to salt away. But as the trees were being cleared, W.W. began looking for other business.

'Sides sheep raising and farming, the biggest business around Cadiz was coal mining. Already his eldest son, Will, was a trapper boy in Mine Number Five. The next two boys, Charlie and Clarence, barely old enough to count money, were helping by gathering branches stripped from hewed tree trunks and caring for the two mules used to haul the posts. In a few years they'd be trappers, too. W.W. was plenty strong and supple from years of labor, and his sons were growing muscular from work. His hands, toughened by horse handling or farm and mine labor, held his five younger ones (two boys, three girls) like iron pincers might hold a feather pillow. Because he didn't feel sufficiently gentle with the "young'uns," he seldom embraced them. Becky realized that her husband was not a fondling-man toward their children, but she had reason to believe he was right comfortable caressing ladies, even when day was breaking.

Tom trotted him to sundry, familiar places that morning of 1891, as W.W. watched how dawn came subtly—by shades quicker than a wink.

Somehow, with long time passing, years also can pass quicker than a blink. Tom trotted his master three thousand more mornings until being put to pasture. Now in 1900, at the turn of the century, W.W. was driving a buggy around Mt. Pleasant, a hamlet some miles southeast of Cadiz but in Jefferson County, where he'd moved his family. Though Gideon, who replaced Tom, occasionally carried him on his saddle, W.W.'s horseback days were almost over.

Having cut down all the top-of-slope trees that Anna allowed, he'd ridden around Harrison, Belmont, and Jefferson Counties finding only a few dozen more swamp white oaks fit for mine posts. It was sometime in '93 that he finagled eighty-five acres of Mt. Pleasant farmland from the land owner, a Mr. Smith. Smith was having some big kind of money woes and was close to losing his property, W.W. had heard while riding Tom around the countryside. So little rain that the droughts took a heavy toll. And the bankruptcy of Reading Railroad and other troubles had folks talking about "the Panic." He "happened" to drop in on Smith. "Sir," he said to Smith, "I know this land . . . know it considerably . . . an' I be a pretty fair farm manager. I got some idees how crops can grow here and make a profit." W.W. was a shrewd bargainer. So when he rode away from Smith's failing property, he had full control of the farm and structures large enough to house his family. He'd shared the hard-earned farm profits with the landowner these past seven years.

Since '93 he'd seen Fleet Walker twice. First when Fleet's mother died before the Christmas of '93; second when Fleet's wife, Bella, passed away in '95. Newspapers and folks like Anna, however, acquainted him with Fleet's goings-on. He shut his eyes for an instant while Gideon, full of git-go and smart as any hoss, knowingly pulled the buggy across the slope toward the Mt. Pleasant mine. A thought made him shake his head. His own life had been crowded during the nineties—but Fleet's had been way more a tarnation, yea indeed!

Because of dips and rises and holes, Gideon's pace was slow—giving W.W. time to mull things over. He and Fleetwood had grown apart, living different kinds of lives. This made him think of his three older sons. These boys, working in the Mt. Pleasant mine, didn't see eye-to-eye with him, either—especially Charlie and Clarence, who were a bit younger than twenty-year-old Will. Their minds were now on what Booker T. Washington was telling folks, talking about yielding one's own self for the benefit of the many through organizations. He, W.W., had tried something like this some years ago, but that "Afro-American League" had failed. "First, ev'ry tub's gotta stand on its own bottom," he said to his boys. It was his opinion that progress for the colored race depended on each man standing up by himself, for himself.

From the wagon he saw some young fellows, Charlie and Clarence's age they seemed, rassling there on the hillside when they should be in the fields or down in the coal mines. "Hey, there!" he called out. "What you'uns doin'?" They looked his way, giggled, and kept on rassling. He mumbled, "No account whippersnappers, they be." Gideon kept his wagon rolling past them, but W.W. figured that Charlie and Clarence could whip all four of them. When he was their age, every young man around these hills was either too busy farming or mining—as his sons were doing this day. 'Course his sons would be happy fraternizing with others. That was the problem with this younger generation: too ready to gang together and fussing and nothing gets done. He thought of the smart chaps of his generation or older, such as Frederick Douglass and politician Blanche Bruce and even the young Booker T.—who rose up by themselves, not through some group. Individual responsibility, he contended—the responsibility he himself was showing.

He wasn't antisocial, though. Mostly to content Becky, to appease her fierce religious spirit, he served as an A.M.E. deacon—using his people management skills. Right now he was on the way to the mine where he'd been made deputy to a section boss. Well, it was just on a part-time shift, but his sons and all other colored miners were proud of his position—'specially because he was the only colored boss. He was breaking open the door for others. This was how one man, using his own feet to stride through snags, could make a way for his kinsmen.

Becky looked at "black folks rising" through the A.M.E. church. Her folks, Nelson and Harriet Thomas, plus their eldest children, had made their home in this black church before even Becky and her twin sister, Martha, were born. To Becky a man's gains were all about Jesus Christ and the Holy Ghost—nary a man's own powers. Well, he did fear the Lord God and respect the church; however, he believed it took a lion—not just a parishioner—to go ahead of and protect the pride. That was what he'd been doing, Lord knows.

Now at a trot, Gideon pulled the buggy into a flat-ground road leading to the mine's entrance. W.W. would pick up two of his sons finishing their early shifts, so they could do some farm chores before supper. He saw the giant breaker building's top ascending above patches of pine and buckeye trees. The building seemed to grow in the blink of his eye, reminding him of the subtly changing sky.

He was still thinking of himself as a leader—as well as father and husband, but mostly as leader. And he was comparing himself to Fleet Walker. Fleetwood was school-educated. Had been a great ballplayer, too. His name was known over half the nation, wherever professional baseball teams drew crowds. He, W.W. couldn't match this—no way. Yet, somehow, he'd match his leadership with Fleet. Yes, indeed. They both had miles to travel down the road of life. Someday he'd make just as good a fist as Fleet. Tears spurting up from the soul made his eyes go salty-wet. "Whoa, boy!" The buggy at a halt, he drew a big ol' blue bandana from his overalls, rubbed the weep from his face, rinsed his parched throat with whiskey . . . then urged Gideon on to the entrance.

CHAPTER 13

*R*iding on winter's sunshine, the twentieth century descended upon Jefferson County and the snow-sheathed hills of Steubenville. "Husband, were you this distracted at home with 'Missus A'?" Ednah asked him. Since they married nearly two years ago, Ednah had been referring to his first wife as "Missus A." Somehow she couldn't bring herself to use the name "Arabella." The deep grief of Fleet and the children bothered her. By using the term "Missus A," she kept a distance that was less emotional . . .

Fleet was sitting at his small, hardwood desk and drawing shapes on paper—amid ruler, protractor, compass, and other drafting tools. She wouldn't have minded his concentration, except that the attention paid to her, or his children, seemed less and less. "Sir!" She began to repeat her question.

"'Fraid so, Ednah," he grumbled, indicating he'd heard her the first time.

But his demeanor—his personality, too—had changed since his Bella had passed. Also, probably since the second anguish—his conviction and imprisonment. He felt some guilt over Bella. Following the "ghost" baby, and after each of their three children, he should have paid more attention to her frequent bodily complaints or miasmas. Now he finally had his long-sought-after Ednah by his side—but not even this satisfied him.

Ednah—every bit as cool, handsome, and graceful as she was during the '80s when Fleet first courted her, even when he was with Arabella—strolled into another room to contemplate her marriage to Fleetwood. On this Monday, the New Year's holiday, Fleet's daughter and sons were out on a sleigh ride with their Uncle Weldy.

Edna watched gusts of loose snow outside blowing across the windowpane. Unlike what folks said about Arabella, she seldom wept. Yet she stood before the window with wet eyes. "That Walker lad," Oberlinians

79

had told her some eighteen years past, "will make you a fittin' mate." But her feelings for the ball-playing Fleetwood were so-so. Tall and handsome he was, and popular. She, though, had a higher education and other things to claim. He surely worshiped her, Lord, yes. But then there was Arabella twinkling his eyes . . . then the *ghost* baby. She did find him intriguing, so they met each other a few times before she left Ohio to teach in Kentucky, then to operate a store in Chicago where she met her first husband, Mr. Price.

From afar off she seemed to hear young voices. Ednah, who'd looked after Linda, Tom, and George during this last year when Fleet was incarcerated, expected they'd be home soon. Then Linda would help her prepare dinner. She slid a linen kerchief out of her calico dress pocket, wiping her eyes, remembering. In Chicago in '95, she'd received a telegram announcing the death of Mrs. Fleetwood Walker in Ohio.

"Hey, hon, I need more ink. Have you seen a cruse of India ink hereabouts?"

"I believe it's in here, in the old box of your desk things." She turned, pointed to the corner, and watched him pass by her. As he opened the box, snatching out the cruse in an abrupt fashion, Ednah thought of how brusque he'd become. After their wedding, he'd never pass her by without either bussing her or patting her buttocks in ingenious ways. Immediately after his release from prison, he was quite passionate, but it seemed his passion was waning now—as was hers. Was this her fault? No, indeed! She was trying hard to keep the light of love burning between them. She was guessing that "Missus A's" illness and dying had left a hole in his heart—though he had professed a great love for her, Ednah, and insisted they join, finally, in matrimony. She also felt sorry for Arabella's losing struggle with the cancer, and especially the children's loss. But she was now his wife. She deserved some warmth from him. And his imprisonment, which had surprised her only four months following their marriage, certainly had nothing to do with her.

It was in September of '98 that the law picked up her new husband. She heard of this from a United States Marshal. Fleetwood's job for years had been riding a railroad mail car with a few other postal clerks. He was the registered mail clerk, however, with the more important position. In fact, Ednah recalled, only a month before his arrest Fleetwood had let her peek into his mail car. The train, Wellsville & Bellaire Line, sorting mail for the Cleveland & Pittsburgh Railroad, was sitting on the side rails for some repair. He briefly sneaked her on board and proudly showed her where he worked. Huge canvas bins were fastened side-by-side on each side of the car; big boxes were fixed likewise below the car's ceiling. Clerks did their jobs standing and sorting mail in the too narrow aisle. Fleetwood had a desk at one end for handling letters, packages, and pouches of the registered stuff. Among all the paper and inked stamps and tie-sacks, she could understand why railway post office clerks had to be trained hard and tested often—their sorting and stamping was complex and furiously fast, and their minds had to be so nimble! Her new husband was so proud of his position, and of the eighty dollars monthly he earned.

"This be serious," he had told her from the county jail. "The government laid a trap for me. Of course I'm not guilty, honey." She lingered at the snow-flaked window, thinking of his use of the word "honey." Before, and surely after, he and his Arabella were married, she had snubbed his use of the pet name "honey" for herself, Ednah. But like persons never addicted to sweets, after years of tasting honey it finally dawns on them that they've come to need this nectar.

Anyhow, following his arrest she learned that some postal inspectors did, in fact, ensnare him. Seems that pieces of registered mail had gone missing, mainly those that had been Fleet Walker's responsibility. So these inspectors registered a decoy letter containing seven dollars and planted it in a tie-sack bound for Wellsville. The inspectors met Fleet's mail car at the Wellsville station. When the decoy letter was demanded, he "found" the envelope, in a trash can by his desk, torn open, money missing, and the envelope's face with this inscription: "Received in bad order." The Post Office Department was using this evidence against him. Fleet told her, "They're out to get me . . . because of my color, my fame, my notoriety." Despite needing to believe in her new husband, as Arabella had done in '91, she debated first with herself, then God.

Anyway, Fleet was judged guilty and sentenced to prison for one year. Now he was back home, and the "Year of Our Lord 1900" had finally arrived.

"There they are!" Ednah called out. The excitement in her voice prompted Fleet to interrupt his drafting to come to her window. "About time," he grumbled. He did hang one arm over her shoulder. They stood watching, at a distance, G-Bob, Weldy's fancy draft horse, a gray Gypsy breed gelding with feathered fetlocks, easily tow the two-bench sleigh as if the roads weren't covered by snow. They saw Tom and George cutting didos with Linda in their seats, and Weldy trying to wave them still from his driver's seat. Ednah felt good hearing Fleet chuckling at her side. At least his spirits were still high when it came to his teenage youngsters. And his arm *was* warm and gentle on her shoulder.

But before Ednah could get snug there with him, Fleet said, "I'll go see to them," then strode out of the room. He pulled on his wool-lined cap, great coat, and galoshes, then stepped out into the snow. Ednah, seeing him trudging toward G-Bob and the sleigh, felt odd. What did he mean by "see to them?" She noticed that Weldy had good control of the sleigh. And the children's pranks were not disturbing G-Bob, whose hooves were true, steadily flaying snow down the gentle slope.

Fleet met them when G-Bob eased to a halt. George and Tom leapt out laughing. Linda let her father help her to the ground. "They's a bit wild t'day, but we had fun." Weldy giggled, then drove G-Bob with the sleigh to the barn. After a few words to his boys, Fleet threw his arms 'round Linda. Just as her literal name, given by Arabella, implied, Cleodolinda was indeed *his princess*. Tall, lithesome, and lovely, she made him proud. She was nearly eighteen now and young fellows were after her like prowling wolves. He had to safeguard her. Tom, going on sixteen, was tenderhearted like his mother, but clever enough to take care of himself. George, nearly fourteen, was athletic like his pappy and quite handy with his fists—more interested in the sport of boxing than baseball.

"Father," Linda asked while she and he slogged arm-in-arm toward the house, "what you been doing all afternoon at your desk?" This made Fleet grin proudly at her. "Coming up with another invention, gal. First one of this year." She chuckled with him, this being January the first. She felt commiseration for him—not just due to his spending a year in jail, but also 'cause none of his inventions had ever panned out. "Good, Pa." Last evening, when her family attended the Watch Night Service, the usual New Year's Eve program at the A.M.E. church to celebrate the end of slavery, she noticed that her father seemed unhappy and restless. She nuzzled him.

Ednah gazed through the window, feeling a little left out, seeing Fleet and Linda tramping so intertwined through the snow. She noted their smiles—particularly her husband's. Maybe Linda was taking her mother's place? Maybe not, Ednah consoled herself, maybe Fleetwood, out of his guilt over "Missus A," was simply showering the girl with his repentance. Ever since he had wed Arabella but professed his love for her, Ednah, she'd wondered how a sun's heart could equally abide two moons. Quietly she'd accepted his word that he loved her more. But now?

The boys hastened to their winter afternoon chores. Linda began helping her stepmother complete the New Year's dinner. Fleet returned to his drawings. But already his interest in architecture was sliding away. His pen was making only doodles. He studied his hands, those battered and warped twenty years ago on baseball diamonds. All for a sacrifice for a measure of fame and fortune . . .

"Hell, yeah, I got to the top of the baseball world. The 'Dark Adonis,' some called me. The 'Lion of Home Plate,' and other ravings. Me, and Weldy to some extent, the only colored chaps in the majors! Then they shut us down . . . they did."

He reflected on his days, then and now. Oh . . . then there were such lovely ladies, even white ladies, trailing and sneaking him lurid notes! The newspapers and *Sporting Life* articles. The big money in his pocket. And mostly the raising of himself, a Negro, to such high status in spite of all the prejudice and bigotry abounding. He was riding the wind, until . . . until the racists drove him clear out of the majors. And afterward the game caused so many batters and bruises that he lost his bounce—and his playing job. The evenings in tie and tails when he took Bella, also Ednah twice "on the sly," to fancy balls. The killing of Curly and that itchy trial. The sad years of Bella's sickness, then Ednah's agreement to become his wife—all followed by 395 days of his life as a prisoner.

But in April of '95, nearly five years past now and just two months before Bella expired, he was the most celebrated citizen in town. Fleet pulled his desk drawer open and found a yellowing newspaper page. He recalled how the congregation of Quinn A.M.E. Church had swelled and there was hardly room for the other folks anxious to hear his memorial speech on the death of Frederick Douglass. This yellowing page was neatly wrapped in Edison waxed paper. He slid it out to examine once again.

Hearing the tread of her Oxford buttoned shoes, Fleet looked up, a bit startled. "You must be hungry, husband," remarked Ednah. She began kneading his shoulder and peering down at the page. The caption read FREDERICK DOUGLASS—Statesman and Diplomat—Address by M.F. Walker—Sunday, April 7, 1895. Steubenville Weekly Gazette. She'd never before read a speech composed and given by Fleet. One phrase so struck her that she read it aloud: "By forceful argument, dignified and majestic bearing coupled with a Roman eloquence, he electrified the nation's heart as only heroes are permitted to do . . ."

"Fleetwood, this memorial is wonderfully written! You must exercise this ability!"

Yea, surely he could write on the story of his people that Douglass had lived and told so fiercely. He beamed, drew her face down to his, then kissed her lips most deeply. Ednah was so stunned, so pleased with this moment of passion, that she stumbled from the room saying, "Oh . . . I must tend to dinner." But she did a quick turn, a pirouette. "Thank ye, husband."

Elation burst in his breast, and a rare smile came wriggling across his face. He realized he hadn't shown Ednah much love lately. She was much more deserving than this. Why had he been so miserable and unloving? He resumed pondering. He thought of Willy doing well over in Cadiz according to Anna, and formed a true grin. Willie Brown, now called W.W., never became a big name like himself but had pretty well passed him in business. He was glad for Willie, and he'd told that to Anna. She'd replied, "You prob-ly could do well in business, too, if you watch yerself." The grin now left his face.

"Watch yerself," Anna had said before he was jailed for stabbing Curly, and she said the same to him before his arrest years later by the federal government. He hadn't seen Anna for a couple of years now. Well, her terrible wisdom scared him. Yet he had *heard* her words about his business possibilities . . .

Intruding into his thoughts were the aromas of a feast. And this call from Ednah: "Dinner is gotten ready!"

On his way to the dining room, Fleet glanced out a window. Stiff snow had cloaked the pane. His eyes discerned a stark whiteness covering the ground like he knew an alabaster cloth would be covering the dinner table. His step was lighter. This was his family's first dinner of this nineteen-hundredth year since the birth of Savior Jesus. He would be a new man in this new century! Itching his mind now were these three endeavors: mechanical inventions, essays on the status of Negroes, and some sort of business doings. He felt good again.

Tom and George were in the side parlor busy using a stereoscope to look at peculiar side-by-side pictures that magically changed into real scenes. Fleet peeked into the parlor saying, "Let's go eat, fellows." In the dining room Weldy carried a huge platter of roasted turkey to the table. Ednah was placing other platters of food out. Linda, looking just like Bella, was making room for the plates. And Sarah Richmond, the Irish charwoman who helped Ednah keep house, was still busy at the stove. "Happy New Year's, folks!" Fleet chirped, surprising them all with his wide smile. Then he took his seat at the table's head. The table, its alabaster spread flowing over like a sheet of snow, held a royal feast.

CHAPTER 14

W.W. met this great turn of the century with several promises to himself. These promises included looking for greater opportunities in northern parts of Ohio. He was thinking of Elyria, where, twenty years before, he had helped construct the Lorain County Courthouse. Another intention was to hook up with Fleetwood Walker, whom Anna said had just been let out of jail and now had joined his brother Weldy in some sort of business in Steubenville. But today he took up yet another promise: to reconcile with the kinfolk from whom he was estranged.

Many Browns lived here and around Cadiz, some true blood, some whom he couldn't be sure were related by blood, and a few to whom he'd rather not be related. Of course he had to begin with his pappy, ol' George Brown. Pappy and ol' Reuben Brown were two town codgers he needed to come to terms with.

"Naw, husband!" Becky ranted in her strongest alto voice. "You shan't be goin' out t'night—be it kinfolk or not." Becky was annoyed with him coming home after midnight, reeking of liquor, and she not knowing where he'd been or whom he'd been with. "You got all these children here who seldom see their Pappy. Seems they only see me, their Ma. An' I been like mother an' father to 'em. You an' I talked on this—now I'm taking a stand here, yessir. Tod, you be stayin' home tonight with us!"

W.W. frowned while also grinning to himself. When Becky got stirred, she could near about whip her weight in wildcats. Well, his thick, strong, and robust wife was telling the truth—causing him to feel a great pride in her. She was on his case fer sure. He fixed himself a toddy, strode into the front room, and plopped down amongst the younger children, who looked surprised. This was not how he'd planned to spend this evening.

Harriet, all of age ten, was teaching three of her younger sisters—Sarah, Hester, and Mary Margaret—how to make a stuffed doll. Clarabelle, almost eleven, was putting away the bucket after scrubbing the kitchen. Ottie and Clinton, ages fourteen and twelve, were cleaning the wood dust off themselves from toting in stacks for the stove. They would next study their reader, The Pilgrim's Progress. A few minutes later, Charlie and Clarence, ages seventeen and fifteen, arrived home from the mine, after working the second shift. Becky completed her ironing as little Martha Emma, nearly three, sat licking her stick of peppermint. Their mother welcomed the coal-dirty boys. They were muscular and strong. She silently thanked the Lord when seeing them every evening. "Thank Ye, Jesus, fer bringin' 'em outta that hellish mine."

"When's Willie finish his shift?" Becky asked the boys. "Ma, he wanted to work the 'graveyard shift,' too," Charlie answered. "Won't be home 'til after Pappy begins his shift, after morning light." Willie, age twenty, was her firstborn, and she quietly was closer to him than to her ten others. "Well now, after y'all wash up, you kin get some greens, ham an' corn bread from the oven safe."

"Don't spill nuthin' on this floor. I scrubbed," Clarabelle warned.

Becky clasped little Marth'emma's hand and traipsed into the front room, where she was surprised. W.W. had gathered the youngsters in a semicircle and was kneeling on the floor facing them—telling tales! "Wa-a-ll, I jus' want you young'uns t'know . . ." Becky smiled as she plopped into the Queen Anne chair. Her husband, his toddy mug in hand, was amusing the children—flabbergasting them, really—with stories of his greenhorn years. Eight of their youngsters stared wide-eyed, at attention because Pappy almost never was home talking with them like he was tonight: "Y'all never been far yonder from these hills 'n' coal mines. Yer Pappy, yer grand-Pappy, yer uncles, an' yer big brothers a-movin' coal—tons an' tons of black rocks. Where to?"

Setting his toddy mug on the floor, he took little Marth'emma into his hard-muscled arms. "Twenty years ago, yer Pappy was living up in the northlands of Ohio, an' seen mountains of coal bein' shipped. Place called Lorain County, alongside Lake Erie."

"Is that one of the seas?" Harriet asked.

"Yea, girl. A great sea of freshwater. Only called a lake, 'cause it's not an ocean with saltwater such as the Atlantic or the Pacific. Lake Erie, then, an' where I saw them humongous piles bein' transported was in the busy town named Lorain. I done tol' you I was stayin' with my Aunt Julia Moore an' family in Elyria, only nine miles from Lorain—"

"Pappy was a hostler in E-leer-ya. He knows all about horses," said Hester, proud that she remembered hearing of this.

Maybe because he'd been thinking lately of opportunities in Lorain County, W.W. eagerly began retracing his long-ago lakeside experience. Growing up not much more than an hour's horseback ride to the wide Ohio, he was familiar with sidewheeler steamships and riverboats hauling freight. But those lake steamers—so tall, long, and sleek—docked at Lake Erie attracted him like a magnet. Now the images, still wet and windy, were coming back easily.

Back in '80 he managed to take time out from driving workhorses between Lorain and Elyria so he could prowl the lakefront piers. The sea of unending water, the smells of the lake, the seagulls cavorting up in the sky, the wind, the men and a few women tramping around the wet docks in their galoshes—all of it fascinated him. His bright face and ready smile made him fast friends with merchants, peddlers, dockworkers, and sailors. Especially sailors. On at least three occasions they took him on board their idled steamer, where he met the first mate and once even the ship's master. He'd never before witnessed such a complicated shebang—and with such transfixing machinery!

He was led up near the big boat's bow to a shed standing above the deck. "This be the fo'c's'le," one sailor said, then pointing to a higher structure. "This's the pilothouse." Each visit the vessel bobbed and he planted his feet while looking beyond the piers at the great, greenish sea that sailors said stretched all the way to "Minn-ah-sotah." To W.W. that seemed almost like to the end of the world, or almost to Jerusalem. On his first visit a deckhand told him the steamer had begun its route at a dock city named Duluth in Minnesota, where seven thousand long tons of iron ore were loaded on and carried east to Cleveland, Ohio. Then, after the ore was unloaded, the freighter ship turned 'round and steamed west to Lorain. W.W.'s ears had picked up when the deckhand said, "She's 'bout ta be filled with Ohio black an' we'll head back to Duluth." W.W. knew that "Ohio black" meant soft coal, probably mined around his home county down in Cadiz. He wanted to see this!

Noises of all sorts crammed the docks, so he hadn't separated the hum of a coal dumper's start. Suddenly, though, he heard something like rolling thunder. He scurried to the boat's aft. What resembled a towering jackleg monster made of wood and iron was vomiting coal gulped out of railway cars into the vessel's hold—tons and tons of coal rumbling down. Thunderous noise and the shaking of this ship's hull unsettled him, but he watched the coal's cascade awhile longer. "Could be," he told himself, "the same rock Pappy an' others in Harrison County carved out of a hole just a fortnight ago." Sensing that this boat would be departing soon, after deck-hands finished shoveling up the coal-spill on deck, he teetered over to his sailor buddy.

The mate grabbed his arm. "Let's go into the fo'c's'le." The large, sturdy, but battered fo'c's'le (forecastle) buzzed with mates exchanging news, departure directions, and port gossip. W.W. was ushered to the First Mate, who was always looking to hire a deckhand or porter. First Mate Hansen tried to recruit him there on the spot. But the ship began rocking more than usual, striking W.W. with fear. Noticing his quiver, Hansen assured him, "'Tis just thuh big windlass workin',' movin' thuh boat to an' fro so's tuh even out her coal cargo—makes fer safer sailin', ye know." W.W. didn't know. All he knew at that moment was that he wanted off this boat. Five minutes later he was climbing down a ladder to the dock. He made haste up Fifteenth Street to the horse stables.

The youngsters, eyes wide open, were fascinated with his tale of big ships and the Great Lakes. Hester was the first to speak. "Pappy, you were so fearless! How many trips did you make on those seas?"

W.W. hesitated, then grinned. "None. Truth be that yer Pappy was always fit to be tied when feelin' that 'ere boat wobble. When it shook, *my* heart well-nigh shook up t'my throat . . ."

"A-a-a-a," sounded the Brown children.

"I'd skedaddle off that boat, yea indeed! Yer Pappy was more snug on a wild hoss than on a ship." The youngsters, even W.W. and Becky, burst into laughter. This evening was a delight. Pappy was seldom at home, and they rarely could hear his tales and laugh with him. But soon Becky let them know it was time to retire for the night.

This night Becky was pleased. In their bedroom she closed the door. That was a now-and-then signal which her husband well understood, so W.W. was pleased, too. They embraced and she jokingly mumbled something about not being ready for yet another baby. They had four sons and six daughters in the house this night—and their eldest son, Will, was working the night shift in the mine. Becky put out the coal oil lamp as he slid into their featherbed before she disrobed. W.W. jokingly wondered why women always saw fit to undress in the darkness. "So y'know 'bout other women doin' this, huh?" He wisely didn't answer her. Becky, in an amorous mood, let him slide. The moon was full . . .

Moonlight floated eastward and was shining directly above the Browns' home just outside the tiny village of Mt. Pleasant when heavy footsteps hit the front porch. Becky and the youngsters were sound asleep, but W.W., who was a light sleeper, heard the boots, then the rap. He jumped up and straightened out his nightshirt while making his way to the door. The caller was a neighbor, grimy-faced and still in his miner's garb. "Uh, wanted to warn you . . . Maria's on its way tah yer home! 'Tain't good."

W.W. understood immediately. "Will got hurt!" The neighbor nodded and said, "God knows, I'm sorry, Tod."

"Black Maria" was, of course, the name coal families gave to the wagon or makeshift ambulance carrying a badly injured or killed miner to a hospital or to his home—whichever was closer. The only hospital was a long, hard way over steep hills to distant Steubenville along the river. "I kin stay 'n' help y'all," said the neighbor, but W.W. thanked him and told him to get on home to his own family. W.W. lit the outside gas lantern, wondering whether to alert Becky. But Becky was already at the door.

To the sound of hooves clip-clopping, Black Maria rolled up to W.W. and Becky's home. No greeting, no unnecessary conversation—just Becky's cry as she tried pushing past her husband. The driver and a mine foreman gently, carefully lifted Will from the wagon. A full moon, glowing along with the gaslight, pierced the menacing blackness that pushed against the five figures outside. Becky let out a sharp wail when she saw her son's crumpled body. Some youngsters were rushing from the house, but W.W. halted them, allowing only Charlie and Clarence to approach their brother.

A folded, gray cotton blanket, blood-soaked, stuck to Will's left side. The driver and foreman lowered Will to a part of the porch where his brothers had hastily laid a clean quilt. Will's eyes were drawn shut. Becky bent and kissed his cold, still face. She leaned her head on W.W.'s shoulder, sobbing. In a shivering voice, the foreman explained that Will had been crushed between a coal car and the "rib," or wall, of the mining room. As his next-to-last function this night, the foreman pulled from his pocket a crumpled slip of paper. Under a gas lamp he began to read a standard prayer: "Heavenly Father, this here miner has been taken . . . ." Shocked, neither Becky nor the others—now most of her family was collected 'round the porch—was really paying much attention. Will was Becky's firstborn child. For his twenty years he had . . . would always have . . . a special place in her heart, though she'd never admitted it. The foreman turned to leave and Becky began to shout: "No, Lord, no, not any more of my boys! We got to leave these *damned* mines. We got to get away from here!" Her daughters took her and ushered her inside.

W.W. figured the undertaker, who was being notified by the foreman, would not arrive until sometime in the morning. Meanwhile he and two sons would clean and wrap Will's body. He stepped off the porch, ambled off by himself, and studied the heavens. In an unbelievably short twinkling, the moon was yielding to a glimmer of pale daylight.

CHAPTER 15

*S*he toted, she hoisted, she shoved large wooden boxes around the roomy hall. Boxelder chests containing opera house accoutrements. Living with Fleetwood, Ednah had learned in these six years of this second marriage for each of them, was like riding a steam-powered carousel. Yes, spinnings with sudden ups and downs came weekly, it seemed to her. Now Fleet had just purchased this Cadiz Opera House from Ed M. Brown, and Ednah's thoughts swirled as she prepared a bedroom for them on the second floor. "Durn!" she screeched when a flat, a disconnected frame of stage scenery, fell as she was pushing it aside. "Durn it!" She was glad, though, of her strength, which allowed her to do work that Arabella could not have done. She was recalling previous happenings in these six years.

In "nineteen-aught-aught" [1900], Fleet decided to relocate his family from their High Street home, where they had lived since '98, to 105 Market Street in Steubenville. She had not been thrilled about the move. This Market Street place was the Union Hotel, which he and brother Weldy leased. Ednah was not pleased because the hotel, with its saloon, would attract those ruffians anxious to hang around the famous ex-baseball catcher and embolden his own drinking. "You're drinking more'n ever. Why?" she recollected saying to him.

"Girl, look at my tribulations!" Fleet had hotly replied.

She was aware of four "tribulations": his slide from baseball fame and the sour this caused, albeit that was ten years past; his murder charge in New York; the sickness and death of Arabella; and his being jailed for a year on a federal offense. But she'd been through trials too—and being his missus *was* a trial! Whisky, beer—'sides drinking in his own saloon, he got into trouble drinking in other places, like the Dewey Hotel's bar. And all the Liberia fuss! He got into the "black versus white" issue, dashing ideas onto paper, flirting with emigration to Africa for colored folk. These ideas made up the little newspaper, *The Equator*, that Fleet and Weldy composed, printed, and distributed.

Ednah poured hot water into a pail, then took a mop to the floor. This was more hard cleaning than she had ever done. (Ednah was used to having a chambermaid.)

She recalled reading a column in the *Herald Star* about her husband's paper. Must have been in "aught-one" or "aught-two." It went something like this: ". . . M. Fleet Walker, a well-known Negro resident of Steubenville, has accepted an invitation from Senator Wright of Liberia to move to Liberia with his paper . . . and, with his family, will remove there as soon as he can arrange his affairs." Fleetwood's name was often in the papers, but she'd read this that day and had a real conniption! Her husband had never told her about deciding to go live, "with his family," in Africa! He had argued in *The Equator* that emigration by his people made sense. She, in fact, disagreed with him! And although he'd mentioned a letter from Liberia, she'd never read this, thinking it just more fodder for his paper. This *Herald Star* column led that evening to their first great ruckus! As she'd railed, Fleet was "a haunted *Fury* drawing thunder and lightning." She was not about to pick up and move to Africa; neither did Linda, Tom, nor George cotton to the idea. Still, her husband was a charmer. He had charmed her—oh, 'twas nineteen aught-two, just two years ago, yes?—into appearing with him over in Mr. Brown's Cadiz Opera House as comic "talkers" alongside the new moving picture shows. Land sakes, they were good entertainers, too! Matter of fact, they went on the road with their act to Pennsylvania and West Virginia—as well as in churches and on city hall stages—showing these new-fangled kinetoscopes. Now Fleet had his own stage to run pictures and "talk." Betwixt a smile and a frown she got on her knees to scrub the floor.

Joining with her husband as a "talker" (or a "lecturer," as this was formerly labeled) was a welcome thing, Ednah thought. It pulled out her creative side. After all she'd been an *honored* graduate of Oberlin College, a schoolteacher and ran her own business—until she got a divorce, then returned to Ohio to marry Moses Fleetwood Walker. When he asked her help in presenting these silent moving pictures, she'd hesitated. But then she found that she could emote, and even sing in the background, as well as he—only he could also play the piano.

So now they, but not his children, would be living above the stage featuring light operas, small theater plays, and motion pictures, not to mention things like vaudeville, dances, and high school graduations. Ednah was anxious to finish her scrubbing.

Ednah heard the side door open and close. It was Fleet coming back; she knew his footsteps like she knew the tenor of his voice. He hustled up the stairs. "Ednah, my dear—I'm here!" She was glad to see him; this was late afternoon and he'd been gone since early morning. "What things you been into today, Fleetwood?"

"Shucks, I've been chatting business with several folks . . . got some news, too." Fleet snatched her, bending his wiry frame to kiss her lips. "Goin' to fetch someone to do this cleaning for you," Fleet chirped as he took the scrub brush out of her hand and pointed to a bench. "Let's sit so's I can relate what I was doing." She knew he'd set out to meet with some Cadiz bigwigs, so he began with that. Three businessmen and a town official were pleased that an opera company from Pittsburgh had planned to put *El Capitan* on next month, the middle of May. Because operettas seldom played at Cadiz, the bigwigs thought this could raise the town's cultural level—yet they had not told Fleet of it. "I welcome the opera company . . . but they never contacted me. I'm running this house!"

Soft, sardonic smiles slid onto the faces of the four white men. Fleet felt his fury about to erupt, so he forced himself into a momentary silence. Anger rose inside him because all the previous indignities, going way back to his baseball days, suddenly returned. He'd borrowed cash, he'd signed papers of ownership, he'd obtained licenses and prepared to pay taxes, his name was now stamped on this opera house—yet he was made to feel unequal, a flunky, a plug of shit! But he was sitting here as, also, an ex-convict, a beleaguered creature. Logic told him this was not the time to roar!

The mayor's man quietly advised him that he was the "caretaker" of this "community hall" and beholden to the townspeople. "This opera company," the mayor's man said, "does not know you yet, so they got ahold of us. They know we've always had a hand in what's presented in this opera house." Fleet was seething inside. Then one of the business fellows, a retailer, instructed Fleet that Cadiz's business circle had an interest in opera house shows that also were good for commerce. "We can tell you which programs attract folks, who have shopping money, into town." And another bigwig warned Fleet that there were certain forms of entertainment that the town wouldn't tolerate. This piqued Fleet even further— What's he think, I'd bring in *nigger hoedown* shows? he wondered. The mayor's man butted in to explain: "You do understand, Mr. Walker—I'm sure you know—how Cadiz tries to stay Christian in deed an' attitude.

93

This 'Women's Temperence' sniffs for liquor an' they patrol as diligently as our police. They get upset 'bout things of carnal nature, too." Fleet nodded. He kept his own whiskey hidden, like all fellows in town did. Even sweetened his breath with *Sen-Sen*. The mayor's man settled him down—for a moment.

"One more thing," a bigwig said. "We're fixin' ta bring in a minstrel. Minstrels always attract a crowd, 'specially the lodge fellas."

This was more than a cudgel; it hit Fleet like a sledgehammer!

"What'd you say, sir?" The man began telling how a minstrel would boost the house's coffers, but Fleet went deaf. He was visualizing white men in blackface poking fun at Negro ways. Words written by Frederick Douglass about minstrels, words so heated that they burnt into his memory, shouted now through his brain: ". . . the filthy scum of white society, who have stolen from us a complexion denied to them by nature, in which to make money and pander to the corrupt taste of their white fellow citizens." Fleet abruptly got to his feet and snatched from his trousers a pocket watch. "If you'll excuse me, gentlemen, I'm late for another appointment." He would figure out a scheme to keep minstrels out of his theater without creating more trouble for his furious self.

Fleet stared blankly in the direction of his wife and sighed. "Anyway, we've got to ready this place for a town spelling bee and some affair by the Masonic Lodge and the opera company from Pittsburgh."

Ednah noticed that he slouched, looking weary and much different from the brash, young baseball phenomenon who had pursued her at Oberlin more than twenty-five years ago. "Well, where did you travel after this morning's meeting, Fleetwood?"

He paused for a couple of seconds . . . "I felt strongly that I needed tah visit Anna over on the slope." Ednah's eyebrows raised. Who was Anna?

Late that morning he'd bowed out of the meeting, leaving the other men puzzled. He was forlorn and angry. He needed to break away, lest he explode or give in to violence. Second only to Jesus, Anna was just the one he could tell his troubles to and walk away with his spirits lifted.

His carriage doddered westward, as the horse carefully avoided rocks and ruts along the foothills. "Whoa!" Fleet barked as they neared Anna's little cabin on the slope. She was out hanging her wash on lines. "Ho, Moses Fleetwood!" Anna sang out joyfully. She hadn't seen him in a bunch of years—although she'd heard he was taking over the opera house in town. He walked over to her, and they embraced and kissed like old times. "I hankered to talk with you, if I'm not imposing on your work schedule."

"Come in the house an' rest yerself. I always got time tuh catch up on you. Ain't seen you since you remarried. Have some tea, or you got a taste fer some mount'n dew?" He grinned, saying, "Tea sounds good."

After a half hour's chitchat, he told her what he wanted to discuss with her. He was feeling sort of lost in ways that Ednah, refined by her "proper" upbringing and Oberlin College and her former city life, just wouldn't understand. He'd gotten himself into trouble too many times and now was vulnerable—afraid his "colored man's anger" could lead to his complete ruin. "Let us study on these here bad feelin's," Anna suggested. Anna was calm, understanding, steady, and wise—a special kind of friend, he knew. "Puts me in mind of the goldfish," she said with a slight smile.

"What do you mean, Anna?"

"The big river once broke into separate streams. Palefish swum in one stream, an' darkfish swum in t'other. But one of the darkfish was the color of brass, so he was called goldfish—an' he landed in the palefish stream. Goldfish, he swum faster an' jump higher than all the palefish. Lawd, he was sump'n! Palefish, they got so jealous they gang up on him an' force him in t'other stream with his own kind. But he was still cut'n didos an' actin' like he don't know if he belong to palefish or darkfish. Tryin' tah swim in both streams at the same time. When finally he settled in the darkfish stream he realize that stream is muddy. Well, sir, that made he mad. He blame the palefish for this. That be why he organized the darkfish to get some clear water out t'other stream."

Fleet looked at Anna, whose eyes had a mischievous glint. He burst out laughing. "Gal, are you telling me I'm the goldfish?" Anna's deep brown eyes widened. "I want you tah tell me who Moses Fleetwood Walker truly is these days." He shut his own eyes and took a deep breath. This is how she counsels folk, he recalled, often answering a question with a question. But she was plumbing his mind now. The *who* of him was something he needed to ponder, yes. Was he a "goldfish?" It was the morning meeting that had caused him to come to Anna, so he described how this had burdened him—his lack of control at the Opera House, being dictated to by Cadiz bigwigs, the matter of minstrels, which was angering him and insulting his race and presenting a quandry. He could not reject these shows they wanted and still have a profit-making house. Furthermore, Mayor W.T. Perry and the town officials, if annoyed, might look into his past and mess with his licensing. On the other hand, he wanted to set the place on a course that raised his people up, not ridiculed them. 'Twas almost like serving two masters!

"Can you think on Jesus and the Roman coin?" Anna asked. Seeing his perplexity, she told of Jesus pointing to Caesar's coined image and saying, "Render unto Caesar the things that are Caesar's, and unto God the things that are God's." But could he satisfy the white folks of Cadiz and still turn his building into a place where coloreds could celebrate?

"How many white men sat 'round you?" Anna asked. "Four," he said. "Now, why you need to haggle with yer tormentors by yerself? Even Lord Jesus picked twelve good men tuh help Him do His mission. They's good, strong folk in town willin' tuh stand by you. No?"

It occurred to him that he'd been too much of a lone wolf going about his new Cadiz business. This was his fault—being too self-centered, too cocksure of his own prowess. Anna was right. "Gal, you feed me truth!"

"Not from me, Moses Fleetwood, but from the Holy Ghost, from thuh Scriptures. You oughta try this." She grinned.

Fleet moved to Anna and kissed her. In Steubenville he'd reached a high order in the Knights of Pythias Lodge. "I'll contact the lodges here—Pythians, Masons. Also, the pastor of Saint James A.M.E. I'll get some *other* town strength at my side . . ."

Anna nodded, then remarked: "I'm thinkin' that you're burdened, too, by our overall racial sit-see-ations." Before he could rush to agree, she added, "I did read yer paper, The Equator, an' I appreciate yer writing. Now seems tuh me that you've got more to say, so a book 'bout what's in yer heart might be in order—might turn yer burden into thoughts to be shared with all folks. Might lessen yer burden!" Ideas laced him.

Ednah listened. After six years of wedlock, she was still learning who Fleet was. And now, learning about this stranger woman named Anna. She didn't know whether to be jealous of or thankful for this Anna. Maybe both. But Ednah grasped her man, pulling him close to her body. She felt a fire in him again. And she felt his arousal for the first time in a while. Outside, an April storm stirred, winds whipping and pelting raindrops against the opera house's tall windows. While they scrambled to the rug floor, Ednah knew their lives would be changing.

CHAPTER 16

*J*efferson County, Ohio, November 1907. Two sturdy wagons, each one filled with Browns and pulled by a workhorse, plodded along snaking, sloshy country roads from Cadiz over to Smithfield in Jefferson County. Pappy, W.W. Brown, drove one wagon, and his next older son, Clarence, drove the other. The family—except for eldest son, Charlie, who'd married this year and moved to another town where he and wife, Ella Jane, were living—was coming home from Grandma Bell's funeral.

Isabelle Lawrence Brown—she left many sons and daughters, with William Wesley being the oldest. As he held the reins for the lead wagon, W.W. thought of his mother. And, even more, he thought of his Pappy George.

"Yer mammy an' I am glad you come back so's we could reconcile, son," George had spoken some years back. "Reconciled," because George and "Willie" were on different tracks ever since his eldest was just a boy. These different tracks were now on W.W.'s grieving mind. Pappy George, he muttered to himself, was a man of mystery. W.W. kept driving in silence. First of all, Pappy, he guessed, never tried to know him and he didn't know Pappy near as well as he should. Becky, this minute riding quietly next to him on the wagon bench, had accused *him* of the same thing. "You don't really know yer children," she'd said, "an' they don't really know you!" Well, he figured, they do know their father came out of Cadiz. He only knew that his Pappy had made his way to Ohio from Baltimore in Maryland, nothing else. Who was Pappy before Cadiz? Who were Pappy's people? He wasn't certain of these things because Pappy kept them to hisself—mysteriously. And his Ma, "Bell," wouldn't talk about this. Over the years he'd learned things about Pappy, but certain things he still hadn't resolved.

For example, particularly in W.W.'s early years, why did Pappy George seem so offish?

Maybe it was the war. From his earliest childhood days, as a four- or five-year-old, he remembered men in uniforms running around town. Later his mother told him how there was much confusion in Jefferson and Harrison Counties because of so many Quakers being against the fighting. His Pappy was obligated to the Quakers, who'd helped him settle safely in Ohio in 1859, the year before their "Willie" was born. So George Brown stayed out of the way of government officials and kept his own family half-hidden.

But probably Pappy's peculiarities had more to do with his slavery days. W.W. didn't know much about his Pappy's life before coming to live free in Ohio, except that he came from Baltimore, where officials were trying to hunt him down like he was a got-loose animal. Those days some slave catchers even came into Ohio, captured runaways, and also, illegally, some free Negroes living there without papers. So Pappy, same as other fretful coloreds, laid low in town. He never seemed to get over this fretful feeling, despite the end of slavery. By the by, Pappy became so close-mouthed and sulky that it affected his otherwise frisky children. Ma Bell was the one who kept her young'uns in sunny spirits.

Usually Pappy seemed somewhat uneasy around his Isabell, whom he and the family called "Bell." Ma Bell had her own Lawrence spirit. The Lawrence folks had been living out of bondage in Ohio for many years and had ways different from those people fleeing slavery in years just before the war. Pappy was one of the newcomers, whose way of dress and talk and habits lacked Ohio's refinement. He looked up to Bell, appreciated his wife. But he surely felt a little lack in himself. Compared to Ma, Pappy came of a "one-horse" background and was as "savage as a meat ax."

Maw was friendly, outgoing. Pappy, holding to himself, was not all somber, yet his smile was a dark one. Pappy said little, so . . . very few folks knew what he was thinking. Nobody took him lightly, though—he had a hiss about him, something on the order of a rattlesnake. He was quiet, seemingly gentle, yet at the same time, hard as a nail.

As W.W. drove the wagon on this sad day, while Becky shut her tired eyes and nodded, one other thing about his parents was on his mind. He recalled Aunt Julia, his mother's sister, whom he was staying with as a young buck up in Elyria, telling him about George and Isabell's marriage. They wed in 1868, when he was only eight and too young to remember now. "Oh, they were actually wed years earlier, jus' they 'jumped the broom' like slaves did, tho they were in free territory," Aunt Julia said. Well, Aunt Julia seemed to indicate the reason was that they were keeping quiet and out of sight—avoiding all government officials, including those census-riders. Then in '68 they decided to make their marriage official. Somehow he'd never discussed this matter with either Pappy or Ma. He felt it was just too personal, not his business.

Anyhow, Pappy George and him sort of made up before Pappy passed away. For years Pappy had grunted about "Willie" being a "dreamer," but that eased up when he realized that some of W.W.'s business deals made a good profit and kept his family fed and clothed. W.W. didn't understand why Pappy thought dreaming was wrong. He was now still trying to fathom Pappy's peculiar ways. How was Pappy molded before he come running to Ohio? What things had Pappy faced? he wondered.

Saturday morning, August 22, 1857, Montgomery County, Maryland.

George noted the five-point silver badge on mastah Charles Brown's chest. This meant the mastah had either been deputized by Montgomery County's Sheriff or had deputized himself (which was usually the case). Either way it was serious. Mastah was readying himself and other white men to go catch Big Ben and Warren, who'd run away overnight. From the cornfield George watched three men, two carrying Baker rifles and one a shotgun, ride up to mastah, who was on his big roan stallion. Mastah held leashes to three "nigger dogs" and a pure bloodhound loaned to him by a neighbor. These "nigger dogs," George knew, were kept chained out of sight, trained just to scent and hunt Negroes— they were so fierce they'd tear a man to pieces if not curbed. The bloodhound was a true tracker, but the big, blue-hound "nigger dogs" made his skin scream! They were growling and ready to rip. He hoped Big Ben and Warren were far away.

They had planned their escape for a week, including his being part of it. Tobacco planting had shrunk due to soil gone poor, though the Quakers now had ways of making earth rich enough for oats, wheat, and corn. Since mastah's farming was slackening, rumors were that at least the two older, Ben and Warren, were to be sold down South—a terrible outcome. They all had kin in nearby Georgetown and mastah knew this. So the plan was to start toward District of Columbia, fooling slave hunters, then make a run north to Pennsylvania using the "railroad." George, however, had his own plan, which first connected with Levi, the Quaker boy.

Three years ago, when George was sixteen, mastah had him join the Saturday evening sport in the County. Folks called this the "Battle Royal." Tough, colored slave-boys fighting each other in a cleared circle of ground, while crowds of folk, mostly white men, whooped and hollered them on. They fought bare-knuckled in a "free-for-all" until only two were standing. The next Saturday these two fought for a prize. The winner's owner got a fistful of cash, but throughout the fight, pennies and nickels were thrown on the ground for the fighters themselves to gather. George was short but strong, and he would earn some coins. He liked the applause—even some white boys would praise both the winner and loser afterward. That's how he met Levi. One day, a fortnight ago, he saw Levi at the Farmers' Market where he accompanied mastah. Levi whispered to him, "Mine Papa is a 'Friend.' Papa wants you to know that whenever you need a 'ride,' we will take you." George now knew the "Friends" were Quakers and a "ride" meant some help toward freedom. Levi's father, named Nahum, was saying, "We trust you, now you must trust us." Besides, Nahum and Ol' Ezekiel were friends. George several times had been loaned by mastah to a tobacco plantation over in Prince George's County. Ol' Ezekiel was a free Negro with his own little ground, but he also helped out at the plantation. He told George he would get him to Baltimore "right quick" whenever he made up his mind to flee.

So, on the sly, George commenced working out his own plan. From Levi, Nahum made arrangements with Ezekiel. About ten o'clock on August 22, Nahum and Levi would be taking a wagon with their crops east to the Chesapeake's western shore. They'd slow down the wagon, near the gully just past Sandy Springs, long enough for George to board, then take him to the big fork over in Prince George's County. At the fork, Ezekiel'd be waiting with his wagon of tobacco bound for the twenty miles north to Baltimore. George would need to be smart, swift, and timely . . .

Picking corn and watching mastah, he glimpsed the sky reckoning it was about eight o'clock. (He didn't dare to draw out his pocket watch.) His mastah had quickly assembled men and dogs this morning, like a sharp deputy should. He was thinking—mastah's efficacy was obliging George's own schedule. "Stop yer dreamin', boy!" Mastah called out to him. "No time fer a no'count dreamer. Git that corn picked and ready for market by evenin'!" Then the dogs, having sniffed Big Ben and Warren's bed cots, were loosed and the riders dashed away. Well, George was no dreamer. His croker sack, full of his belongings, was hid nearby. Seeing the horses and dogs rush southwest through the hills, he grabbed his sack, canteen, and walking stick. His heart was beating fast. He headed across the cornfield. Picked his way eastward among briar patches and trees. Before ten o'clock he arrived at the gully just past Sandy Springs. A smiling Nahum and Levi met and rode him as far as the big fork, then bade him God-speed.

He waited behind a tree. Ezekiel, his trusted old friend, and a wagon pulled by six mules lumbered up shortly under a sky turned sun-honey gold. Ezekiel, walking alongside, motioned the wagon to a halt, then looked around. Then he turned a circle silently beckoning a ghost out of the woods. George stepped forward from the trees. Ezekiel smiled, but no greetings were exchanged. "Okay. I got these made up," Ezekiel whispered and handed George two folded sheets of counterfeit "free papers." "Show 'em, if we get stopped." He led George over to the large wagon. Three pairs of mules were strung out ahead of the wagon. A young fellow, George knew he was the mule skinner, sat on the left mule of the pair closest to the wagon, holding the long rein, or "jerk line." A second husky fellow leaned on the rear wagonside. "This be Rome an' Britt," Ezekiel mumbled, pointing to the mule driver and the other colored. "They good, strong men, he'pin' me. You, Britt an' me be walking 'longside or ridin' the wagon sometimes. Let's git goin'. We got twenty more miles tuh travel."

George understood from his days working on the Scaggs plantation with Ol' Ezekiel. The huge wagon carried several hogsheads containing pressed tobacco leaves and weighing a "load" (around 500 pounds) each. At the wagon's rear there was feed grain and a barrel of water for the mules. Ol' Ezekiel made this trip to Baltimore whenever a planter had hogsheads of cured tobacco ready for market. So the road patrols, agents of plantation owners, sheriffs, and constables knew he was on legitimate business and rarely stopped his wagon. And Ezekiel was not in the habit of smuggling slaves, either.

The big, heavy wagon rolled and shook all day, going first on a trail next to Patuxent River, then on the North Trail toward Baltimore City. No fellows or officers stopped the wagon, so it harmlessly reached Baltimore.

George, though, had his eyes open. He peered at every thicket opening and every bend of the river and wherever pursuers might come riding over the horizon. He watched the mule team—the lead pair in front, the swing pair in the center, the wheel pair directly in front of the wagon where Rome rode one of the mules and drove the six. Rome shouted "Haw!" to bear them left, and "Gee!" to bear them right, but it was the "Whoa!" George listened for. "Whoa!" could signal horse riders bearing down on them. He'd never run away before; he was nervous, though he was putting his trust in Ol' Ezekiel and, more, in God Almighty! He kept praying.

"Stay strong," said Ezekiel. "Thuh Browns, who'll be takin' you in at Baltimore City, be they kin?"

George slowly hunched his shoulders. "Dunno, sir. But I hear they's good people."

Ezekiel assured him they were, indeed, good folks who would see him safe 'til his next step North.

Late that afternoon the mule wagon pulled into tobacco market stalls. A crowd was busy doing business. However, a tall, white man with piercing eyes stood watching the wagon arriving. George would never forget this man's scrutiny. "J'in the crowd here, then sneak off. Do what I tol' you," Ezekiel whispered. George Brown drifted away, soon to be free, whatever "freedom" meant.

Clip-clopping was a steady, humdrum sound, but now W.W. heard the whistle. He looked behind him. Clarence, driving the following wagon, was blowing a coach whistle to signal his Pappy. Clarence was slowing the horse. W.W. pulled the reins to steer his wagon to a halt just off the road, realizing that the young folks riding the following wagon needed to stop for a while.

W.W. himself strode privately into the woods. Where he was standing, the oak and hickory trees gave way to a thicket. He quickly saw the briars, their prickly thorns threatening. He thought of old tales about the cunning rabbit and briar patches, and wondered if his Pappy ran away from bondage through patches such as these. Pappy, he told himself, must've gone through hell getting from Maryland to Ohio—if he'd been a slave back when slaves were hunted down like criminals. Maybe he'd made his way partly among such razor-sharp briar patches, which most sane pursuers would avoid. Or otherwise he might have been living half-free in Baltimore City and just snuck into Ohio . . .

He pictured his Pappy as being a toughie as a youngster—not a rowdy, but a short, strong, mannerly fellow with fists of iron which he could use if he had to. He, W.W., didn't take much after his Pappy—being taller, more jocular, and more quick-witted, he recognized. Of course it was their natures where they'd really differed. Pappy was wary of all government officials and white men (except for Quaker folk, who had aided him when he came to Ohio). But W.W. was ready to cotton to most anyone, white or colored—and he was a smooth talker. He was more like Ma Bell that way. Ma would accept his plan to trek north with Becky and their young'uns in search of opportunities, whereas his Pappy would question this. Well, both Pappy and Ma were gone now. Gone to be with the Lord, he figured. He strode back to his own family ones, who were boarding the two wagons again now.

CHAPTER 17

August 1908. Fleet and Ednah sat in their kitchen, having breakfast in the "City of the Gauls"—a phrase that was the meaning of the name, Gallipolis, Ohio. Gallipolis was not their fixed home. They were only there for a short while. Fleet had suspended the opera house operations in Cadiz while pursuing his latest venture.

Ednah saw that his plate was heaped with eggs and bacon and hominy grits. "Don't be wolfing your breakfast down, husband," Ednah begged him. "You've got time." The hackney taking him to the Baltimore train was not due for an hour and a half, so he had time to even finish the morning paper. "What're they saying about Springfield?" she asked.

Unlike his joking grin when he sat down to face her, his face was now shaping a fierce grimace. "Whites went on a rampage—killing some Negroes and wounding many more. A terrible time there in Illinois—you hear me, Ednah?—this is a goddamn shame!" Fleet slammed his fist atop a news page on the table. Months ago he had cursed about the riot in Springfield, Ohio—but this one, in Abe Lincoln's old hometown, was worse. Words spilling out through his lips were ugly, bitter . . .

Elegant and refined, Ednah winced from his language. She reached out and touched his arm. She was sorry she'd asked him about Springfield. "What time, honey, will you be arriving in Baltimore?" Her gentle touch and her "honey" interrupted his tirade—her voice instantly reminding him of the sweet and husky sounds she'd uttered earlier in their bed.

Fleet answered, then loaded his fork with food. He knew why she'd blurted the question. He knew what she was doing. He'd just started on a hairy path. So he stopped talking. He chewed his vittles and called to mind disturbing things. At times his anger had broken loose like wild water cascading down Rock Hill after a spring flood. And this anger, which had driven the writing of his book, worried Ednah. And she disagreed with his assertion that all Negroes should be transported to the continent where their blood originated. Yet, even as he argued this, a dark, pesky thought nettled his mind: Was his argument sound? *Our Home Colony: The Past, Present, and Future of the Negro Race in America* had recently been published. He'd poured out his soul into this. It was his tour-de-force. He intended to make this a bell whose clang would be heard across the nation, and he would ignore, swallow the pesky thing.

Ednah, sensing his daydreaming and fearing where his mind was likely going, asked, "How's your breakfast, dear?"

"Oh, this is scrumptious! Gal, you can cook up a storm when you take a mind to it!" Ednah smiled, although knowing full well that, though he never said it, her cooking couldn't measure up to Arabella's. And surely it could not match Anna's from the Cadiz slope.

"Well, your belly needs some fortifying—because you wouldn't let me fix a lunch for you to take on the train, and Lord knows when they'll serve you dinner."

He grinned. Then his thoughts drifted again.

With the sun gushing its golden light, Edna later watched him step to the hack. He was toting his overnight bag and copies of his new book. She shared his excitement about meeting the imposing Bishop Walters.

In the coach he fidgeted. Not because of the train's jolts, shrieks, and roars, but because he would soon go face-to-face with a man some regarded a saint. Fleet's gaze out a window was resolute, as if catching glimpses of holy prophets bobbing up out in the summer air. Alexander Walters, he thought, could be one of these afternoon ghosts. Fleet pulled his watch from the fob pocket of his vest. Around two hours now 'til Baltimore . . . While his spirits still burned about the big trouble and blood-letting in Illinois, his blanket rage was over increasing Jim Crow, which often brought on lynchings—even here in the North. Seclusion, insults, persecution, beatings, the horrible spilling of life's bitter red juice. Today he understood why the bishop of the African Methodist Episcopal Church, Henry McNeal Turner, had stated year before last that "hell is an improvement on the United States where the Negro is concerned." This old bishop had declared that blacks must return to Africa—the notion Fleet himself was also putting forth. His book had been spirited by Anna from the slope and his thesis inspired by this old Bishop Turner. What is Bishop Alexander Walters's stance this August day? he wondered. (Three shadowy specters still bobbed out against the sun shining along the railway tracks.)

He already knew that the two bishops had some differences. Maybe the biggest difference, he guessed, was in their stages of life. Turner is old enough to be his father, and Walters—not of the A.M.E., but of A.M.E. *Zion*—is around the same age as himself. Turner represents near about the generation of the great Frederick Douglass who passed away thirteen years ago. Turner was shaped back in the day when the song of Africa was running fresh in his veins, back when the call of that continent was still strong, calling the holy man to come build a nation. Bishop Walters, Booker T. Washington, his youthful crony Willie Brown of Cadiz, and himself are the following generation whose souls have been fully baptized in the American dream. What speaks to him these days is that fellows of his generation are geared to lifting mainly their own selves. Such might have been necessary during the decades following the War Between the States, when colored men had to climb up through briar plots and claws of prejudice by force themselves and make the race proud. But, Fleet mused, now the younger folks are showing that all Negroes can be uplifted at the same time through organization. Bishop Walters, therefore, has been guiding some of these younger folk in establishing the National Afro-American Council. This bishop received a copy of his book and arranged today's meeting. He was excited over meeting Alexander Walters, this man of God, for the first time. As the train neared Baltimore and Union Station, Fleet stood, grabbed his satchel and the sack containing several copies of *Our Home Colony*. He noticed that the bobbing figures had vanished outside the window. Maybe they'd pop up and lead him to the meeting. In his head he heard the old spiritual, *There's a Meeting Here Tonight*.

Bishop Walters's provisional office in Zion's parish house glowed dimly inside high, handsome mahogany-paneled walls surrounding bookcases and desks and chairs and a long table. The tall, robust, and handsome man stood and welcomed Fleet. "America's first colored baseball hero—Moses Fleetwood Walker, the Lion. Pleased to meet you!" Both men's handshake was strong. Two local Zion churchmen also greeted him.

"Sit . . . rest yerself. It's a bit of a journey coming from Ohio," Bishop Walters chirped. "We're here to discuss your book and it's import to us Negroes. Later we'll cross the street an' have some dinner." Fleet smilingly fetched two books from his sack to hand to the others. "Here there's a nice bedroom all set up for you tonight. I prayed for the Holy Ghost Himself to keep you comfortable." The bishop chuckled, then began a powerful prayer.

Besides congratulating Fleet on his book, Bishop Walters spoke at length on his overseas travels for A.M.E. Zion—to England, Europe, Palestine, Egypt. "God has allowed me a fair understanding of how folks mesh and struggle with human evil and bigotry, not just in our land but in fatherlands across the earth." Examining Fleet's face, Walters asked, "Have you traveled likewise, Moses Fleetwood Walker?" Fleet shook his head "No." Walters grunted—a grunt that unhinged Fleet a bit, making him wonder what point the bishop was shrewdly making.

"Now if we may, let's turn to page thirty-one of your book, Mr. Walker . . . It says here, and I read, 'The only practical and permanent solution of the present and future race troubles in the United States is entire separation by Emigration of the Negro from America. *Even forced Emigration would be better for all than the continued present relations of the races*; but there would be no necessity for force if the proper measures are taken and the Negroes are offered reasonable help to return to their native land." Seeing and hearing his own words being read, Fleet swung his head in acknowledgment. He'd heard that Bishop Walters, along with Bishop Turner, was in agreement with "Back to Africa."

Loudly, one of the two Zion fellows sucked in a deep breath. The second one rolled his eyes. "Mr. Walker," said the bishop, "that is a powerful statement! Well, I must admit I had similar ideas—once."

Fleet began feeling warm, and not just from the room's August heat. "Bishop, I'd be obliged if you would just call me Fleet."

"Well, sir, hereafter it shall be 'Fleet.' You know, as a Christian cleric, I am charged with considering even social or political proposals in light of biblical teachings. Now let me read your thoughts from page thirty-nine. I quote: 'Many people of kind heart, rather than of good reason in the matter, believe that the application of Christian principles will right all the difficulties between the races in this country. We do not believe that the Christian principle—Fatherhood of God and Brotherhood of man, or even anything in the Decalogue—teaches that alien races can unite in the same state to their mutual welfare. Furthermore, we believe it in perfect accord with the Divine teachings, that diverse races remain in separate territories. For the Bible says: 'God hath made of one blood all nations of men to dwell on all the face of the earth, and hath determined the time before appointed, and the bounds of their habitation.'

"Fleet, I find myself in disagreement with your sense of the Scriptures. We should consult the book of Deuteronomy." Walters, having his own Bible, reached over to a stand and fetched one for Fleet. The Zion men were already turning pages. "Deuteronomy, chapter thirty-two, verse eight . . . page 138," he noted. "Will you recite this, Fleet?"

Fleet was not liking this moment—interpreting the Scripture in the presence of not only three ministers, but one of them a bishop! His fingers were strangely moist and his heart was quickening. "When the Most High divided to the nations their inheritance, when he separated the sons of Adam, he set the bounds of the people according to to the number of the children of Israel . . ."

"Appreciate your reading, Brother Fleet. You see—Lord, make of us a witness!—all peoples share one blood, that same blood of our Father Adam. But in this passage God, through Moses, is dealing with the *Israelites*—not all folks on earth. God first set boundaries for the line of Abraham, but in time moved these folks to Egypt. Then He delivered them from Pharaoh. As you know, Fleet, neither the Jews nor any other peoples have been locked for all time in the land where they raised up. "So, sir, I cannot see that a 'back to Africa' move is mandated according to the Scriptures. Expense of such a move? Now, I did find your proposal as to how a yearly expatriation in numbers matching just the annual increase in our Negro population can be paid for. Let us turn to the last paragraph, page thirty-three of your book . . . I read: 'By the census of 1900, the population was 8,849,789, an increase during the decade from 1890 to 1900 of 1,352,001, or 12.2 percent. Now to transport this increase of 1,352,001 at twenty dollars would cost $27,040,020. If this task was undertaken by the General Government, the sum would be less by one-half. Who will deny that the great and powerful Government of the United States could not afford to expend even $100,000,000 per year to accomplish an object so fraught with beneficial results to two races, alien and incongruous?'

"You also wrote: 'There is to our mind no other rational plan but Emigration for the Negro . . . The conditions in the United States are opposed to the development of any spirit of independence, either of thought or action, among the members of the subordinate race. High ideals, lofty and noble thoughts, can never enter the brains of a people oppressed.' Well, sir, allow me to air my reactions . . ."

The two Zion ministers folded their arms and leaned back in their chairs. Bishop Alexander could be long-winded. His deep thoughts, his words flowed like glossy pearls in a stream flooding any room. Fleet was looking amazed, while sensing a train of repudiations. He was correct. Bishop Alexander Walters started by linking Fleet's ideas to those of

A.M.E. Bishop Henry McNeal Turner, who once made these statements: "As long as we remain among whites, the Negro will believe that the devil is black . . . that a black person is the devil . . . and the effect of such sentiment is contemptuous and degrading"; also, "Until we have black men in the seat of power, respected, feared, hated, and reverenced, our young men will never rise"; and also, "Africa is the only hope of the Negro race."

Alexander Walters swiveled his big chair to face Fleet directly.

"I am thankful for ol' Bishop Turner. He's one of our saints, you know. Long years past, many of our people—mostly the working class and farmers—tasted and swallowed his message. And, Lord knows, as a younger fellow I, too, entertained this same message. I felt the fire of persecution, of Jim Crow. Today, though, with the years piling up, I have tempered my judgments. Aw, just in aught-five, three years back, Professor DuBois—W.E.B. DuBois—invited me to that meeting held at Niagara Falls, 'tween Canada and New York. I couldn't be at that get-together, yet I joined the now-renowned 'Niagara Movement.' I am in agreement with Professor DuBois and others that, rather than emigration, we need to fight right here for our civil rights. In fact, because of today's news of whites killing blacks in Illinois, I've gotten several telegrams. In the next few days a mighty meeting will be held. We're surely going to pull on, both colored and whites together, battle garments for God . . . we're going to battle!"

Fleet was shaken by the bishop's jarring words. Walters talked of victories needing to be won "right here, right where we stand." He said, "Thousands of our peoples have died—and many thousands maimed—for a cause." His voice trembled with militancy. He mentioned Scripture, Numbers 32:27: "Your servants will cross over, everyone armed for war, to do battle for the Lord . . ." While Walters was quoting Scripture, Fleet thought of a Negro spiritual: "I'm On the Battlefield For My Lord." Fleet wondered suddenly where *he* was.

Looking Fleet squarely in the eyes, Bishop Walters asked, "Have you planned to personally coordinate the emigration?" The question struck hard, and as if Walters knew the truth. Fleet lowered his eyes, then lifted them. "Well . . . uh, yes, Bishop. I would offer my services as the Chief Agent." Fleet realized the paths where he and the bishop were heading—but he had to be truthful. The bishop was nobody to fool with. "And your brother—I believe his name is Weldy?" Fleet could not very well shorten the full truth, which he suspected Walters already knew. "Weldy, yes, would serve as General Agent."

"Uh-huh." The bishop chose not to mention Fleet and Weldy's possible other motives tucked inside *Our Home Colony*. "Fleet, I laud you for your truthfulness." Bishop Walters's point had been made!

"Gentlemen, is it time for dinner to be served us?" Bishop Walters asked in a manner more like a command than a question. Both Zion ministers stood up and one headed for the door to inquire at the eatery across the street. The other man gathered up papers, including a bunch of telegrams for his bishop. "Fleet, shall we close with a prayer?"

Fleet's mind was shattered, its pieces sailing through his head. Why was he here? he wondered. His answer was somewhere among his sailing bits of reasoning. Surely someone was sending information about him to the bishop. Who? Who was this adversary? Could it even be a friend or a kinsman? Even Weldy . . . or Ednah? Maybe the bishop even knew he killed Curly Murray or that he was convicted and jailed by the United States for mail theft. Maybe Walters knew that both Bella and Ednah looked almost white. At this moment, he was a goldfish flipping and flopping out of water, without oxygen. He needed to go to Anna again in Cadiz!

"A prayer, Fleet?" Bishop Walters was restless now—and hungry.

Fleet nodded, and the invocation began. A discombobulated question streaked like greased lightning across his mind: *These three men of God—had he not seen someone like their images bobbing before him on his way into Baltimore?* Afterward Bishop Walters paid tribute to Fleet's amazing baseball years throughout dinner and until he and the three holy men shook hands farewell.

CHAPTER 18

*I*t came like a spit of tobacco chaw into his face. "'Cept maybe fer barbering, you can't actually operate no good business 'round here these days, Tod," the huddled fellows said. "An' even colored barbers done lost their white trade due to the white foreigners come here."

The place was Elyria and this summer was 1913. W.W., or "Tod" as some called him, was in this town with his family for the second time. He was here to once again test "opportunities," and he had new business ventures on his mind.

He studied the fervidness in their eyes and the raising of their brows. "Fellows, I appreciate yer opinion, surely do." Then he shook their hands, grinned, and went on his way.

Elyria was still a strange, new city to Becky Brown. When she heard the clatter of his horse and wagon, she stepped out on the porch. W.W. had been gone since daybreak, telling her, "Today I sure 'nough be snatching a bigger opportunity fer us." Although he'd promised such things before without result, this time she'd felt a certainty in his voice. He grinned at her while climbing out of the wagon.

"Pappy," she called out, using her husband's family handle, "I just toted in the last few bundles of wood. I might need more to complete my cookin' tomorrow. You best go over to Flushing Coal an' have a cord delivered."

From the driveway he caught the aroma of what Becky was baking on her huge, cast-iron range. As usual it nearly took his breath away. The only better cook he knew was Anna from the slope. "Yea, Becky, I'll go to Flushing's now. By the way, gal, we'll be needin' more'n a cord." He chuckled. "Lord knows, you got plenty more cookin' t'do." W.W. winked at her, then climbed back into his wagon—leaving Becky mumbling, "What's this rascal meaning now? Lord, ha' mercy!"

She'd been wondering how long her family would be living in this huge house with room enough for two full families. When they'd moved to Elyria here a year ago, ten of their twelve living children were in the house. But now all the boys and two of the girls, all grown, were on their own, and just six younger daughters were here. Three bedrooms on the third floor were now empty. What was W.W.'s "plenty more cooking" all about? Becky figured he was conniving something. It was his scheming that had brought them to this busy little city close to the shore of Great Lake Erie.

W.W.'s old draw-horse pulled the wagon, clip-clopping down the street, to Flushing on Middle Avenue. Since the coal and wood stalls were located next to the Masonic Temple, there were usually some prominent fellows gathered nearby—talking business. W.W. got out of his wagon, looking around. Two men he saw were ones he needed to speak with. "Gentlemen, how you be today?" The men—Pat, sidekick of Deputy Assessor John Winslow, and Harry, aide to ward leader Henry Beck—swung 'round, surprised. Their eyes took in this Negro, brazen but with a soft voice, who'd interrupted them. He was dressed even more smartly than they—dapper suit, gleaming white collar, neat bow tie, shoes polished into laced-up, black diamond small boats. Was he that rail-straight, proper colored man who several times had silently, stealthily stood along the back wall of their council meetings? "We're fairly well. How do you be, sir?"

"I'm tolerbly well, thank the Lord," W.W. answered the men. Then he began engaging them in conversation. "Have you'uns heard remarks spoken recently by Mr. Booker T. Washington?" They nodded and opined, "Yea, maybe so. Who has not catched Booker Washington's ideas? He's certainly known fer pushing you colored folks into makin' a good account of yourselves."

"Yessir. And pushing the white man, too, into lettin' loose some real opportunities so our pushing has results, I reckon," W.W. retorted with a dry grin.

For ten minutes W.W., Pat, and Harry chatted about Booker T.'s call for business opportunities which Negroes can take advantage of. They talked of the Negro Business League, which Booker T. was heading, but which had no presence in Elyria. Then W.W. laid out his own business plans. Pat and Harry were connected to local authorities in ways that W.W. believed beneficial. The men liked his plans. He shook their hands, saying, "Good day, gentlemen." Plans laid heavy on his mind.

Meantime two automobile drivers had already parked and nearly blocked his horse, "Wicket," and wagon. "Confound it!" He stood figuring the best way to maneuver out onto Middle Avenue. However, Wicket, fifteen years old now and wise of age, carefully picked his way around the two pompous motorcars. W.W. had his horse and wagon clomping up the road when he suddenly remembered why he'd come to the Masonic Temple in the first place. He would have to turn around on a side street and get back to Flushing's, or otherwise hear Becky's mighty jawing. His mind—his soul, too—had gotten crowded: jumbled with pieces of dreams, jiggling shards of mind-light matching the sun sparkle this summer afternoon.

Starting to turn onto Fifth Street, he saw them: one of his sons, Clinton, leaning against a Ford truck, hands stroking his *tootsie's* face. *Whoa!* Hearing Wicket's halt and glimpsing his father staring from the wagon, Clinton scooted away from the girl. "Pap, uh, good afternoon!"

"Bidin' yer time while tryin' to spark a good-lookin' young lady surely is pleasurable, but it's not earning any wages, is it?"

"Pap, I was just finishing my lunch when she walked by," Clinton said sheepishly. "I'll be gettin' back to Mr. Feece's garage, back to work, 'fore long."

W.W. suggested that his son go over to Flushing's and, using his Pappy's credit, load a cord of stove-cut wood in the truck and deliver it because his mother needed it for her cooking.

"Yessir." Pappy's "suggestion" was really a command, Clinton understood.

Wicket, just like the horses he had trained years before, took up W.W.'s other command, "Home, boy," and headed straight to West Avenue. Having just encountered one son, W.W.'s thoughts switched to his others. Charles, Clarence, and Otto were also on their own, working for different employers. Charles, his eldest, was even away with his family, toiling in a clay mine. While not as often as Becky did, once in a while he wondered what sort of father he was. Years back Becky once questioned, "Ain't you be trainin' yer hosses better'n yer sons?" His sons, strong and husky men now, seemed to run counter to their Pappy. He always wanted to be independent, or at least in charge; they seemed content as hired hands. He himself was always figuring; they settled too much for fields as they lay. Other than for their vigor, jubilance and tomfoolery, were they more like their mammy by nature, or was it because he wasn't around them as much as Becky? Anyway, he'd kept them in line when they were cubs. However, now they had grown big, tough and wild. Had the time come when they no longer had any real fear of his prowess? Was his roar the only way he could control them? All his boys were working in different places.

He wondered how he could bring them together under his charge. Wicket pulled up at home.

"Becky, we got some confabulatin' to do," he spoke while bursting into the kitchen.

"Do tell? You order wood, Tod?"

"Aw, I spotted Clinton. He's gettin' a cord and will bring it here."

Seeing her busy with the stove while she cooked, W.W. stepped into another room to pour himself a whiskey out of Becky's view. He was thirsty, but not for water. Usually by afternoon good liquor was giving him a boost, so this drink was late coming. Tasted good. He gulped and swallowed some more. Then the figments in his mind began to take sharper shape. He rested himself, for a minute he thought, in the Bentwood rocking chair. Soft, striated sunlight sneaked in through the wooden shutters and helped make him drowsy.

"Pappy!" He opened his eyes, realizing that Becky stood beside his chair. "I guess you had more'n one dad-blasted whiskey drink. What is it you want tuh talk 'bout?"

He sat up straight. "You know I been sniffing 'round Elyria fer new opportunities. My ice cream parlor's in a fair place—Fifteenth an' Middle—but it's bringing in only a middling amount. I been thinking of owning a hotel in the course of time. But as a start taking in boarders in this here house, to see how it goes. I come across some white fellows connected to City Council an' ran it by them this morning. They liked the idea, knowin' the troubles that arriving colored workers have findin' places to light whilst here on construction. These men said lodgin' and feedin' licenses could be easily arranged. Now we got lodgin' space upstairs. Our girls could help you with the extra cooking. What you think?"

Becky was not fully surprised. After more than thirty years of marriage, she knew her husband's mind. Earlier he'd given her reason to suspect.

She beckoned him into the kitchen, where she had their afternoon dinner heating. "It's more than a notion, you know."

W.W. nodded his head in agreement. "The girls can ready the guest's sleepin' quarters when they're not pullin' shifts at the ice cream place. 'Course, it shall add a few plates to yer dining room table—huh?"

Becky mumbled something as she turned down the stove's damper. The hog hearts for dinner were almost done and needed less heat. "Tod, honey-man, we can talk now 'bout a *sharing* of profits," she said with a serious grin. The aroma of pork was so delicious that W.W.'s next furtive sip of whiskey seemed even tastier to him. But he didn't answer. Becky had rolled each one of the thin slices of smoked hog heart in flour and browned them with chopped onion in hot bacon grease. Now she pulled the large pan from the oven, smothered the slices with biscuit dough and shoved the pan back in to finish cooking. "You reckon one a' these times the money you plan to make might be headed fer me an' the children—who be doin' the work?"

He watched how masterfully she prepared dinner. No wasted motions. This was the smooth way he'd always wanted his hired workers to do their jobs. Becky assembled dishes, silverware, and platters while keeping the casserole heating just right. Her big woodstove—she insisted on applewood for cooking—made food tastier, with a better smoke cachet, than coal stoves. She could manage feeding not just boarders; she could operate an eatery. "You reckon," Becky had just asked, "money . . . might be headed fer me . . . who be doin' the work?" Although her mouth had a grin, he knew Becky wasn't joshing. He remembered what his mother, Isabell, had said—talking of George, who ran loose from bondage—"*Be no slave.*" Was he treating his family like "slaves"?

"Wife, suppose we term this move, 'Becky's Boarding'—an' you collect the money, keep it in yer purse, spend it as you wish? It be yer enterprise." While her back was turned, he took another sip of whiskey.

She turned to face him. "My enterprise? The money coming directly into *my purse*? Tod, that be—das'nt I say, uh, unheard of. What's got into you—'sides the whiskey I just heard you swig?"

His eyes told her that he was serious. She took a deep breath and touched her chest. Though she was the strength of the family, he was the leader for keeping them bread-and-butter sound. He controlled all funds and paid all bills. "Becky's Boarding?" While she was absorbing this, some of the girls came trooping in for dinner.

Of course, Becky's little enterprise, with its money directed to her, got around. Neighbor and Second Methodist A.M.E. "sisters" got fired up. They who only collected coins for washing or ironing or domestic work. They became emboldened enough to think of claiming more control of things in their own homes. W.W. gained greater respect among Elyria's colored women. So he smiled, but couldn't reveal that this new feather in Becky's cap was actually preached to him by Anna living on the slope of Cadiz during his latest trip down to see her.

Autumn, winter and springtime saw boarders come and go. Boarders spread praises of Becky's cooking. So did Second Methodist A.M.E., whose parishioners frequently called upon Becky and her daughters' fine cooking whenever a feast or social event was to be held.

But W.W.'s itch was growing. His ice cream parlor and Becky's Boarding were only steps toward his dream. Dreams of building a prominent and lucrative business that employed and uplifted Elyria Negroes. A firm in which his sons and daughters could be proudly involved. That's why he was noseying around town, sniffing out possibilities, getting the scoop on activities, getting to know business and political people.

Then one day his eldest son, Charles, and his family came to visit.

Charles, powerfully built but slightly shorter than his slender and handsome Pappy, was himself a strong voice in the family. Like his mother, Charles had an imposing presence and, unlike W.W.'s tenor tones, he spoke in a deep baritone. His father's mind was both mercenary and as subtle as a fox. But "Charlie" was just a tough, hard-toiling young ox—less concerned with multiplying money and fame than growing and enjoying nowadays his fresh family of six.

"How things be in the clay industry?" W.W. asked.

"Doing good, Pappy. I've had intentions to talk with you about this."

Charlie Brown lived with wife, Ella, and their four children in Lisbon, where workers scooped fire clay out of low-rising hillsides. This was on the same order, but easier than mining clay's cousin—coal. "Pappy, you heard about a big war taking place way across the pond—those Europe countries. Anyway, some clay companies now beginning to make the fixtures used by foundries that manufacture things needed by our brotherly nations waging war. You know, Pappy, this fire clay can make linings for great big furnaces. Contracts are comin' in." He said this in case Pappy was of the mind now to try the clay industry.

W.W. lit a cigar, nodding that he understood. Both he and son Charlie had grown up in deep, tiny black vaults chiseled out of coal. So W.W. and Charlie knew something about the uses of seams of clay that lay below and above the soft coal veins of Harrison and Jefferson Counties.

In Lisbon, and much of Columbiana County, clay seams thicker than the coal had lain in the ground for hundreds of millions of years—since way *before* ancient times when an early world was hot and swampy. It waited for people who needed this "plastic" earth for making pottery and ceramics and sturdy products such as sewer pipes, bricks, and tiles.

Charlie spoke of new-fangled ceramic items like sparkplug insulators for automobiles and aeroplane engines. W.W. shrugged at these things. Sparkplugs? The meshing of working parts of gasoline buggies and flying machines was too baffling for his contentment. He feared all of this. He was expert at having horses work—men, too—and now he was too old to get expert at the managing of machines. But when Charlie mentioned cement his interest piqued.

Between puffs from his high-priced Havana, he asked, "What cement they be makin' over 'round Lisbon, son?"

"Portland—they say it's the best, Pappy."

Weeks went by before W.W. sprang into action on his idea. However, he hadn't been still; he had been studying local construction jobs—roads and buildings—that white contractors were doing, and he fleshed out his plan. He'd already noticed faults in construction. W.W.'s habit was to hail folks on the street this way, "Fine day, don't you think? How you be?" Five minutes into a chitchat they were baring their souls or telling him things about their circumstances that he hadn't even asked. So, when roaming around town, he'd stopped to jawbone with men who, unawares, complained of cracking foundations or streets crumbling beneath the weight of new gasoline buggies. "Concrete not holdin' up?" he would ask. "Uh-huh, I s'pect they're using weak cement," often was the reply. He learned from Charlie of cement manufacturers doing brisk business. And that there were some "short contracts" where men were hired for a few weeks at a time.

So W.W. assured himself that Becky could take care of the boarders and their meals, while the girls could handle the ice cream parlor, then he headed for Lisbon. He found the pay, on short contracts, quite good. But he was not there so much because of the wages. He was there to study cement making. This was the third part of his plan. As he helped mix clay with limestone, he quietly studied the formulas and methods. He calculated changes that might strengthen the cement.

"Short contracts" required only an extra dozen or so of whiz-bang men who could afford coming to the Lisbon cement works for two weeks at a time. Of these, just two Negroes—crackerjack young Mack from Akron and fifty-six-year-old W.W. from Elyria—were regularly welcomed by the shift foreman. Foreman Alec, a big blond who had no friendliness or high regard for coloreds, had nevertheless taken a liking to the adept and courtly Negro he somehow was moved to call "Mistah Brown." He couldn't help the feeling that "Mistah Brown" brought a wisdom, which he couldn't quite pinpoint, to the shift.

W.W. closely watched limestone and clay being ground and baked into "clinkers"—then the clinkers, along with a chalky stuff called gypsum, were further heated and ground into grayish cement powder. Also he'd studied the behavior of Alec, his foreman, who was the shift chemist, too. Alec was sober, thin-skinned, and jealous of his cement-making skills. So W.W. knew he had to be very careful in offering suggestions to him.

One workday when Alec was in a sociable mood, W.W. sidled up to his foreman. "This here plaster-of-Paris sort of stuff—uh, you term it gypsum?—it does good at holdin' in cement."

Alec shook his head. "Amazin' material, gypsum! It sure keeps our raw cement from setting too quick."

"Sure does. You're a master at the mixin'. Would you say a bit more gypsum might make cement even stronger—I be jus' wonderin . . ."

A warm wine of persuasion made an easy flow into the cool waters of complacency. Alec did not react with jealousy or even resentment. He mulled W.W.'s soft suggestion over in his mechanical-type mind. He could see the point that "Mistah Brown" was making. He thought of reasons why the measure of gypsum used had stayed steady for years.

By shift's end Alec decided to make a "10 percent" mix of augmented cement that he would have a customer, a concrete maker, test. And, following W.W.'s suggestion, he would give this batch a special number. W.W. shook hands with Alec, commending him for this decision. "I s'pect you might jus' be pleased," W.W. said with a grin.

Three days later Alec strode up to W.W., who with two other men was loading and firing up the huge kiln. He took him aside. "Well, Mistah Brown, the concrete maker reports that my new batch of cement held up as strong as any other—maybe stronger. Allows him to use less water in his mixin'. Wanted you t'know I'm giving this recipe a number, 'mix number seventy-seven.' Appreciate your idees on this." Alec smiled at him, then strode off.

W.W. smiled to himself. He didn't need any more recognition than what he'd just gotten, nor any boost in wages. What he had set into motion was now complete. His reason for being on any further "short contracts" had ended.

Now not only was the Lisbon clay industry flourishing, Elyria's factories and foundries were growing strong. This was springtime of "Seventeen"—President Wilson made his declaration against Germany and folks were calling this a *World War*. America was gearing up for the fight to "make the world safe for democracy once again." Workers with their families were coming up from the South into Elyria to help make whatever our Allies overseas and our own army and navy needed in order to fight the enemy. Meanwhile, young fellows—including mechanics and factory and foundry and construction workers—were leaving town to join the military. W.W. Brown, having seen all this coming, set up his employment office at 52 West Avenue.

There were houses and shops to be built. Mainly there were roads to be constructed or widened, requiring cement. So W.W. went looking for contracts, then for workers. Businessmen and politicians recognized this well-dressed, smooth-talking colored gentleman strolling into their offices. With their polished-oak desktops shrieking from the clutter of orders calling for new work, they listened to him. They liked what he was offering, which was low-priced but excellent work by his Negro laborers. They promised him contracts.

This was now the final phase of his plan. Spring was in the Elyria air, and a spring was in his step. Feeling optimistic, he would behold the buckeye trees in green bloom and the Ohio mud, thick and loamy.

W.W. had thought about taking some time for a brief, private trip to Cadiz. He'd heard that Fleetwood Walker was putting on wonderful shows at the Cadiz Opera House, shows that Anna-from-the-slope might want to go see with him. But before he could arrange such a trip, contracts started coming in. Time to hire some men, beginning with a couple of his sons, and order bags of cement from Lisbon—Mix #77.

CHAPTER 19

*H*ere in Cadiz, 1919, Fleet and Ednah were arranging for Negro singers to perform between the feature film showings at their opera house. At his desk this morning, Fleet sat like a mannequin. The thwump-thwump in his chest was keeping time. The meat of his mind was as busy as a whirling dervish. Several times in his sixty-two years he'd outrun the hounds of hell. Now trouble, different this time, was dogging him again. Despite his father's ministry, Fleet had never really learned how to pray. This minute he was trying.

"Fleet, dear, I just went over our ledgers again. We might be able to afford this group, Lieutenant Jim Europe's 'Four Harmony Kings,' if I can schedule them!" Ednah spoke excitedly as she hobbled into the room. Then she noticed the gleaming line of a tear or two on his jaw. "Fleet?"

He had almost never wept, at least outwardly, in their twenty-one years together. His face quickly grew composed. "Good, honey, sounds great! You know, I wish I were as smart as you . . ." He reached out, pulled her slender body to his face, and clasped her gently. Ednah had not been feeling well, so he gestured for her to sit.

Their opera house, still the only one in Cadiz, was steadily running the feature motion pictures that the distributor rented him according to its own choice and schedule. The whites of Cadiz were keeping seats filled. They demanded films starring the Gish sisters or Mary Pickford or Theda Bara or Fatty Arbuckle or Charlie Chaplin. The colored folks, however, were pressing him for plays, not minstrels, they could relate to. He knew that some coloreds even thought that Ednah—she being so proper and looking almost white—was steering him toward Caucasian-type programs. This put him in a pickle: He could not ignore the wishes of his own people, but he needed the white crowds in order to stay in business.

"Just a month past, Fleetwood, you were happily leading folks high-stepping along the stage doin' the *Buck an' Wing*. But lately you been moping around and, I swan, a minute ago you were nearly weeping. What's troubling you?"

"Uh . . . mmm. Just business junk, I guess. But, hey, you just now pulled up my spirits, gal. If we can book 'Four Harmony Kings,' that'll bring sophisticated Negro music to the opera house. This should please both colored and white. Especially on account of the *Kings'* master being murdered—when was it?"

"Two months ago, in May. You read that article saying James Reese Europe, 'Harlem Hellcats' hero of the Great War, was one of America's most distinguished musicians, the equal of any white band leader."

"Yeah. That's right. The 'Four Harmony Kings' could be as big as any attraction we've ever mounted here!"

Ednah clasped, lifted, and kissed his right hand. She suspected that something deeper was bothering him—enough to cause him to shed a tear. Something occurred to her: Why, these days, did he seem so vexed every afternoon when the mailman had come and gone?

Fleet did have feelings he'd not admitted to Ednah. One was about his application to the U.S. Patent Office. He'd had a bone to pick with the Feds ever since his hard work for the Postal Service resulted in his being incarcerated in '98 for a year. Also, his 1891 patent for artillery shells got him no sanction by the government . . .

"Are you still brooding over the 'reel alarm' request?" she sorrowfully asked, bending her face toward his.

Fleet simply shrugged.

Now he realized how his behavior was betraying him. He didn't know why the patent business, the delay in responding to his application, was disturbing him so—but it was. Nine months had passed since September 1918. Even though he was using what he'd invented, he was in a hurry to get that damn patent!

'Twas a year and a half ago, in 1917, when he first took action. The motion picture reels were cumbrous, each a thousand feet of thirty-five-millimeter film. There he was many evenings, in the dim little parlor made into his projection room, hunched over either one of the twin projectors. A feature movie required at least two reels. So the first reel ran for twenty minutes on the first projector, then the movie resumed through the second reel on the second projector. His theater audience always disliked the short time spent between the end of the first reel and the beginning of the second reel. Sometimes

Ednah arranged for a chanteuse to do a song as an interlude. He set about to change this.

Thoughts of sucking fire and inhaling searing smoke also provoked him. He and other operators in the region had often slid open the metal box, the magazine containing a running reel, to see the length of film remaining. This was much danger! Heat from the two carbon rods, with electric current jumping in arcs between them furnishing a bright, white light in a projector, was likely to cause a fire—or an explosion. And the celluloid film could spew poison gas. So, rather than open the fireproof magazine, he had developed a way to determine exactly when the running reel would finish and when he could put in motion the next reel on the second projector, thereby eliminating the awkward changeover period. Fleet called upon his engineering skills.

"Fleetwood?"

"Yes," he said. "That pending patent's on my mind. But it'll work out okay—jus' kind of annoying, you know, sweetheart."

In '17 he was smart enough and able enough to fashion devices that would give the operator two signals: first, a sound indicating that four feet of the running reel remained; and second, an alarm sounding that only a foot remained. Thus, he—or any other operator—could determine precisely when to activate the second projector/reel for a smooth transition. This kept the audience from waiting, and it was much safer because it kept the film from catching fire. No one in the theater business could fail to understand that his inventions were brilliant! So why, he queried, was the government keeping the patent from coming?

He'd previously had a patent search and his inventions were novel, unprecedented, and his application was made through a patent attorney. Might the government be playing tricks with him—on account of his criminal record? He wouldn't mention these thoughts to Ednah. She'd consider them ridiculous, even crazy. Truth was, his greatest worry this moment was not the patent or the opera house fare, but Ednah herself.

"Ah-h be back directly." As Ednah hobbled away, he knew where she was headed. Worry gripped him further. He was witnessing, too, some bodily changes in her that didn't bode well. Her once-shapely legs had swollen. Her creamy skin tone was looking sallow. She at times clutched her midsection as if there was pain, though she admitted nothing.

He listened as the plod-plod of her footsteps finally ceased. From some hidden place, mind glimpses began to burst open for him: a peek into a cloudy day when the opera house had a weak program, so he took to the piano while Ednah sang "I Ain't Got Nobody" to a restless but suddenly appreciative audience. A glimpse of her sitting with five or six youngsters on evenings going over Baldwin's Primer and the Barns reader, mentoring those who were missing or failing classes at primary school in Cadiz. He saw Ednah's bonny eyes seem to shimmer as she called out, "Children, let's all turn to page . . ." A glimpse of her joining colored and white ladies last year to knit woolens for the doughboys "over there" in the Great War. Although knitting was not one of her talents, she stayed with the ladies until after Armistice Day. A glimpse of that foggy-brained Friday morning last month, the day after the Cadiz "Juneteenth" celebration. On Thursday, June 19, a gaggle of colored men played a pickup baseball game in honor of the date slavery had come to a complete end in 1865. Fellows representing Masonic and other lodges played. As usual, they asked Fleet to serve as the head official since he had been not only a professional catcher, but the first Negro to ever play in the now all-white "Majors." He had carried on his celebration into the night, and some fellows had to tote him home, three sheets in the wind, in a wheelbarrow. When he opened his eyes, and he was foggy-brained alright, lovely Ednah was sitting beside their bed. He realized his shame. "Honey, when we married you did promise you'd stay with me through thick 'n' thin." He grinned when he told her this. "Uh-huh, husband, but I was determined that if it got too thick, I'd thin it out." Then she'd cackled like a rebuking hen. Glimpses . . .

The sound he heard roused him and sent him scurrying. He found Ednah sliding to the floor. She was weak and nauseous—and she was panting. "Honey?" he uttered and threw his arms around her.

Her eyes were glassy, but she regained enough composure to whisper, "I'll be okay. Just a dizzy spell." She blamed this spell on rushing about, trying to line up programs for different opera house patrons. He determined that moment to fetch a doctor. Helping her walk to a couch in their next room—she refused to go to bed—he told her, "Beginning right now, I want you to rest, dear. I'm gonna call somebody. Meantime, don't be worked up over what shows to arrange. Forget about these Harmony Kings. I'll get motion pictures that will keep our audience, most of 'em, satisfied."

The physician said that Ednah had a kidney problem. Ednah told Fleet not to worry. Ednah, he knew, was a strong, positive woman, and she went about as sure as ever. But he wasn't convinced that she would be okay.

As he'd assured Ednah, a run of movies fairly satisfied audiences—movies along with town ceremonies such as school graduations. The colored folks seemed contented by the occasional stage shows. While Ednah hobbled about, pretending that she was still strong and efficient, Fleet managed to soothe his worries with spirits from the bottle. Cadiz was "dry" now, but bootleggers were everywhere. Ednah was not pleased about this. However, he was more careful to be charming now even when soused.

The March winds of 1920 hurled snow along the sidewalk in front of his opera house. Fleet not only was keeping the entrance clear, he also wrestled up the billboards and hollered instructions to the hired fellow who helped and sold tickets. Inside, Ednah tried her best, struggling hard to help Fleet. She was ailing worse now, often having to take to bed. Her sickness tormented him. He believed her time with him was growing short.

Up the stairs, Fleet halted. It was just two more steps and then a thirty-second walk to their bedroom, but he had to grab his handkerchief and dab the salty wet out of his eyes. Somehow he'd been stronger twenty-five years ago when Arabella was dying. This thought made him twitch: He loved Ednah deeper than he had Bella! Ednah had given him no children, but he'd loved her first, before Bella, and more profoundly. He just couldn't stand to lose her. As he entered their bedroom, he beheld Ednah lying crosswise, softly moaning.

"Fleet, how are things outside?" Ednah, sitting up now, spoke quicker than he could.

"Oh, cold and windy . . . House lookin' good, though." He understood why Ednah had spoken quickly . . . so he wouldn't ask about the groans she had been making.

"Well, I had my nap, dear, so I'll go make dinner."

How can I relieve her of these trying tasks, without breaking down her spirits completely? he asked himself. His strong arms bolstered Ednah as she swung her swollen legs out and raised to her feet. "Say, how 'bout my fetchin' us something from that fried chicken joint down the road? I 'spect they've wondered why we haven't tried their fare."

"Oh, that's a good thought, dear. I . . . I don't feel like anything heavy, though." She slid one hand over her belly. "Rather than fried chicken, you can order me a bowl of chicken soup if they fix that. Huh?"

"I'll make them stir some up for you, darlin'," he said grinningly. "Must be one tender hen who'd rather be simmered than griddled."

Ednah tilted her head toward him, saying, "All right," then she sighed a bit. Swiftly he headed to his automobile. "Fleetwood, will you be back 'fore long?"

"Of course, darlin'!" his voice rang out.

In the next moment he realized the reason for her odd question. He thought of several reasons. Only six months ago, for instance, was that "night of the fine ladies." He had picked up Ednah out in the country, at a little mansion home of an undertaker's family, where a half dozen of Harrison County's genteel ladies gathered for their usual afternoon tea. All these women, he felt, were as "fine" as Ednah—the choicest of the county. But two of them needed a ride back into town. "I'll be glad to drop you'uns off," he'd said and Ednah smiled. Ednah was not feeling her best, but she didn't want to reveal this. She suggested he take her home first, using the excuse that she wanted to help Demetrius and Susie, their workers, get ready to open up the opera house for the evening. He did that, murmuring to Ednah, "See you shortly." Then as they rode on to Gloria's home, she and Josephine mentioned that as good as tea and biscuits had been, they could've used a bit of liquor. He joined them in their thirst. So these two attractive ladies and Fleet found themselves at Josephine's having a real drink. Three hours later he waddled into the opera house. When the program ended, when everyone had gone, Ednah pitched a fit. She'd wept. She'd threatened to leave him.

He stepped to his motorcar, thinking of other occasions. The tall, mechanical monster, sitting cold in an inch of snow, seemed to be waiting for him. He opened the door, reaching to the wheel, and set the spark and throttle levers. Then he stepped back out and strode to the car's front where the hand crank dangled. He cupped his right palm 'round the crank and grabbed the choke wire from the radiator bottom with his left hand. He powerfully turned the crank, but due to the cold, the engine didn't start. Once again he manipulated the choke wire and crank. This time the engine roared. At such a time Ednah usually was sitting in the front seat to immediately pull the spark lever. This time, however, Fleet had to jump and dash to do this himself before the engine died, forcing him to start all over again. Well, her absence during this tricky automobile task brought to mind two other episodes still bothering Ednah—and himself:

A year or so ago, he'd taken the Model T to the garage for servicing. Some county men, Pullman Car porters, had on an off day brought in a Templar motorcar with a bad engine. The mechanic at this makeshift, colored folks' backyard garage said he could do an overhaul, only it would take a few hours. "We can pass the time with Bid Whist," a man said, "but we'd really like another player." These Pullman fellows were schooled, sharp men, and Fleet was interested. He suspected they were slicksters who welcomed him as their "pigeon." But Fleet had news for them; he was a mighty crafty card player himself. After three hours they were into a tight game, and the engine overhaul was not near done. So they played on, Fleet forgetting to telephone Ednah. She became angry, then worried—never thinking of that backyard garage. He slumped home after nightfall, two sheets into the wind and pockets empty. Ednah was upset for days!

Yet five days afterward, when he went back to pay the mechanic, he discovered Sophie. She was youngest sister of one of last week's Pullman porters, based in Harrison County but now back on the rails. Sophie had traveled from Toledo to visit her brother, and this day she did a favor for him. She drove his Dodge to the garage because its engine was idling badly. The small garage was crowded—with two bustling mechanics and a half-dozen anxious clients who'd arrived earlier. Soon after mincing inside, she heard someone mention his name, and she identified the tall, handsome, aging man as the famous baseball player for Toledo whom her brother had told her about. Fleet was lollygagging with folks, while trying to edge himself out into the easy autumn afternoon air. Sophie just couldn't help herself. "Excuse me, Mr. Walker?" His eyes poured over this comely stranger, this long-legged, chocolate-colored, thirty-ish lady with a bright smile.

"Yes, ma'am?" his voice purred.

"I've always longed to meet you, Mr. Fleet Walker. My older brother, Carl, and I grew up in Toledo. He was able to watch you play when he was a boy. He told me there was no other player with the Toledo Blue Stockings or any other white team who had your genius! Also, being a black man, you were his hero!"

"Carl . . . Carl . . . ?" Yeah, Fleet recalled, last week when he'd spent hours playing Bid Whist and drinking with the Pullman porters, "Carl" was the quiet one, but the one who had remembered his play for Toledo. This Carl had an interesting, fine-looking sister!

"Lady." A mechanic burst in to their chitchat. "We can't git ta yer Dodge right away, 'cause of others who been waitin'. Can you leave it here, an' come back in an hour—we might have it ready then." Fleet took Sophie by the arm.

"I got time to talk with you. We can go in town to a cider press and have a glass an' doughnuts meantime." She smiled, then said to Fleet and the mechanic, "Okay . . . okay." Then he escorted her out to his car.

Ednah had fixed an early dinner. They would eat and make things ready for their evening show. Fleet had promised to be home before three. She glanced at the clock. It was now half past three. In a flap she dialed the switchboard and was connected to a mechanic. "Mr. Fleet went wif Miss

Sophie while I tended to her Dodge. Her car is ready now fer her ta claim it. If he returns wif her, I'll tell him you called."

Fleet and Sophie sat on the wooden bench several yards from this press shack. They laughed, sipped fresh cider, and munched on fried doughnuts. Sophie, much like his Ednah, was an educated, witty lady with a flowing sense of humor. She stirred him, jiggling his mind so their bench time rushed by too fast. How this lady, though quite a bit younger and darker-complexioned, reminded him of Ednah! She even was in the Court of Calanthe! "Oh, your wife is a member, too?" she remarked, having described her "court" activities as fund-raising and good works chairlady of her local organization. "Sure is. Ednah was first fascinated by the classic story of Pythias and Calanthe, his 'foxy' bride. Maybe she compared herself to Calanthe. Like you, Ednah's a pretty woman, you see." He chuckled. "Anyhow, she joined the sisterhood . . ."

Sophie nodded and smiled. "Or perhaps she related you to Pythias, who substituted for his buddy, Damon, in prison."

"Probably not," he shot back, chuckling. "On second thought, maybe she did in a weird way . . . but that's another tale."

Her eyebrows raised in curiosity; he felt mightily attracted to her. "I feel so honored," she half-whispered, her eyes fixed on his, "to be lunching with one of the greatest baseball players of this nation!" [How long since he'd heard that? Twenty-five, thirty years? Since Curly Murray of Syracuse had made him a killer, since the Postal Service had called him a thief?]

"O-o-oh." Sophie grunted. "But I suppose I had better get back to that garage, yes?"

Fleet pulled out his watch. He was jolted by his time-promise to Ednah! Four o'clock, *an hour past his pledge to be home*! While the hug Sophie gave him at the garage heated his heart, his mind was on Ednah. The mechanic who'd spoken to Ednah was busy and didn't deliver her message. Fleet hurried home, prepared to please her by telling her about this young lady who was also a member of the Court of Calanthe. Ednah was readying the evening show, but shaking with sobs. She wouldn't talk to him; she only screamed, "Why, Fleetwood . . . you promised!" In tears she trembled. "Why . . . ?"

These were the harsh memories on his mind as he headed for soup and shack-fried chicken this cold March afternoon. His peccadilloes, though, slipped back into the past now as the engine responded with a promising *VARO-O-OM*. This day Fleet determined to get back home promptly, exactly as he'd given Ednah his word. The chicken shack did prepare for him some tasty consomme, though it took a half hour. He thankfully paid, saying "much obliged," for a tin pail of the soup and the bag of fried chicken pieces, then drove straight home. As the Model T rumbled up to Cadiz Opera House, he saw some ladies bustling into the private entrance. This scared him! Nervously he parked and hurried forth. His employee Susie met him at the door. "Got company, sir!" she excitedly whispered. "Three Eastern Star 'sisters' just went upstairs. But after you drove off, a short while ago, Miss Ednah went down. She didn't fall, just sort of sagged. You see, Mistah Fleetwood, I s'pect she is not as well as she lets on." Susie's eyes were dewy.

Fleet thanked Susie—told her he would have the doctor to see Ednah. Upstairs, he greeted the "sisters." Ednah, a higher degree in Eastern Star than they, was bravely smiling with the ladies. Fleet tried to work his charm on them. "The Lord must've touched me with clairvoyance, sisters. I just bought some shack-fried chicken and this pail of soup—enough for Ednah an' me and you lovely ladies, too. Can we share?"

Of course, they declined. Fleet figured they were on a mission. Very diplomatically they let him know that their Order intended to assist him in the care of Ednah's needs—that the Lord had blest them to do for Ednah what she had previously done for many other "sisters." They put this in such a tactful manner that neither of the two proud Walkers could deny them such a service.

And so it went as the weeks came lurching by. Ednah welcomed the blooming of spring, even while her strength was fading. Looking out and down from a window, she rejoiced over little garden plots across the street where spring flowers seemed to dazzle and dance. And on April's wet, windy days, she enjoyed Fleet's visits—to whatever space she occupied— and the gentle stroking of his rugged but careful hands. Fleet's own spirit rose and sank, dropped and lifted. He stayed concerned about his pending patent, about opera house programs of which Ednah no longer could be involved, and about fading finances. What unsettled him most, however, was the waning of his wife. Some days she sat up strongly alert, knowingly. Other days it seemed she hardly recognized him. Sometimes she astounded him—on these days they talked of their life together, even joked. "Fleet, dear," she said. "One of these days we should go far, far away . . . to that wonderful land, that paradise we used to dream of . . ." He didn't know whether to chuckle or not. "Yes, my darlin'."

Soon the pregnant, potbellied month of May came creeping into 1920. It came creeping in like a famished, uninvited, and unwelcome, then welcomed stranger. During this last afternoon of May, here on the slope, Anna sipped her tea mixed with wild honey, while Fleet sipped from a mug of coffee. Once or twice a year, or when his soul was quite troubled, he'd visit Anna out here on the slope. This moment she sat watching him. His eyes were wet. "Have you learnt to talk with God, Fleetwood?" He mumbled yes. "Well, then, it surely must've helped you in her passing." Last Wednesday, the twenty-sixth of May, Ednah's spirit suddenly vanished—way above miles and minutes and pride and pain—into the Beyond. Anna was among the multitude attending her service. Today, Monday, he and Anna talked.

"Yeah, Anna, I finally got the hang of praying." Anna knew that his Pappy, the Reverend Moses Walker, had trained his youngsters in ways of the Lord. "I mean, I'd mostly given up prayer for fifty years. Then, when I learned my wife had a fatal kidney disease—interstitial nephritis, her doctor calls it—prayer words began to come out of my heart." Anna clutched his hand.

"Fleetwood, aint nuthin' wrong with speakin' to God Almighty every time we need His attention. Not jus' in troubled times. Fer me, it be's night an' day." Fleet believed her, believed this was one more valuable lesson—for years there had been many—that she was giving him. His respect for her was even stronger than the gripping of their hands.

"I know yer burdens now be heavy. Y'know Ednah an' I never spoke at length. Howsoever, I gauged her to be a ref— yea, a refined an' beauteous woman. Days came when she suffered so much she weren't the same woman, but struggled not tuh reveal this. Uh-huh. So now you must find solace that she's not sufferin'—that she's finally at peace. An', Fleetwood, you surely cared fer her lovingly till thuh end . . ."

He admitted this by a slight nod, while oozing a breath of relief. "An' as far as the opera house, I s'pect it'll be a strain managing by yerself. Don't you fret 'bout this. Don't be thinkin' that givin' up the business right soon would forsake Ednah. If she's lookin' down at you, it be with true understandin'. You hear me?"

"Yes, I am hearing you."

In a twinkling, Anna's words lifted his spirits. How could Anna, this longtime friend of his, this Anna-from-out-on-the-slope, know such real truth about the intimate circumstances 'tween him and Ednah? He wondered, while his mind and heart jumped forward. Anna was on the mark: There were changes he needed to make now—not to be locked in grief or fruitless sentiment. Feeling consoled, he stood up. Anna wiped the weep from his eyes, said a little prayer, and gave him a gentle, "Now take good care of yourself" kiss.

Fleet stepped out the door, his head tilted upward. He didn't exactly know what he'd do next, but he would do something. Also unbeknownst to him was that the Post Office was about to deliver the U.S. Patent Office confirmation of his approved motion-picture-film reel patents.

CHAPTER 20

One hundred and thirty miles northwest of Cadiz, as the crow flies, W.W. Brown was preparing to hire young colored men for new jobs. "Pappy?" Myrtle, his youngest daughter who served as secretary and bookkeeper, called out. "You received a letter from Cadiz from your sister. It says Mr. M.F. Walker's wife died last week. Aunt Pearl wrote that he . . . uh . . . Mister 'Fleetwood' . . . is an old friend of yours. Pappy, isn't he that famous old baseball player?"

"Sure 'nough is," W.W. answered from his desk in the next room. "I had heard that Ednah was ailing. Lord, ha' mercy . . ." The business phone call he'd started to make had to wait for a few minutes, while he absorbed this bad news. He had not seen Fleet Walker for many years. And he hadn't seen Ednah since maybe 1880. She'd been Fleetwood's heartthrob at Oberlin College back then, but Fleet first married a gal named Arabella who was just as downright pretty as Ednah. "Myrtle, ring the operator an' see if she can connect us with Cadiz. I'd sure like ta talk to Fleetwood a bit. Been a long while . . ." Myrtle tried, but Cadiz was not able to reach Mister Walker. W.W. had Myrtle draft a short condolence note for a telegram to Fleetwood.

They had kept missing each other. When he and Becky were young and raising a family in Cadiz, Fleet was playing baseball or starting his family with Arabella in different cities. When Fleet came to Cadiz with second wife, Ednah, he and Becky were elsewhere. Also, their lives were certainly not alike—Fleet being a college man and a renowned athlete, while W.W. was just a farmer, miner, and small-time manager. But they both had a business sense. W.W. felt sorry about Fleet losing his Arabella and, now, Ednah. His heart this late morning was already heavy—yesterday he'd learned that tired, old Wicket had been put to sleep.

"It ain't like a human loved one dying," he conjectured, "but it can ache jus' the same!" He sat by the window, not seeing anything outside his own thoughts. Becky once told him that he gave more attention to training his horses than to rearing his sons. Well, he got hold of Wicket as a two-year-old, just after the scalpel changed him from a young stallion to a frisky young gelding looking "soon." Yeah, even Wicket's big brown eyes couldn't soften his "soon" look—a flashing of quick intelligence and curiosity! W.W. set out to train him, with skills honed by training more than a dozen horses before. He knew how important it was to quickly gain an animal's respect and trust. In Wicket, though, he finally realized that the creature also trains its master. He'd learned to respect and trust Wicket. On several nighttime occasions, when he'd had too much to drink, he pulled himself into the buggy, then dozed off. Wicket trotted him home, then whinnied or stomped hard enough to wake him. Moreover, Wicket had taught him patience and caring. For eighteen years Wicket had hauled him around, following his lead or leading him when necessary. By 1918 Wicket had begun to slow down. He and W.W. could talk to each other, so that each neigh, snort, and whinny—each slant of the horse's ears, each cast of his big brown eyes—sent a message. "I'm sorry, boss," Wicket snorted. Because of this and because W.W. was now being chauffeured around by one of his sons, he'd decided to put Wicket out to pasture on the Kilgore farm. And for these last two years he'd visited Wicket almost every other day . . . until now. Now his heart was twice heavy.

Shortly he finally placed a call. "Howdy, this is W.W. Brown. Hope yer havin' a fine day? . . . Glad yer keepin' busy. I was jus' wondering if our contract is solid." The builder paused, then whined about bank loans being held in abeyance until the economy came out of its slump. He explained what W.W. was already sniffing about jobs and industry: that huge government contracts granted for the Great War were ending here in this spring of 1920—so industry was temporarily at a slowdown. That meant W.W. would not be hiring those fellows hoping for work.

No, he wasn't surprised that the economy was slowing, except that he'd thought he'd have a few more months of brisk contracts. A dozen men, however, were still in his employ, so some money would continue to flow. On his desktop, in one of the two small rooms arranged as his office, in this huge house at 52 West Avenue where Becky and some of his family and occasional boarders resided, was a sketch of a building project. He put this aside for Myrtle to file in the other room. The project would have to wait for a better time . . .

Months later, just before new contracts started coming, he and Becky received a family thunderbolt. With eyes perhaps half-closed, they saw their sons and daughters differently. W.W. knew that he and Becky had unlike visions, particularly about their sons. Becky had wanted them to be strong but humble Christian soldiers, good fathers and steady wage earners. He himself wanted to see them also as men with vision, fellows desiring to raise themselves and families way above the common circumstances of coloreds bound by Jim Crow, segregation, and the wiles of the white man. He'd wanted to see them as men of enterprise, far thinkers, dreamers. Well now, the boys moved more like Becky's idea than his. Oh, they were tough, a bit wild—especially Clinton—hard workers, but seemingly content with a middling life.

One day that autumn, Charlie, their eldest living son, came from Lisbon to visit. With Charlie was wife, Ella, their son, and three little daughters. As a gas lamp flickered light in the living room that chatty evening after supper, Charlie politely raised his arm for quiet, then began to explain to W.W. and Becky the real reason for his visit. In his heavy but melodic tones, this is what he rumbled:

"Somethin' powerful happened to me last month . . . August. Well, it changed me and demands your knowing. That day my crew had hewed out another chamber down in the mine. I was alone there cutting clay in the dark, only a lantern to see before me. Suddenly a real strong sound—I knew 'twas the voice of God—came to me seeming from an east corner of the room. The whole chamber came aglow. A light brighter, it seemed, than the sun! This voice and this light changed me, changed everything around me! I've got to get outta the mine—to travel aboveground and preach the Gospel!"

After further describing God's "call" to him, his mother, filled with joy and pride, beckoned him to her and hugged him mightily. W.W. lit a cigar, puffed, and uttered, "Lord bless you, son." He didn't know quite how to receive Charlie's revelation. Charlie would never be an ambitious businessman, he'd decided. But Charlie was a goodhearted, strong-minded fellow—sincere, faithful, and dependable. He could make a solid minister.

Charlie, a bear of a man, had always been formidable like harnessed thunder—but mostly he showed gentleness and kindness. In fact, Becky depended on Charlie to tame the wildness of his younger brothers, Clarence, Ottie, and Clinton—particularly Clinton. Now Charlie was making plans to rejoin the Browns in Elyria. While needing study and ordination as a minister, he would need employment. He and his Ella had three younger daughters and a son to finish rearing.

So the next day W.W. went about providing for his eldest son. Charlie was not a qualified carpenter or plasterer or plumber—the sort of workmen he was now employing—but Charlie was as sturdy as an ox. Not bothering with big firms such as Elyria Lumber and Coal or Parsch Lumber or Spaulding Concrete, W.W. sauntered up to some white contractors who already had a few, small paving job contracts. "Would it be easier on you if I furnished and delivered top-quality raw material, say cement, sand, an' gravel for ye?" he inquired. One fellow, Sol, called to mind W.W. edging him out of a small contract last year. As a white man he'd expected to land any matching contract over a Negro, but he suspicioned that because he himself was Jewish he got no preference. He recalled that Brown's men did a fine job, just as fine as his crew would have done. "It would save strain on my guys, 'n' save me some valuable time," Sol said. "What's your terms? I'm Sol Morris."

W.W. hesitated only because Sol's reply was so much quicker than the previous two fellows he'd approached. He and Sol negotiated for just a few minutes and a deal was made on the spot. W.W. was to have some heavy materials delivered in a month or so, including Cement Mix #77—which Sol would learn was better than any in town. When Charlie and family arrived, W.W. had a job ready. Charlie would be in charge of the hauling of cement and other heavy materials.

Even as Becky gave him credit for Charlie's job, she began pressuring him more about the church. Second Methodist A.M.E. appreciated her work and her daughters' activities, but wondered why her husband and sons were not often faithful to the church. Now, Precious Lord, one son had gotten ordained as a preacher—yet his brothers, and, mostly, his Pappy, needed to join the family in devotion to the Lord. She got on Pappy.

"Becky, you know I go tuh services most every Sunday . . ."

She glared at him, standing bold and steamy. "Tod, you barely can stay 'round after service—runnin' off to some business meetin' or 'nother, such as that there Residence Association—or whatever it's called. Always some meetin', not church business. And I ain't never sure how true the 'meetin' is, either."

"Woman, these days if it's not foolin' 'round home like some trifling fellow, it's got to be business. Keepin' up a home an' a full family is a large task. Keep in mind my way of rising above the sea is 'business'."

W.W. was riding above his sea. Becky and their daughters kept fixing and catering succulent dinners for the church. Two daughters arranged various social functions. Charlie, now connected to a Baptist church, began preaching. But Becky fussed about her husband's loose ties to Second Methodist. She fussed until after the big fire . . .

At Saturday supper—it was May 7, 1921—Becky was slightly vexed, once more, that "Pappy" had not joined this family meal prepared so heartily. None of her sons or sons-in-law were there, either. Across town W.W. had just finished an informal meeting arranged to form an Afro-Mutual Benevolent Association of Elyria, Lorain, and Oberlin.

He arrived in front of his house about seven o'clock, sober and ready for a toddy. A rush of whisper and a flash of light caused him to raise his head. He took a few steps backward to get a better view. There was fire on the roof! Only a fistful of flames that he could see, but a vigorous little bundle nevertheless! Bursting into the house, he called the family, those who were there, together. "I want all you'ns tah file out of this house past me—RIGHT NOW! There be a small fire up on the roof. Scoot outside NOW!" His eyes, and the urgency in Pappy's voice, caused them to obey smartly. He glanced about him, satisfied that the kitchen stove and all else was in order, then stepped to the telephone and rang the central firehouse, which was just a few blocks away. His family members stood on the devil's strip, or on the sidewalk, gazing at the roof. Becky wrapped her arms around li'l William, the grandson she and W.W. had been rearing since their daughter Harriet died. The boy wanted to dash to Pappy's side. One or two minutes whipped by, then they heard the clanging from a fire engine coming. Medium height, slender, standing straight and strong as an I-beam, W.W. moved his eyes up, across, and down the building—and the adjacent buildings. "I don't see no other burnin' area," he barked to the Deputy Chief who jumped off the truck, shaking his head in acknowledgment. Right behind the pumper, a 750-gallon Robinson, followed an aerial ladder, a sixty-five-foot Seagrave. Within ten minutes the six firemen had the blaze out, with the small area cleaned and the entire roof inspected. "Had to be caused by some incendiary blown to yer roof from somewhere else," the Deputy Chief supposed. "Not much damage, only some shingles needing replaced." W.W., in thanking the men for their quick work, added, "We need tah know where that 'incendiary' came from, don'tcha figure?" The Deputy agreed. "We'll follow up on this." He and W.W. began discussing, along with a Broad Street beat patrolman drawn by noise and excitement, what exactly "follow up" would mean. Their daughters went back inside, but Becky remained while li'l William watched in fascination the ladder on the Seagrave folding back onto the truck. This shiny, puzzling truck sort of reminded him of a crazy circus wagon.

Becky said nothing, just watched the three men. She had never seen her husband in such command—with city emergency officials, no less. W.W. was saying, "I s'pect you'll canvass or take stock of the neighborhood this evenin', fellahs. Makin' certain there's no firebrands 'round here." The fire Deputy described his procedures. "You'll see to it, too, from yer perspective, officer?" W.W. asked the uniformed cop. The policeman replied, "Yessir." Becky was surprised. Both officials, these white men, showing W.W. such respect!

Neighbors, alerted by fire trucks on West Avenue, began stepping back inside their homes. Though conversing, the Deputy and the cop and W.W. each had kept sharp eyes on the small crowd. They'd each noticed a strange-looking man standing on the sidewalk. To W.W., this fellow was also "strange" for two reasons: his face was not familiar, because W.W. had gotten to know all the neighborhood residents, and this fellow had already smoked three cigarettes while standing there. W.W. hissed to the officials, "That fellow bears watching."

As the fire trucks, onlookers, and two officials departed, Becky and li'l William walked over to W.W. "Could've been worse," he remarked. "I b'lieve God just showed us His mercy. Our home will be safe, but I s'pect there be some work tah find this fire's cause. You reckon I kin have some supper now?" Becky smiled and nodded.

"Supper's real good, Pappy. You know it always is," li'l William said.

Becky was suddenly feeling overjoyed. W.W. had been sober and in command. He even mentioned God. She was so glad he'd arrived home when he did. She grabbed his hand, for the first time in a while, and stepped into their house.

Next day, Sunday, W.W. not only accompanied the family to church, but he stayed afterward to "fellowship" with the congregation. Becky didn't know whether this was because he felt she and their daughters were shaken by the fire, or because he'd decided to make his presence stronger in their family church. Anyway, they had a good dinner, with even a couple of sons and their families in the house. By a quarter of seven, the Browns' home had gotten quiet. Then they heard a fire engine's wail. "Oh Lord!" Becky cried out.

W.W., who'd begun to relax and sip his toddy, hustled to open the door. "Whatever it is," he grunted aloud, "is down thuh street." By the time the others reached the door, W.W. had snatched his waistcoat and stepped out.

Firemen were spraying water along the top of Elyria Vulcanizing Company, located a few buildings down West Avenue. The Deputy Chief whom W.W. had talked to the previous evening was there again. He spotted W.W. and strode over. "Another alarm, Mr. Brown. But hardly any flame. I'm tryin' to figure where the sparks, the incendiary, are comin' from. We checked this neighborhood today—but, y'know the commercial places were closed 'til tomorrah. No neighbors I talked to, nor any patrolman talked to, had any idea. We'll speak with shop owners in the morning."

W.W., gazing upward and around at adjacent buildings, grunted, "Things could burn down 'fore then." The Deputy agreed. "They's a breeze blowin' south," W.W. said. "Reckon sparks might be traveling from a high spot on one of the buildings sittin' north?"

"Might be. The truck's headed back to our station now, but I'm not finished here. Just waitin' for a policeman to get here. Then we'll try getting into buildings toward the north end. Sparks would have to be coming intermittently from some nearby source." He shook his head.

"Remember last evening," W.W. asked, "when a fellow in thuh little crowd at Fifty-Two was smoking one cigarette after 'nother, strange-lookin'?"

"Yeah . . . maybe English or Irish, with flighty eyes. You make a good point, Mr. Brown, he was lighting smokes with book matches . . . not stick matches. I looked unsuccessful on the ground for used matches, but found no evidence."

W.W. had a thought. "Might be sparks arose from cigarette stubs, y'think?" Now as the Deputy began thinking along the same lines as W.W., a Broad Street policeman walked up to them.

No one knew who the flighty-eyed man was. They discussed this and decided to look for him among the roomers upstairs nearby on West Avenue. "Come with us, Mr. Brown," the Deputy Chief requested. "We can use your alertness." So the three began their canvass, which went slowly—entering, wherever possible, building by building; and, where anybody answered, room after room, talking with neighbors. One door was half-open, so they were about to call to whoever was inside. However, they heard a fire engine siren and a clang! "The boys got another alarm, and it's hereabout!" screeched the Deputy. Then they saw the roomer named "Mahoney," the one with the flighty eyes. "Where's the fire this time?"

Mahoney asked them. They rushed into his room. They discovered that this nervous fellow had sometimes been tossing cigarette butts out his window. In fact it was from this northerly window, slightly hoisted, that a smoldering butt had landed on the shop awning below! The patrolman and Deputy Chief walked Mahoney to the police station, where he got a severe reprimand. He was ordered to pay some costs, including the replacement of W.W.'s wood shingles.

A note from the Fire Chief reached W.W. two days afterward, in thanks for his help in solving the firebrand problem. The family was proud and, at least for the moment, Becky had no gripe with Pappy. But W.W. decided to move the family away from 52 West Avenue, out to the countryside. Making big money now, he could afford an estate.

CHAPTER 21

*T*his mattress and these springs, on his cane panel iron bed, never felt better. What day of the week was it? It had slipped his mind. Fleet stared at the wall. From its calendar he decided this was Sunday, May 11—1924. Trucks and automobiles were making noises outside his bedroom in Cleveland, Ohio.

He coughed, then again, bringing up a quarter cup of phlegm.

Four years ago, when Ednah had died, Anna from the slope had told him right. "Don't be thinkin' that givin' up the business right soon would forsake Ednah," Anna had said. "I s'pect it'll be a strain managing by yerself."

Fleet descended into old thoughts and memories.

Ednah was gone. Her clothes hanging there sang to his heart about her coming back, but certainly he knew better. The bills coming due, the programs to be worked out, the tickets to be sold—he was like a big jungle cat suddenly in deep, chilly water. Now he was beginning to fully realize how much he'd depended upon her. Ednah once called him a "romanticist." Truth is, he's more creative and more restless than her. She is . . . was . . . more pragmatic than he. Her practical, mathematical mind better allowed her to take care of the opera house daily business.

"Fleetwood?" He jerked. Did she summon him? Uh-h, *no*.

Anna was right. He wasn't of the mind or temperament to continue with the opera house. So that cold day, that March of 1922, he sat down with R.H. Minteer and O.C. Gray and signed papers of ownership over to them. They didn't see it, but before and after that hour he wept. He packed up his belongings—even Ednah's handbag, which he could not bear to open in the past two years, even though she wouldn't need it.

He cracked a smile to himself . . . then he gagged, coughed, and spit into the bedroom's old brass cuspidor . . . and he kept remembering . . .

Of his two sons, only George had seriously tried playing baseball. But only for a hot minute. George liked boxing better and fancied himself a fearsome fighter. Remember when George—just age twenty-one then, around 1907—attempted to become sparring partner of the great Jack Johnson? Of course, that was before Johnson got to be heavyweight champion, the days when Jack was still chasing Champion Tommy Burns all over the world. Chasing Burns because a Negro fighter, no matter how great or famous, was not supposed to fight a white champion for his title. Now, George was only a little larger than Tommy Burns, who was smaller than Johnson, so George figured he was just right as a sparmate. He never caught up with Johnson—Jack was fighting and whipping, several times, such powerful black battlers as Sam Langford and Joe Jeanette. Fleet remembered and chuckled over how stout-hearted George was.

And where is his precious daughter Cleodolinda this cloudy, springtime morning. . . ?

Never mind that her brother Thomas is monkeying around with his Uncle Weldy in their joint Steubenville businesses, and that brother George is somewhere on the road. Cleodolinda must still be breathing that Pacific air between Hollywood, California, and those San Gabriel Mountains. Her married name is Mills; nevertheless, she's his Linda.

He'd never told her how very precious she is to him—both as a bright-eyed little girl and as a statuesque, silken-haired woman. Linda had tried to take Bella's place in their home at age thirteen, but when Ednah moved in . . .

He'd been dozing. Seems that when he snoozes the sky turns deep cobalt blue, yet the images, people and places 'round him are bright as ever. Anyways, he was snoozing-tired after a stupefying time last night.

More so this morning, but for weeks, months perhaps, his mind was groggy and he knew it. Time was—aw, six or seven years past—when his grasp of mechanics especially was so sharp that he'd compared himself to Granville Woods and Garrett Morgan, these Negro inventors. Last year, right here in Cleveland, Garrett got his patent for a three-way automatic traffic light, which General Electric was paying big money for. And before he died a dozen or more years ago, Granville Woods made a name for himself by all his inventions on electric trolley cars. Oh, he was something! Running electric better to trains . . . designing the "third rail" . . . contriving effective automatic air brakes . . . Granville wrestled with Thomas Edison and George Westinghouse over several inventions. Since his death, folks now were remembering Granville Woods as the "Black Edison." Aww, well, people have forgotten Fleetwood Walker's patent for a gun cartridge, and will probably forget his motion picture reel improvements. Huh? He could remember one patent number: "1,308"—no, "1,328,408."

He heard a loud rap on the door beyond his bedroom. "Who is that?" No answer. Again the knocking. Is it Weldy? Thomas maybe . . . or even George? Like himself with Weldy, Granville, the "Black Edison," had a close brother named Lyates. Lyates helped his brother with his brilliant inventions. While Weldy had always marched in step with big brother Fleetwood—attending the same colleges, playing baseball, and taking over his Steubenville business—Weldy was no help with his inventions. "Who is it?" Feeling chilly, he pulled the blanket above his neck. But his skin felt hot, as if he were a live lobster set into a broiling pot.

Imagining a cellar beneath a basement, he made a grin. A hatch in the center of the cement basement floor opened. Some steps led down into the cellar. He'd never before witnessed anything like this. He wondered what was in that cellar. Darkness could be seen from the opening—a pool of utter blackness. He grinned because other steps led him back up to his bedroom—where he'd never left. What a vision!

Lord knows, he'd worked hard on his inventions, particularly the new motion picture reel—just himself and patent attorney Lacey. Looked good that his patented reel would bring him considerable wealth. He'd contracted with Cleveland's Globe Machine & Stamping Company, which set about manufacturing and marketing the reel—the best on the world market. The royalties for this seemed to be slow in coming, confound it. Fact is . . . it's costing him money to defend his patents. Smarter and richer men were trying to make his inventions their own. So it goes. All this tangled business inflamed his anger. He, the angry visionary, was surely missing Ednah's calm, practical sense.

Fleet, hearing a ruckus outside on East 49th Street, turned over in bed.

Somehow East 49th is different from where he lived a couple years back—East 55th Street. Not only the street of Temple Theater, East 55th is where Hooper Field sits—the rugged ballpark where Rube Foster's Negro National League teams (mostly the Cleveland Browns) play baseball. He'd resided at the Temple Theater address because, for a few months, he had operated that theater.

Though shivering like a pup, he forced himself to sit up in bed. Under the blanket, he was fully dressed. Besides bringing him a bowl of warm noodle soup, his kindly neighbor has insisted on calling the hospital wagon for him. He looked around, making sure his brogues were there on the floor for him and his jacket and cap hanging on the door. City hospital, more'n likely, would give him some strong medicine and send him back home to East 49th.

Harry Smith had introduced him to Temple Theater. After he sold the Cadiz Opera House, he'd visited his old crony. "Harry," he'd said then, "I just retired—same as most other fellows age sixty-five." His crony, six years younger than he, refused to believe him, saying, "Fleet, you've still got too much to offer our people." Harry was serious, even when he seemed to be kidding. Harry Clay Smith, everybody knew, was a force of God—one of God's righteous lions. Famous longtime boss, editor, and publisher of the influential Cleveland Gazette. Former member of the Ohio state legislature, where he put his name on the Smith Act that grants the kin of lynched Negroes the right to sue county governments. He recalls meeting Harry back in "nineteen aught-two." Brother Weldy and himself had started putting together and publishing their Negro paper, The Equator. As editor of Cleveland's Gazette, Harry encouraged him in the newspaper business and they became friends. But then Harry read his Our Home Colony book a few years later and disagreed with his racial ideas. Harry Smith had told him then, "Fleet, if you're gonna send a flock of our folks back to Africa, don't save a seat for me. I ain't going, that's for dadblamed sure!" [Now Fleet chuckled and coughed.] Actually, Harry was as furious over Jim Crow as he. Anyhow, two years ago Harry took him to Temple Theater, where he met the Bolasnys. These Bolasny brothers, being aware of the fine vaudeville acts and motion pictures his Cadiz Opera House had presented, talked him into a "tryout," a short-term lease of their Cleveland playhouse. Harry boasted about this in the Gazette. But after a couple of months he was missing Ednah so terribly, and the expenses promised to be so great, his efforts so taxing, that he turned the theater back over to the Bolasnys.

A little sunshine apparently was now gnawing through the gray sky, but his limbs seemed almost too tired to raise him up toward the window to verify this.

Time was when his limbs were snappy steel-like strops. Yes, indeed! Playing baseball, his legs could take him from here to there like greased lightning. And his catcher's arm rifled that little horsehide sphere to second base with a bullet's speed, to snare any base-stealer. And he could hit, too. Himself, Bud Fowler, George Stovey, and Frank Grant were labeled the "colored wonders" back in the eighties. One newspaper's sports page—

Bella had gushed over it, causing him to commit it to memory—accentuated this poem:

"There is a catcher named Walker
Who behind the bat is a corker,
He throws to a base
With ease and grace,
And steals 'round the bag like a stalker."

But, oh, his playing grabbed attention even before he and Weldy got on the Oberlin College varsity team in '81. Maybe young Willie from Cadiz—folks now knew him as W.W. Brown—was the first to really get him rolling. While Willie, who was working then in Elyria and organizing pickup games, too, introduced him to a white man simply called Major (seems Major was one of those not killed at the Battle of Antietam). Willie was as smart as a steel trap—easily meeting well-to-do white folks, which was why he always had a gainful job in town. Anyhow in 1880 Major, swayed by Willie, got him to catch for that tiptop white team called *The Elyrias*. That Elyria club was independent, but once in a while it played teams that were part of the upstart National League. So, in '80 he and the Akron club's Ed Johnson were among the first coloreds to break the color line! Yessir, on that hot day—sure, it was July 16, 1880, he could recall—Elyria played Akron at Akron's new grandstand on Perkins Street. He snatched balls barehanded for Elyria; Ed dazzled at first base for Akron. That broiling Wednesday, he and Ed fomented their teams into raving demons. Akron did win, 7 to 3, before a crowd of 400, but folks say it was "the best game ever played in Akron."

He barked, choked, and retched. His back pained as he reached for the dark bottle on the bedside table. A gulp or two would halt his cough for a while. 'Twould pacify his lungs. 'Twould keep his memories flowing—these rolling fancies . . .

Whatever happened to "*the Elyrias*"? All he knew was the Elyria team faded when he played for Oberlin College in '81. Willie Brown had gone back to Cadiz then . . .

His hand trembled, but he grasped the dark-brown bottle with label reading PISO'S for Coughs & Colds, shook it several times, and took a couple of swallows.

Whenever he was severely bothered in his chest, he used PISO'S (Py-so-z), knowing it contained cannabis and chloroform. This potion also

142

served as his balm of Gilead and allowed him these visions, or twisted dreams. He slumped back into the mattress . . .

The other day, here in the city of Cleveland, 1924, Rube Foster had paid him a visit. Rube—everybody following baseball, particularly Negro teams, is familiar with Rube Foster—stepped out of his chauffeured Packard limousine, which he'd probably hired. Neighbors, the nosy ones, watched him stomp up the stairs. Big and black and oh-so-shrewd, Rube drew more attention these days than he, himself did when he played for major league Toledo forty years ago. Well, Rube was called the "best black pitcher ever" for his playing with Negro clubs in the nineteen aughts and teens. Rube is today owner of teams and, more than this, ruler of the Negro National League. He'd come with a notion. "Fleetwood, I s'pect you been approached before and turned down the white men. I'm here as a fellow Negro . . . a fellow former player. You know the NNL is having financial problems. Attendance would jump up if you and other old-time stars could help us promote games . . . stir up the crowds." He reminded Rube of why he'd turned away from baseball years ago. First the decision to bar him and the few other colored big-leaguers from the major leagues in the 1880s put a lasting hurt on him. Second, when the colored teams were formed, not just the white owners but also the Negro managers and players, deliberately ignored the old-time players, as if they were jealous of the legend he, his brother Weldy, and others like Bud Fowler, Frank Grant, and George Stovey had built. No, he didn't want to be used or manipulated—or serve as a shill—for any present team—black or white. However, since Rube, who is based in Chicago, was so entreating he said, "I'll think on it."

PISO'S Cough Syrup works fairly fast. His landlady entered, but Fleet already was settling deeper into his reverie. "You gotta eat *something*, Mr. Walker. I'll be bringin' some soup."

He winced, then grunted, then wheezed . . .

Anna from the slope. He wanted to see her. All these years—the last time being four years ago when Ednah died—Anna had tapped good things way down in his soul and drawn them up like a woman delicately pumping water from a well. Even more, like a *diviner* locating a fresh water source running underground and causing some of this to be lifted to the surface. Anna is special! His father once preached about the meaning of angels—and one time about Jacob and the angel. Well, Anna was the closest one to an angel he'd ever met. Often they even had discussions about heaven and hell. He decided to go see her.

He touched his chest, trying to ease his misery.

Lord!—she'd come to see him! But she attacked him by her mouth. Neither as silver-tongued as Ednah, nor as passionate as Bella, Anna nevertheless is deeper—more forceful. Her words and his words are clashing with each other. In their clashing, Anna keeps asking, "What measure is your faith?" His answer is not an answer, so they keep on contending . . . on and on and on. At times his tone's heavy as a Leo's roar; hers as permeating as the sun's sweet song. He yields. Finally, she touches his chest, and she's gone . . .

CHAPTER 22

From a rear window of Anna's cottage, W.W. could see almost all the way down the slope. Splotches of spoonwood, whose pinkish-white flowers climbed up the hillsides, could be seen. Even the tops of mighty evergreen trees, standing far down at the gorge's bottom, had nearly reached heights across from the window.

Anna was taking hot biscuits out of tins. His Becky's biscuits were much desired by folks in Elyria, but here in Cadiz Anna's biscuits were the world's best. He gazed over to the bedroom where the four-poster was handsomely covered by Anna's quilt work. Her quilts, especially those mounted on the walls to keep out winter chills, were so colorful and wonderfully stitched. Again, this talent overshone Becky's fine quilting. The bed quilt prompted a question, which he held back. A delicious smoked ham scent filled her house. Anna was serving him ham and scrambled eggs and biscuits and honey. She rested a hot skillet of thick ham slices on the table. Somehow it suddenly seemed a third person was in her home.

"Cleveland's just twenty-odd miles from Elyria," W.W. spoke. "'Tis a shame I didn't realize how nearby he was in his last days. I could've—no, should have—looked in on him. When last did you see Fleetwood, Anna?"

She hesitated a long moment. "My soul visited his'n 'fore his last breath." W.W. knew that Anna was not jesting! She was strange this way. He wondered what exactly she meant.

"Uh . . . Was you in his Cleveland room when he passed, gal?"

"My soul was." Anna gave him one of her strange smiles. Then she motioned for him to say a prayer of blessing before he began eating.

"Lord, I thank Ye, this mornin'. Bless these wunnerful nourishing morsels prepared by my 'sister' Anna. In the sweet name of Jesus, I pray . . ." Anna joined him with an "amen."

Then abruptly she spoke the answer to a question W.W. was about to ask. "His son Thomas, also his brother Weldy, journeyed to Cleveland an' claimed the body. Fleetwood's buried, 'course, over there in Steubenville."

Between fork-fulls he glimpsed her. Though her hair, silken braids crowning her head, was graying now, her face was still smooth and tight as a girl's. Her deep-set eyes still sparkled, even if they hinted of unspoken sorrows. Her lips were always ready to form words from the Scriptures. This was Anna-the-strange. "In the gospel of Luke, Christ tol' the thief: 'Today shalt thou be with me in paradise.' Uh-huh."

W.W. got shocked, almost jarred out of his skin! How did she know that in thinking of Fleet he was wondering whether a sinner, much like himself, could repent and be saved—on his deathbed?

"Anna . . . Anna, how . . . ?" Her eyes seemed to narrow, as with vexation, so he shut up.

She sat down across from him. She sipped some tea, took a flaking biscuit off the platter, and placed it on a saucer before her and wiped a hand on her apron. "Willie? . . . You mind if we talk . . . 'bout yerself now, me 'big brother'?"

Chewing a small chunk of pearwood-smoked ham, W.W. nodded. "Lately," he spoke slowly, "work in Elyria has picked up. I been hiring more 'n' more young men. The County . . . Lorain County . . . bigshots, they be called County Commissioners, got a pledge from the state gov'ment in Columbus for $48,000—so some new roads kin be built. This here is forty thousand dollars—a whole kit 'n' caboodle of new jobs! I shall be drawin' some of these jobs!" This prospect roused him—so much so that the hand holding his fork shook and his breakfast plate wobbled as he emphatically recited his plans.

Anna noted his fervor. For a long while she'd encouraged him in his business undertakings. Her mind and spirit told her that the Lord had gifted Willie with exceptional abilities for enterprise. And she had personally seen him turn her upper slope's little grove of trees into good profits, furnishing mine posts. She also understood that he mystified white men by hustling along—even if like walking barefoot on red-hot cinders—the same business paths that only whites had trod. But she had one qualm. "I feel a harvest comin'!" Yet, in her voice was a frown.

"Reckon it be a big harvest—finally," he chirped with a smile.

"Hope so. Now how's Becky an' yer family?" As she expected, W.W. was only middling about his large family. He returned to what he was accomplishing with his enterprises.

Anna reached and curled her fingers 'round his hand. "By harvest I speak 'bout more'n money, 'bout more'n yer family's welfare. I speak 'bout godly things, too. Willie, I'm hopin' you be using yer gifts for enterprise to develop the same talents among yer sons an' daughters. I hope you're also workin' to strengthen them in yer strong ways of bearin' the Lord's harvest." Looking at her, he tried to figure what she meant. "In that ol' Bible of mine, it say . . . uh, in the book of Luke, Jesus says, 'The harvest is great, but the laborers are few . . .' Think on that."

On this visit she gave him much to think on—regarding Fleet and himself and herself and also the Word of God.

CHAPTER 23

$\mathcal{W}$.W. tramped around a part of the southern skirt of Elyria once called Carlisle Township. While mostly green and country-lush, the land surrounding his own estate was speckled with storage sheds, tool shops, and spur tracks. Yonder were gravel beds and the Baltimore & Ohio Railroad tracks. He eyed the tracks, also the rumbling freight cars, with two fresh vexations.

First, not long ago he'd hoped young William had not hopped into a B & O boxcar. That day Becky had been beside herself. When their daughter Harriet had died in '11, Becky and he took her only child to rear. These days young William was "feeling his oats"—like an oats-fed colt kicking crazily 'round his pen. "Pappy," Becky had warned him, "I swear, you'd best have a talk with Willie. He's gittin' too big fer his britches, and I'm 'bout at my wits' end in dealing with the boy." W.W. had replied, "Okay, woman," but then ignored it. Becky had tended to their sons back when they were young William's age, while he was off plunging into one business or another. However, that was thirty years ago. Youngsters now are more rebellious, and Becky not the force she used to be. Then, a couple of Saturdays past, it happened! W.W. strode into the house to find Becky arguing with the boy. He ushered Willie to the backyard. Willie, preferring William as his name, was age sixteen and fuming. "Boy, don't you ever again be shoutin' at yer Grandma!" W.W. growled. "Or it be yer last time fussin' with anyone!" Ordinarily, W.W. was not a terrifying man, yet when enraged he got even more dangerous than a roaring lion . . . more of a coiled, hissing viper! Still, he had a realization and a particular ache in his heart for this boy whose father was untold, with his mother's soothing voice and loving embrace all he could barely recall. Young William's soul was hot. Something was burning inside him, had been since he got old enough for an orphan's natural questions, ones neither W.W. nor Becky,

148

nor anybody, wanted to answer. He dared not air what was in his angry soul. Instead, he mumbled, "Yessir." W.W. could see fury in the boy's narrowed eyes.

Eight hours after, on early Sunday morning, Becky watched Willie head for their Second Methodist Church. However, when she and W.W. got to church, Willie was nowhere in sight. After service Becky realized that Willie had mysteriously taken off somewhere. So W.W. made calls to his brood and their offspring throughout Lorain County, all fifty or more folk. They'd not seen young William. Where had the boy fled? Becky was having a fit, fearing that in his state of mind Willie could hurt himself.

Monday morning W.W. called the police. Next day young William came dragging home. Becky and W.W. were so relieved that, instead of asking questions, they sat down with him for a scrumptious supper. Young William was tuckered out. His hitchhiked sally to Cleveland had left him penniless, ashamed, and sorry.

Some of his uncles and aunts, who'd been recruited by W.W. and Becky to search for him, were seeing red. If they'd done, at Willie's age, what this nephew had just done, their parents would've half-killed them—not greeted them to supper! Though humbled by his experience and appreciating that his grandparents, without questions, had welcomed him back, young William still was feeling uncomfortable at home. W.W. recognized the boy's uneasiness. The boy would surely drop out of school, so he resolved to provide young William with a job so as to keep him busy. That's why Willie now was working with the W.W. Brown road crew, even though he really wanted to be away on his own.

W.W.'s second vexation had to do with this B&O line stretching from southern and Allegheny coalfields, toting stuff all the way here north to nearby Lake Erie. His business delivering road building materials for highway construction jobs was going well. Very well. But he, W.W., was dreaming of his own million-dollar projects—projects as unlikely for Negroes as plow-team ownership is for mules. The dream was big and wide. Yet things kept getting in the way. He was trying to become manager of a goods station, or sidings, where material would be loaded onto or unloaded off of the swelling number of freight cars. "No," he was told, "we already got someone to handle these cars." That "someone," making more and more money, was always white. He was not one to yield easily, though. He did not stare dumbly at the tracks. He was not just a daydreamer. W.W. was quietly inspecting the space between the rails, wondering if this gauge truly kept constant and whether a narrower gauge would help the cars run more soundly. Whether the crushed rock, the ballast, was allowing a firmer run. Whether some changes along the track would invite the building of a better siding or goods station. Mostly he studied the incoming freight traffic—the number of cars, boxcars, and coal hopper cars—affecting his contracts.

Then he turned 'round and headed back toward his and Becky's recently acquired, spacious Italianate-Victorian house.

They could now afford this sprawl of a mansion. Not only are the New York Central and B&O railroads bringing in stuff for construction jobs, the state and county governments are spending money on building projects—not to mention the work of local sandstone quarries. Besides a couple of main contracts, he was getting about a dozen subcontracts.

W.W. trudged over to the front of his big house. Becky had young William scrubbing the steps. "So, Willie, I s'pect you're not goin' back to thuh high school. Son, I'm taking you off thuh road crew an' makin' you one a my cement baggers come t'morrow. A ton of Mix #77 be waitin' at a New York Central siding. I'll want it mixed in portions accordin' to the different concrete jobs planned, then each portion sacked special. So you be earning more greenbacks." He tapped the boy's arm muscle. "You're already strong as a man."

Young William couldn't help grinning. "Yessir, I'll be ready."

Contracts came steadily. W.W. had crews delivering materials to road builders whose projects ran all the way to Michigan, other men plastering new Elyria houses and buildings, and contracts to unload arriving railroad hopper cars—tough, backbreaking jobs that called for hard-muscled men. Some crews were headed by sons Charlie, Clarence, Ottie, and Clinton. Young Myrtle and some of her older sisters were also involved at times with W.W.'s contracts. Myrtle served as his regular bookkeeper/secretary.

But W.W. himself now seldom bent his back or dirtied his hands. He'd heard of a young fellow from Oberlin named Ernie who could make an automobile engine murmur like a hummingbird. So he hired Ernie Johnson as mechanic for his crew vehicles and to chauffeur him around in the new Packard he'd purchased.

By '29 he was paying his crew members good wages. White laborers in town were earning $35 weekly—so for his men W.W. matched those wages. He knew that, after wages and expenses, his net was lower than what white businessmen pocketed. However, his personal profit was 500 dollars a week and he was proud of it! Half a thousand per week! He thought not only of his Pappy, but other men like Pappy George who busted out from slavery to earn just a dollar or two for each day's toil in them dark and damp and dusty and dangerous coal mines. Pappy George, he who once called his son a "dreamer," would be amazed now!

He had to tell Anna of his good fortune—some of it coming from her wisdom. He boarded a train bound for Cadiz, as always trying to avoid its dust and grime. Anna, though moving slower these days, scampered to hug him at her opened door. "Lord, how princely you look, Willie—in that-ere ribbed silk mornin' coat with silk-covered buttons. An' look at yer high-polished shoes. 'Kin almos' see my face in 'em!"

W.W. had a Cheshire-cat grin. She pushed him maybe twelve inches away from her body, but still held tightly to his arms. "I 'spect yer gittin' even more handsome. Prosperous an' elegant, hey? Tell me why . . ."

She motioned and he took a seat. She fixed him a cup of honeyed tea, which he laced with bourbon from his flask. "Today, Anna, I be here in gratitude fer the wisdom you laid on me with yer tongue. Remember what you tol' me 'bout gaining prosperity—long time ago?"

Anna's smile was sure, yet thin, 'neath her narrowed eyes. "What I 'member, Willie, are words from thuh Bible. An' 'specially a reminder: 'Humility and thuh fear of the Lord bring riches, honor, and life.' Says this in Proverbs 22, I b'lieve."

He nodded. But he went on to describe the shrewdness of the business maneuvers he'd made. His good timing in planning jobs. His seasoned know-how in handling workers.

Anna rubbed his forearm while listening intently. She was proud of him, but maybe not as proud as Willie was of himself. The more sips of toddy, the more he talked. Then, suddenly, her listening halted. Her hand grew hot and slid off his forearm. She was coming into a vision. Although her limbs were burning, a coldness ran across her mind. Her chill was laden with icy pictures.

"Anna, why you frownin'? I say somethin' wrong?"

"Jus' some pictures in my head. I tell you, Willie, oftentimes thuh Lord tests us. Get ready to be tested. 'Member what thuh Good Book say 'bout hu . . . humility. You doin' good now, real good . . . but you get ready for trials and troubles, man." She reached his hand with hers. Her look was one of woe.

He took a big swallow from the cup. The honey and tea mixed with bourbon was treating him well. Anna? She's a sweet woman . . . except that she looks for too many bothersome things in the Scriptures . . .

CHAPTER 24

With the calendar having changed to 1930, a new decade and a new spring now in the air, W.W. smiled happily. He had fresh unloading contracts. The money-men around town, though, were grumbling or moaning. For nigh on to six months they'd slogged into and out of brokers' offices, looking at those glass-domed ticker-tape machines. The money-men had reason for their long faces. Those tickers kept spitting out flat ribbons of bad news. Messages carried on these tapes were gibberish to W.W., yet he understood their effect. Stock traders were losing money, and this could hurt business. But while the tickers seemed like the ominous timber rattlers he'd avoided in Ohio's woods, they'd not troubled him. His only problem was fitting twelve busy hours into fleeting daylight.

Becky was busy, too. Her house still had some boarders to be fed. More than this, church circles and committees begged for the first-rate casseroles and cobblers she furnished—usually with the help of two or three daughters. And there were the prayer meetings or revivals lasting well after nine o'clock into the night. Becky didn't mind W.W.'s absence in these activities. Oft-times, though, she wondered where he was.

While being chauffeured around town, folks—white folks, too— were awestruck by W.W.'s big, shiny-new Packard. He visited businessmen with whom he'd secured contracts. And he oversaw the jobs managed by his sons. W.W. was riding high.

Then the sun goes dark. Silvery skies turn midnight, and blood spurts across a crooked moon. O-o-o Lord. 1930 . . . 1930 . . . 1930 . . . !

On Saturday evening, April 6, Becky was preparing for Sunday's church activities. W.W. was polishing his shoes. "Pappy," she said, "I got a feeling we might not make it to church t'morra . . ." She was right. Early Sunday morning they were notified that their ailing daughter Alberta had gotten worse. Instead of to Second Methodist, they were taken to this daughter's home on Oberlin Road. Alberta DeJarnett died at home that day, leaving her husband, George, and their little girl, Edna.

Alberta's death staggered W.W. and Becky. When years before they had lost their daughter Harriet, they expected the remaining eleven sons and daughters to surely outlive them. W.W. and Becky's family gathered and showed great strength, which was what the training Becky had given them demanded.

While Alberta's coffin was placed in the ground, W.W., his mind very gray and a tear trickling down alongside his nose, looked around at the parched earth and sniffed. Differently he sniffed again. This air of Lorain County was far too dry, especially for April. The next few weeks he heard farmers complaining. A scorching heat blistered fields and pastures, causing the worst drought in many years. Grains were drying up in dusty fields, and plants were rotting. He saw new trouble coming.

The new month of May brought other troubles in the county. Industry and business started sagging. Willys-Overland, the automobile factory, closed its Elyria plant. Other fearful plant owners canceled orders for parts, postponed plans for new ventures, and began laying off workers. Even road-building and house-building activities slowed. Suddenly some of W.W.'s sturdy subcontracts felt as fragile as toilet tissue.

Thank the Lord he had more than subcontracts. He possessed three direct contracts. This, though, was turning out to be a worrisome 1930 springtime—businesswise. Maybe it was even a good thing that one of his sons and his brother Henry were working now for other employers.

June arrived on a Sunday—still hot and dry. After service at Second A.M.E., W.W. and Becky looked in on Henry with joy. Henry Brown—called "Hence" by most folk—had followed a long time back his eldest brother to Elyria. "Hence" was happy-go-lucky as usual, but he didn't let on that he was ill. On Tuesday, "Hence" dropped dead. W.W.'s heart was stirred. He recalled his little brother bounding around the steep Cadiz crags over fifty years ago, and "Hence" trying to tag along behind him whenever he came home to visit. W.W. quickly fixed the same strong toddy he took when Alberta passed last month—a mug half-full of bourbon.

Two weeks later W.W. and Becky were notified about their son Ottie, who was on a job at Geneva against Lake Erie about seventy miles northeast of Elyria. He was as a wheat stalk abruptly cut from its roots. Ottie's wife and three children, his parents—no, the whole family—was stunned! W.W. gathered Becky into his arms. He sensed Becky's feeling that her own immense spiritual strength was being sorely tested. And he could no longer look beyond the loss of Harriet and "Hence"—and now Ottie—particularly Ottie, who was so robust! W.W. trembled in his soul. Yet he held steady.

Summer 1930, at least to him, was the beastly, burnt-blood side of the sun. Up close he'd already seen Death stalking the land. This summer, too, he was seeing farmers suffering from droughts, industries shutting their doors, more workers being laid off. He began letting men go himself. And by late summer the bank that held most of his money was in trouble.

One of his plastering contracts was definitely solid, though. And he could depend upon his son Clinton to finish this job in good stead. He'd seen Clinton change from a fitful worker, too often in silly troubles with the law, to a most reliable and talented plasterer. Despite his uncertain construction contracts, he was thankful for this one that Clinton was completing rapidly. He need not inspect this job. Clinton was an expert!

He weighed his work situation. Charlie and Clarence, the other two of his three sons still alive, lacked Clinton's skill. But they had always been more dependable, more helpful to him. Charlie, as burly and strong as an ox, had charge of crews delivering heavy cement bags Monday through Friday, then pastored Shiloh Baptist Church on Saturday and Sunday. Clarence was the one now working in a steel mill. If he needed Clarence, he felt he could get him back. However, with jobs fading each week, he wasn't needing Clarence or the handy buddies of Clarence who were also in his back pocket in case of a pinch. He'd employed dozens of fellows, many who'd come up from the South, and helped them get a hold in Lorain County over the years. He'd hired them when white employers shunned them in favor of Polish, Hungarian, and other men from "across the pond" with white faces. In fact, several of his colored hirelings, including a son-in-law or two, had started little businesses of their own. One even furnished his favorite toddy bourbon in this time of Prohibition and bootleg corn whiskey . . .

W.W. sat in his office shuffling through some papers Myrtle had laid on his desk. One typed, legal-sized sheet snatched his attention. This was page one of his "Brown Ditch Improvement No. 269" proposal listing Clinton's name as petitioner. W.W. grinned. They had talked this over; with his son's name being the lead, Clinton would be branching out from plastering and heading new projects. This petition was submitted to the Lorain County Auditor's Office. Clinton was a serious fellow now; no longer was he his tom-foolish, prankster boy. This Wednesday morning Clinton was plastering for his subcontract with Feinknop Construction.

But while standing on a wood scaffold plank, Clinton attempted to swivel and lost his balance. He fell nine feet, landing awkwardly in a twist. A fellow workman ran to the scene. An ambulance was summoned, which whisked him to Elyria Memorial Hospital. Myrtle took the call from the hospital. She rushed into her father's office room. "Pappy . . . !" Her urgent message came with a weak quaver.

Her Pappy rose from his chair like, she thought, a thunderbolt—almost too straight for a man who'd reached age seventy a month ago. For an instant his figure seemed to be a shining silver shaft. "Myrtle, order my car. I be goin' to the hospital. Don'tcha notify yer mother—let me do that!" As he rode down Broad Street, his mind fastened on Becky: These months they'd already lost daughter Alberta, son Ottie, and "Hence"—so how would she take another family ordeal? He had to be there to support her in case she went faint.

Clinton lasted until Friday night, when he gave up his ghost. By then Clinton's wife and son and the entire family was forearmed, somewhat, for his passing. W.W., trembling inside yet steeled-up on the outside, watched closely Becky's lean on God's everlasting arms.

After funeral and burial services, and a special repast feast, many of the expansive Brown family gathered out at W.W. and Becky's mansion. There were many because of the compounded losses of four family members this hard, terrible year. On this chilly November evening they chased away their sadness by prayers and hymns, with their preacher Charlie's basso cadence leading both. Starting low and slow, above the crackling stove fires, a swirling thunder of Brown voices sang a train of songs. Soul-stirring hallelujah songs. Goin' home music moving evening into midnight . . .

Then, "Will the circle be unbroken . . . by and by, Lord, by and by . . . ?"

Finally, "Wade in the water, children . . . wade in the water . . . God's a-gonna trouble the wa-a-ter . . ." W.W. silently remembered the healing "trouble" from John 5:4. And he also remembered Anna telling him, "You get ready for trials and troubles, man. Get ready to be tested." Well, Anna always told him the truth—even if mysteriously. This year, 1930, he'd been—all his family been—tested.

CHAPTER 25

On the B&O tracks and the NY Central tracks the twenty freighter car became fifteen-car, then twelve-car, then ten-car trains. And the half-loaded boxcars began carrying an illegal, hidden human cargo—laid-off men, called hoboes, sneaking rides to strange places, looking for jobs. In Elyria, same as half a hundred other towns, fifty laid-off men became 100, then 500, then more. Factories shut down, foundries slowed down, businesses closed. Familes went hungry all over the land. Folks began using this term: "the Depression." Although Depression was a term used by economists, an unsettling, deep-gray misery—sometimes a *funk*—was seeping into America's bones.

W.W. was among the employers with fewer and fewer employees. His workers, black men most often termed Negroes, were the "first fired and last hired" by white employers—so W.W. kept on payroll as many as he could, but finally only two or three were left. This, then, signified the end of his business bloom—the same as that of other tycoons in town.

However, a new kind of life, for this skein of years in this new decade, was dawning for him. A new kind of activity rising out of this bean-and-corn-bread-poor Depression. Maybe it was also rising from his and Becky's personal heartrending year of 1930. Instead of cavorting about town for meetings with big businessmen and contractors—often involving liquor and bid whist card sessions—he settled on just dropping in for friendly chats with prominent town folks. W.W. became a welcomed raconteur, popular in Elyria's downtown commercial and professional districts, as well as among social, religious, and fraternal circles. Wearing a stylish gray wool suit and matching spats stretched over polished, laced, high-top brogues and a fur felt fedora, he was a familiar and elegant figure strolling Broad Street. Now invisible was the wiry son of a slave who wore denim overalls and plowed fields, mined coal, shaped timber for mine posts, and rode horseback and chewed tobacco back in the hills.

He got more and more subtle while having Cuban cigars and sparse swallows of bourbon over quiet chats with influential friends. Without definition these chats drifted into politics. Gradually he learned which fellows currently sided with President Roosevelt's Democrat policies and which fellows were holding on to the Republican aims. "Which party are you supporting, Tod?" A Board of Education member asked.

W.W. took a puff, then laid his cigar to rest on the ashtray. "'Twix an' between," he answered. "I be still president of the Carlisle Citizen's Protective Welfare League—out past South End." He explained that this league, which he had helped establish where he lived close to Oberlin Road, had no political affiliation.

The board member was not satisfied. "It's my understanding, Tod, that most coloreds are switching from their longstanding connection with Republicans—the party of ol' Abe Lincoln—to Roosevelt and the Democrats."

"Uh-huh, that's the way I view it, too. And there's some good reason, don'tcha see?" He grasped his Cuban for some more puffs.

"Yessir (even white men had often begun addressing him as 'sir'), Tod, FDR's moves—the so-called New Deal—seem good for coloreds. Glad you recognize this."

W.W. did recognize that this man was feeling him out and, also, that this fellow was himself a Democrat. In their conversation W.W. began to steer this man as he'd once delicately guided his more balky horses—then repeated such a tack with other friendly politicians. His purpose was providing for Elyria's unemployed coloreds, especially his own kin.

The board member soon introduced him to Otto Mischka, an attorney and politician who knew his son, Charlie Brown. W.W. had an idea that he thought Otto might find interesting. "About the elections coming up this fall, I gather you'll be a candidate for Township Justice of the Peace, among other folks. Is this so?" These two studied each other's faces, as the old black man, dressed to the teeth, poured words like molasses on the white, younger man. Attorney Mischka, who had served as Elyria Township Clerk, smilingly agreed that he was thinking of running for Justice. "Well, they's never been a *colored* holdin' a Township office, I s'pect. How do you feel about my Charlie being on the ballot along with you—for the job of constable?" He knew that if any politician would consider breaking ground to put a Negro in office, out in the township, it would be Mr. Mischka—if only to entice and build up the colored vote for himself. Too, Mr. Mischka was an honest and fair-minded lawyer, popular with Negroes.

Mischka was flabbergasted, yet interested. So the aged businessman and the lawyer-politician put their heads together. Certainly there were many Negroes and poor whites calling for a right-minded, sympathetic constable. Straightaway they recognized they were but gusts of wind whooshing over an unwary rock that they were contriving to move. Reverend Charlie Brown would need to be not just willing but excited. He would need to be willing and excited about becoming a lawman—while being a *man of God* at the same time! They both sat down with Reverend Charlie, whose Shiloh Baptist Church had, as had other small congregations, faded due to lack of funds in this Depression.

Charlie, who had recently landed a precious job at Elyria Foundry to support Ella and their four daughters still living at home, listened but wasn't anxious to become a constable—though he could use the extra money. Mischka made his case: Besides the pastors and Doctor Sutton, Elyria Negroes, grown-ups, and children would benefit in their hearts by having a colored official whom they could look up to—surely a constable.

Charlie appeared unmoved. Charlie's father studied his son. "You need tuh take this into account, son," W.W. interjected. "One of us has got to be the first—for others to follow. Y'know, I was one a the first of us to run a business here. But at seventy-seven now, y'all know I be way too old for the constable job." His thin voice rippled in jest, Mischka chuckled, and Charlie grinned. "Son, you're still strong as a bull, you carry a Bible, an' all folks—colored and white—respect you. Yea, indeed!"

Reverend Charlie stared at them both. Then his eyes seemed to sweep the floor. He kept them waiting. His pause was so heavy that it became as ominous as a silent thunder. To W.W. and Mischka, it felt like being bulled into a cranny by a squat, heavy ox, his heart engine's thumping growing greater and greater.

Finally, Charlie's deep voice rumbled, "Y'all let me think on it."

While Reverend Charlie pondered for days, Becky said to W.W., "Tod, I b'lieve you've laid an unjust burden on our Charlie. He's been trying to be a good shepherd for the Lord, but these white officials might want him to be their darky sheepdog—to round up the uppity coloreds an' tattle on those insolent white hillbillies . . ."

W.W. snorted. It was not his way to immediately tie racial causes to relations between colored and white. He saw the constable job as progress for Charlie. In fact, he'd been eager to make Charlie's entry into township government a gift for Becky. He'd wanted this to raise her spirits—considering what she'd suffered seven years ago in that almost unbearable nineteen hundred and thirty, and she was still suffering.

"I guess you have a sound point, Becky. I reckon, though, that Charlie has the high bearing to make the job a welcome surprise for both white and colored." From deep in her throat Becky gurgled a *Lord-ha'-mercy* groan. She was fearful of another son—only two were left—falling into harm's way. Even in these parts, even in these new times, a lynching was still possible—especially for a *black* constable.

One week later, Thursday morning, September 2, 1937, Reverend Charlie met with W.W. and Attorney Mischka. His face was somber. His wide body, sitting rigid, filled a Mischka conference chair. Usually Charlie was affable and quick to jest. This morning, however, he was very serious. Neither his father nor the attorney/politician could guess what his decision would be.

"So, Reverend Charlie, you thought long on this, yes?" Mischka inquired.

"Well, my thoughts've come as now-and-then drizzles . . . whereas I prayed steady for seven days and seven nights." He bent forward and his voice began a deep rumble. "The Holy Ghost tells me to help somebody— tells me now to go ahead. So I'll enter this here race. Lord, be with us in this resolution."

Mischka leaped to his feet, stepped over, and threw his arms around Charlie. "We're in this race together, my friend!" W.W. watched and smiled. His ambition for Charlie was working so far. He'd get other folks, particularly the colored, to start boosting Charlie. Becky, though, might never share his political enthusiasm for their eldest son.

Meanwhile, he had another ambition. In these lean, hard Depression days, W.W.'s motive was to help all of Elyria's coloreds to obtain steady jobs—including his own grandsons, sons-in-law, and grandsons-in-law. So he strode through colored neighborhoods, greeting and speaking with people out of work. He talked to leaders of church, civic and fraternal organizations, suggesting work programs. He found none lazy. Those able but unemployed offered themselves for any kind of labor and only when rejected did they turn to unlawful activities such as running street numbers or bootlegging. Some plants were slowed by labor strikes, yet another can of worms. Yet here and there he manipulated a meager contract—worth enough for him to hire a few fellows. One contract was for unloading coal cars arriving alongside small factories.

Most younger men were listening to W.W.'s whisperings. And to them he was a wise, ol', gray-haired cat, steadily purring into their ears. Now trusting in President Roosevelt's new second-term administration, with more men coming off WPA jobs for regular employment, some fellows managed to open their own tiny business: a couple of new barber shops, a trash-removal truck, and a two-man taxi service, for instance. Even one of W.W.'s sons-in-law started a small restaurant out on Middle Avenue.

Swirling cold air and occasional snowflakes rushed in with November. Tuesday, November 2nd, voters cast their ballots. Otto Mischka was right; Charlie's name on the township ballot drew out the colored vote.

Having spent the early evening on telephones, Mischka hurried to Charlie's home on West River Sreet when darkness was settling. Ella and her two youngest daughters had fixed a hearty meal because Reverend Charlie had told them that "Mister Mischka" might be coming by. After the greetings, and before supper, his exact reason for visiting was revealed.

"Ella," he began, "and girls . . . Your husband and your father is the new constable!" This night the full family cheered and Reverend Charlie prayed.

Next day those Negroes who'd scoffed earlier at Charlie's candidacy ("He oughtta know that no black man can put on a constable's badge") were stunned. W.W. strolled up Broad Street, where folks rushed to shake his hand for his efforts in getting his son, the first official colored lawman, elected. Both white and colored, including the scoffers, grabbed his hand. He stepped into Mischka's office first to thank the lawyer for clearing the way for Charlie—then to commiserate with him. Otto Mischka lost his race for Justice of Peace. Since a Justice normally advises and works closely with a constable, this part of Mischka's and W.W.'s plan had fallen through. In the township office, Reverend Charlie would be without a seaoned attorney-at-law as a friend, and without a colleague he could really trust! Nevertheless, on the Monday following his election, Reverend Charlie had a brief article in the Elyria newspaper. He thanked voters and declared this a win over any racial prejudice.

Some days he enjoyed riding a city bus between Carlisle Township, where his mansion stood, and downtown Elyria. Traveling back home this day, W.W. peered through the bus window at the streets rolling by where some of his offspring now lived. Clarence, his other remaining son, came to his mind. As he'd been promoting Charlie, Becky was gingerly pushing

Clarence toward formal ordination as a minister. W.W.'s face crinkled from amusement. Maybe because he was their eldest, Charlie had always been the more responsible and righteous—whereas Clinton had been a rascal at times, a hotheaded firebrand. Now, this day, Charlie's become a law officer—while Clarence, several times arrested by law officers years ago, was preaching the Gospel! What a rub this was!

Carefully he climbed off the bus, then nodded at some passersby who waved at him. Almost everyone instantly recognized this well-dressed old man, stepping plumb-straight like a potentate but leaning slightly on a cane. He'd begun using his walking stick, tooled brass head fitted on polished walnut shaft, more often these days. "Tetch of arthritis," he would say if asked. He had arthritis, but figured this might have also been an aggravation of the bruised right shoulder and arm he had suffered when accidentally struck by a car half a dozen years ago. He'd been knocked down at Broad Street and East Avenue. Anyhow, his cane was useful. Nearing his home, he stepped along Hadaway Court, looking ahead. There was a black automobile, a Model T, beside the driveway.

Closer he saw a pudgy, dark-skinned man sitting on the veranda, talking with Becky. Of their several dozen friends and acquaintances, none resembled this fellow. Who could this stranger be?

"Oy, boss-mon . . . Meesta Brown!" the stranger called out, rising and bellying up to him.

W.W. shifted his cane to shake the stranger's hand. The stranger had the wide grin and the easy eyes of somebody familiar to him. W.W. suddenly felt a recognition. "Herm . . . Herm Dudley?"

"Yes . . . yessir, boss-mon." Indeed. The same Herman Dudley who was one of the men who'd come from elsewhere to work on W.W.'s road crew ten years ago. Just before the jobs ended in '29.

"This day I come from Cleveland to visit an' ta beseech ya, sir." As Dudley grasped his arm and helped him climb the few steps up to the veranda, W.W. was thinking. Dudley, leaner and strong back then, had not been a particularly steady worker—too much mouth, too little focus on what he was being paid for. Always talking about the great Marcus Garvey, a Jamaican same as Herm. Becky, not feeling well, slipped back into the house.

W.W. eased into Becky's wide chair, motioning for Herm to sit on the porch bench beside him. "Good to see you again, Herm, after all this while. Yes. What be the purpose of your visit?"

"You look in fine fettle, meesta boss-mon, sir. Well, sir, I come to mek your help in melding all black people in Lorain County . . . for progressing our race. See, in Cleveland the UNIA's (Universal Negro Improvement Association) still working and we have large plans. We need a UNIA established in Lorain and next-door counties to help Ohio move the national plan. That's why our Cleveland office, where Mr. Jim Stewart is in charge, is contacting this area's men of influence such like you, sir."

W.W. was listening, but also had called something out to one of his daughters inside. A daughter came with a glass of tea for Herm and him— only his was laced with whiskey. "Thank ye, daughter." Then he turned to Herm. "I'd surely like to know your society's plan, Herm." Herm Dudley sipped and grinned anxiously. Ten years of UNIA toil had prepared him to tell W.W. about what was now exciting his mind.

From a Kingston Market, *mento* singer and disciple of "Black Moses" Marcus Garvey in the 1920s, Herm had grown into something more. He still promoted Garvey, but now, in these 1930s, he was also a Rastafarian— a "stone" Rasta, although his hair wasn't dreadlocked. And his Jamaican brogue had been suppressed. "Meesta boss-mon, do you know of the Lion of Judah, Haile Selassie?" he asked.

W.W. shook his head. "Don't know exactly."

Herm leaned forward, sipped tea, and eagerly acquainted W.W. with Haile Selassie. How Selassie came from a straight line of Ethiopian emperors, directly down from King Solomon and the Queen of Sheba and their son. How Haile was crowned emperor and Lion of Judah in 1930—the same "Lion of the tribe of Judah" foretold in Revelation 5:5. How his original name was Tafari, and how this, combined with the title "Ras" (nobleman), became Rastafari. How some Rastafarians believed that Emperor Selassie was God's king on earth. How Italy had invaded Ethiopia several years ago and driven Haile Salassie into exile. And why Rastas were joined to Garvey's "Black Pride" or "Back to Africa" movement.

"Where are them two leaders today?" W.W. queried, over a swallow of toddy. He was a businessman, not a Bible man or a race advocate. But he did recall the book his old friend Fleetwood Walker had published some thirty years ago—that "Back to Africa" foolishness.

"Both in England now, both sort of expatriates. That's what I wish to discuss with you . . . an' beseech of you, boss-mon, sir. Truth is, they're in different camps, not associating with one another. Emperor Salassie seeming too regal for 'Black Moses.' An' leader Garvey not agreeing with 'the Lion's' trust in white British officials and his lack of identity with other blacks. Our UNIA wants to bring these two giants together, you see. We're thinking of a serious conference in Canada, maybe Toronto. Howsoever, such a conference would be most costly. In order to sit both leader Garvey an' 'the Lion' down, face-to-face, we need to build up UNIA, and our resources. That's why I'm beseeching your organizing help in Lorain County. I've got some literature to give you, sir, about UNIA—"

"Hold yer horses!" W.W. cut in. He had too many questions, too many doubts about where this man was attempting to lead him. "In recent years, 'fore you, some fellas came by here lookin' to build up 'N-double A-CP' . . . then the 'Urban League,' I do believe. Now I wonder how these organizations—them an' yours—fit the aims of all our folks, Herm."

"Yessir, boss-mon, I understand what you mean. You see, UNIA— we, uh, seek to lead all black people in marching together—as one."

"What'd you say 'bout two big leaders not dealing with each other? Might skin color an' money-standing be gettin' in their way, too?" He wasn't familiar with imperial Selassie, but he recalled Marcus Garvey's insistence on blackness.

Herm sipped at his tea. He closed his eyes. He wished the boss-mon hadn't raised this particular question. Finally, he said, "Leader Garvey, he's a shepherd. He appeals mostly to the masses—the poor, the pure Africans. Whilst Selassie 'the Lion' is busy depending on European forces to get Mussolini's troops out of Ethiopia, leader Garvey's in contact with Senator Bilbo for the government to pay for relocating twelve million willing Negroes from America to the nation of Liberia in Africa . . ."

"What? The Senator Bilbo of Mississippi? That segregationist?" W.W., surprised, didn't know whether to believe this. Garvey in cahoots with the notorious anti-black senator? Like a red fox sitting side by side with a gray wolf, both scheming over a coop full of chickens?

"Yeah, boss-mon. Senator Bilbo. This legislation he's proposing is called the 'Greater Liberia Act of 1939.' I got papers over in my car for you, sir."

"Herm, I reckon you oughta let them papers rest." W.W. didn't want him traipsing to his car to fetch a sheaf of papers that would not be read, only stand neglected on his rolltop desk. He was particular these later years, which seemed to go by faster and faster . . .

Monthly pages were swiftly melting from his calendar—the large wall calendar whose dates were rushing toward his eightieth year. In his seventy-nine years he'd known about many ships, some real but most just someone's dream, laden with Negroes bound for Africa. When he, W.W., was still a young man, Frederick Douglass—the "raging lion of black America"—roared against the Back-to-Africa movement. He felt the same as Douglass, that "we came as captives, but now America is our home, too." Fleet Walker didn't discuss this with him when writing the book Our Home Colony, but he would have argued against Fleet's "black emigration" ideas. And he rejected Marcus Garvey's plan to move African Americans back to the Motherland. Herm Dudley was about to try persuading him that the papers in the car were important.

"Don't you bother, Herm. Though I hope them two leaders, Garvey an' Seh—or the king of Ethiopia—can meet and maybe work together, I won't be organizing for your, uh, UNIA. Herm, are you familiar with a colored leader named Asa Randolph?"

"A. Philip Randolph? Yessir. Brotherhood of Sleeping Car Porters. He's sure organizing up lowly porters an' scaring the mighty Pullman Company. Fact is, he's unsettling industrialists an' powerful whites—even FDR! Him with the bass voice like your minister son—by the way, I hope Reverend Charlie and his family are doing okay—when he speaks ev'ry word sounds like velvet thunder. Folks are imagining Randolph as John calling out from the wilderness . . ."

"Yes, indeed!" W.W. bent forward in Becky's big porch chair, as if coming alive. A half dozen years ago he'd heard A. Philip Randolph as the head of the Citizens Protective Leagues gathered in the city of Lorain, only nine miles distant on the Lake Erie shore. Asa spoke not about labor initiatives for Negroes, but about coloreds and whites learning to work together. Asa's voice was indeed a deep, buttery-sounding trumpet. His words, his thoughts, however, conveyed the most stirring message—that racial integration is the key, "for ye are all one in Christ Jesus"; that interracial solidarity is necessary for making a better society and stronger neighborhoods. Asa was a fierce general, but not a conductor of violence. "Yes, indeed. But I would organize only under the banner of Asa Randolph, Herm."

With a smile of final understanding, the chubby follower of Garvey stood and extended his right hand to his still-seated, old "boss-mon."

Then the old man made the gesture of salute. "Herm, I 'ppreciate your mention of Reverend Charlie. I'm goin' tuh give my son your regards. By the by, Charlie was elected and is serving as a local constable."

Well, it was a mild little boast—a small leaking of Pappy's true pride. Yet shortly after this day, Charlie and Attorney Mischka came to meet with him, to confirm what Becky had anticipated.

164

Sounding like a freight train jolting to a stop, Reverend Charlie announced that he'd resigned as constable. As W.W. knew well, when his son had thought on it and made a decision, his mind was unshakable. Mischka had accompanied him only to assure that legal or political measures were attended to. "Turned out, Pappy," Charlie rumbled, "what the job calls for just don't square with me an' the Lord." W.W. learned that his preacher son had had to struggle with evicting some folks he'd ministered to during this Depression. But, also, Mischka was hinting at political ploys, behind the scenes, that neither Charlie nor he could countenance.

They talked—W.W., Reverend Charlie and Attorney Mischka—for a bit. Then Mischka shook W.W.'s hand, while Charlie went to kiss his mother's cheek. Alone next with his wife, who was growing frail, W.W. uttered in his increasingly wispy voice, "Becky, you been right 'bout Charlie and the constableship."

Becky nodded and commented, "You know, an' Lord knows . . . he tried. But our Charlie's too much a *lawyer from God* t'be always bound to carry out man's fickle laws. 'Sides, too many white men 'round here'd rather him make fool. Charlie's no fool!"

Settling in his living room chair, W.W. sipped toddy while mulling over Charlie's decision. He chided his own self for initiating this constable election move through Mischka. Sure 'nough, he was ambitious for Charlie. In fact, he'd been ambitious for all his sons. None quite had his hunger for personal gain, at least in business. None of his boys quite had his enterprising spirit. None had his dream. Had he wanted Charlie to be zealous like Herm Dudley? Or had he pushed him so's he and Becky would have a big shot to boast of? He felt guilty. Well, he told himself, time would come when Elyria would have a colored fellow running the city, the state—or even the country—Lord willing. Finally, W.W. shut his eyes and let another feeling overcome him. Finally, he realized that Charlie, as a consecrated minister, had already reached a mighty high standing, by the grace of God, in this community.

On another day—the Friday evening, first of September, 1939—W.W. watched the sun set. He was listening to the radio. He heard the announcer report that Hitler's armies had marched into Poland. "This might be," the announcer said, "the beginning of World War Two."

W.W. closed his eyes to all his daydreams. He sipped his toddy and frowned. He tried counting his grandsons and great-grandsons now of, or near to, soldiering age. He felt again the peculiar need to speak to Anna.

CHAPTER 26

*B*ells and bugles from distant wars flowed into town. While trickles of young men slipped out of town to become soldiers and sailors. Factories and foundries began full-time operations; merchants also got busy. W.W., retired to his Carlisle Township estate, smelled contracts.

"Tod, what you plannin' t'day?" Becky asked, seeing him dressing in a freshly starched shirt and a silky necktie. She anticipated his answer before it tumbled off his lips. "Yer too old for taking on work in town. There's enough to be done right here on this property."

"We've got these boarders to paint, clean, an' fix what needs fixin'." By "boarders" he meant their son-in-law, daughters, and a couple of grandchildren living with Becky and him. "There's money to be made now with all the war talk. Money that our young folks can use, y'know. That's the managing I be needed for."

He admitted to himself that Becky was right. At age eighty he was really too old for dashing about and finagling contracts. But he'd been restless just staying around home. All his life he'd been a hustler. He had to be out managing. He summoned a driver, one of his grandsons, and began making stops downtown. Some factory heads and other industry captains were still around; most, though, were younger and had replaced the bosses he'd known. City officials who had power over building contracts were mostly new in office, too. So there he found himself, dressed like an old prince and doffing his expensive Adam hat, greeting strangers. So much had changed in just eight or ten years! Because of wars overseas, new businesses had come to town and new fellows to manage them! But he knew where some friends with power still were. One was responsible for unloading freight. Thus, he took a contract for emptying gondola coal cars for industries at a railway spur laying at the north end of East Avenue, between a stocking factory and a golf ball factory. His hired laborers—one or two at a time—shoveled the black rocks into sturdy carts and dumped these into adjacent factory coal bins. Now and then W.W. stood by the railroad gondola, supervising. Really, he enjoyed that neighborhood.

Twenty-five yards from the spur's bed of tracks was probably the most distinct neighborhood in the city: An isolated yet lively rectangle of houses surrounded on all sides by factories and industrial lots. This was further encircled by the big Black River and the main New York Central Railroad line. Folks called their neighborhood "the pocket." Town folks had lived on this land since Heman Ely and partners had gouged it out of forest and founded Elyria in 1817. Colored folks, either freeborn or former slaves, had lived there from the time the city was a striving village. W.W. knew many folks in "the pocket"—they included Reverend Charlie, Charlie's son, and their families. He would amble around three of the four streets, visiting a few homes or just chatting with people on sidewalks.

One summer day a door on Pine Street opened. He recognized the husband and wife, friends who invited him inside. After a merry hour spent in their home, he sauntered 'round the corner onto Center Street and to Reverend Charlie's home, across the street from Harshaw Chemical Company. Standing outside chitchatting were two of the three daughters living in their parents' house. "Grandpap!" one called out. W.W. smiled more broadly than usual. From the old man's gait, like a tall, slender penguin wielding a cane, they could tell he'd been sipping something. "Howdy-do, girls." He pretended to poke them with his cane. His grandaughters jumped away, these teenagers giggling loud enough for Reverend Charlie to notice. He stomped to the door, saw W.W.'s hijinks, and grunted.

Before Reverend Charlie uttered any words, the girls knew what he'd say. Grandpap was at least two sheets in the wind. This always angered their father. "Pappy!" Reverend Charlie uttered. "Will you come on in here? I wanna have a word or two with you!" His sound could curl one's hair.

Reverend Charlie ordinarily was affable. He even liked to joke. But in a time like this he could be most stern. His mother worried about Pappy wandering around town half-drunk. He, himself, had chastised Pappy.

As W.W. stepped into the house, he gave the girls a wink and a grin. They grinned back at him. They figured their Pap would take Grandpap into a room and close the door. In days when fathers took errant sons into a woodshed to discipline them, this was as if Pappy was beckoned to the woodshed by his son. Grandpap, though, went in half-amused.

Outside his family, W.W. was beckoned by young and old folks for his wisdom, knowledge, and experience. In 1941 even Herm Dudley, over in Cleveland, remembered his visit with W.W., who had foreseen what was taking place now. The UNIA was fading fast and Marcus Garvey had already died in London, never having met with Dudley's Rastafarians or Haile Selassie. Emperor Selassie, under the wing of British forces fighting Italy, forces mostly made of African troops, had now reclaimed his Ethiopian throne. Asa Philip Randolph had troubled FDR so much that President Roosevelt had just issued Executive Order 8802 opening up war plant jobs to colored folks. Herm Dudley now had one of these jobs.

Offerings of war plant jobs pleased W.W. His two sons and all his older grandsons were now working. Also, his coal unloading activity had increased, allowing him to hire a couple more fellows.

As Sundays came, he more often accompanied Becky to Second Methodist A.M.E. She'd warned him to "git drunk on God." A certain Sunday afternoon—an afternoon of wind, cold, and dark clouds—he and Becky rested at home after church service and an early dinner. He turned WTAM on, having forgotten that his favorite radio newsman, Lowell Thomas, was on the air weekdays. But another broadcaster interrupted the regular news program. "This morning over a thousand were killed, wounded, or gone missing! Japanese forces attacked Pearl Harbor. World War Two has reached American territory!" W.W. leaned forward in his chair. He didn't know where Pearl Harbor was. Within a half hour the phone was ringing. A neighbor knocked on the door. "I'm going around notifying folks who don't have their radios on! I'll go on to the next house." Becky shut the door to the sharp chill and the quick-falling darkness. "Lord, ha' mercy!" she groaned.

Becky was certainly not by herself. Cities, hamlets, and farmlands all over the country soon filled with "grannies" begging for God's mercy. Nervous fathers saw sons off to war. Mothers committed their sewing and baking and nursing skills to the "war effort." Daughters took the factory jobs their brothers left. Midwestern city boys and girls rode in trucks out to farms during summertime to help the harvesters. In Carlisle Township, W.W. was among the senior citizens lending their organizing and managing experience to the Civilian Defense Service. On December 15, 1941, just eight days after Pearl Harbor was bombed, the Lorain County Civilian Defense Committee called a meeting of all towns and townships now on watch. W.W. put on a gun-metal gray suit, dark tie, spats, and polished high-top shoes. Civilian Defense volunteers were assigned to functions such as air raid wardens, road repair, auxiliary firemen, fire watchers, and emergency medical service. With his past experience, W.W. chose to help those discussing Township "CD" ideas for any wartime emergency road repair. No enemy planes ever roared through Midwestern skies, no towns were bombed or roads smashed, but Civilian Defense was ready. And W.W. himself proudly stayed alert.

Furious months blew by. This Second World War, he sensed, was already bigger than the first one, twenty-five years ago, that he remembered so well. Much bigger. Four of his grandsons were in the army, and one great-grandson was in the navy. All these young fellows of his seemed proud of serving—although they fretted about both the segregation in the camps and the Jim Crow still going on back home. Becky grumbled over this. "Tod, you think our boys fightin' Hitler and Tojo 'cross the seas, can make a difference back here?" Becky wanted to know.

Nowadays Becky was feeling poorly. W.W. now paid more attention to his wife of sixty-four years than probably he ever had. He was taking her to church services when she felt up to it. A few times they were even able to attend special events—recitals by Luther King and Roland Hayes, the famous colored vocalists, and the program at Bethany Baptist when Rev. Glenn T. Settle came over from Cleveland bringing his nationally celebrated choir, Wings Over Jordan.

Just when winter morning's sunlight overcame the dark chill, one of W.W. and Becky's daughters scurried. W.W. sat up straight while waiting in the kitchen for breakfast. "Pappy, she's gone." Hands of the big grandfather clock pointed to 10 a.m. this Monday, January 21, 1944. W.W. sagged. No use to make it to the bedroom. Becky would be lying just where he'd left her—only cold now. Another daughter clutched him. His cupped hands froze together. Two weeks ago she'd embraced him on her eighty-first birthday. They'd been together sixty-five years. Becky had born him nineteen babies, though some didn't live. Now Becky is with the Lord, and with their eleven already-buried sons and daughters. His eyes flooded. She was his anchor. Yea, indeed, she was the family's anchor . . .

As was his nature, he continued walking alone. He had two projects before him. The loaded coal cars still arrived downtown at "the pocket's" edge. And his daughters insisted that work needed done in the family mansion to keep it nice like Becky would want. Few men, or women, were available—almost all were either away fighting the war, or busy in war plants. So he employed some of his great-grandsons.

The two oldest were able to unload gondolas, though one was about to enter the navy. A younger boy worked at the mansion. These great-grandsons became the ears for W.W.'s whispers from the past. Their shovels working, the older gondola boys saw W.W. stand by the car and begin, "When I was yer age . . ." From work tips his lecture changed to memories of jobs he'd done in the 1800s. In his foxy way he was trying to instruct them on ambition and techniques and pride. They respected their forefather. They kept nodding "yessir" and shoveling, hoping he'd pull out his gold pocket watch and say, "Time for y'all tuh have a bite of lunch, I s'pect." Some other days he sat at home, supervising, as the younger boy cleaned the family mansion's fancy-papered walls.

Sitting in his great chair at home, he puffed on a Cuban and sipped a toddy while seeing that the walls were properly freed of dust and grime. Ofttimes he listened to news from his large, polished wood console radio. "You hear that, boy?" he called to his younger great-grandson. "Our troops have crossed the water into France. They call it 'D-Day.' Now Hitler an' the Nazis be truly on the run!" The boy stopped and listened. "Yessir, Grandpap, maybe the war be over soon."

He followed Grandpap's orders, moving and climbing the stepladder so he could reach the ceiling. The high walls of the dining room, living room, and parlor were dressed with heavy, richly colored paper—looking like leatherwork, the embossed patterns printed on a gilded background. The boy took more cleaner putty out of a can of Absorene and shaped a new patty from the pink dough. He lightly rubbed away the wallpaper spots coated with soot from the coal furnace. For spots he couldn't erase, he plied a bit of cornstarch, then brushed away the dirt. W.W. watched closely as the boy obeyed his instructions and was quite satisfied. He decided that this boy was one who paid attention and listened to him. So he began his remembering. He had tales stored up that he needed to release—to somebody. He talked about his boyhood in Cadiz, about helping Isabell rear his younger brothers and sisters as George mined coal, about flocks of sheep up in the hills of Harrison County that provided good wool, about butchering hogs in October for meat during winter. Occasionally the boy dared to pause his rubbing to ask his great-grandpap a question or three. W.W. welcomed the questions, even as he scrutinized this boy's work skills. When his great-grandson came the next week to clean another room, both he and Great-Grandpap were anxious for more memories. W.W. told him about the horses he'd trained and rode, including ol' Jack, his Pappy's Standardbred. The boy's mind was now set on fire. As a city boy, except for the circus, he'd only seen horse riders in cowboy movies at Lincoln Theater. By the time all three rooms had clean and brightened walls, W.W. halted his memories. He thought the boy was too callow for his great-grandpap's further stories.

One year later the soldier and sailor boys began coming home, only they were boys no longer. Terrors of war had made them *men* now. They returned in bunches or they came straggling back, three or four at a time. They arrived at NY Central Railroad Station from the East and West Coasts. Or they arrived at the Greyhound station, having "rode the dog" from Chicago or New York or D.C. or Baltimore or dozens of other places. W.W., dressed as usual like a gentleman, sat on a bench at Ely Park, seeing them proudly display their uniforms one last time. They were members of the "52-20 club" (paid $20 per week for a year by the government), but were eager for a regular job. A handful of colored veterans, including his grandsons, approached him for his connections, in order to steer them to desirable employment. In the interim, W.W. himself arranged for the unloading of a couple of coal cars.

But after this he retired, really, to his mansion. Seeing only a few pavement blocks ahead of him before darkness, he stepped backward on his road of life. Of course his legs wouldn't take him; he had to use his mind to do the trick. The radio announced this: "A Negro, Jackie Robinson, has just been selected to be the first colored to play Major League Baseball!" W.W snorted, then snorted louder. His brain searing now, he backed up sixty-some years—back to when he heard that Fleet Walker was playing for Toledo in the American Association and that Association had become a *major league*. Back further to those days of "on the spot" baseball "teams" that he and Fleet got together. On those days he pitched for one "team" and Fleet was catcher for the other. They played in Oberlin out past the potato beds. Fleetwood Walker was the best he ever saw, but he figured this Jackie Robinson had to be equally amazing! He would now follow Jackie's blessing.

Many other happenings burned within his head as his days and nights hastened by. All provoked in him sensations of color—yellow, crimson, or blue. Lying on his eighty-seven years were regrets he once thought he'd never have. Then there were actions he'd never boasted of, but now felt a wave of joy in. Much was taking place in his mind—much for the better. Six or seven years ago, he and Becky heard a sermon at Second Methodist, where Reverend Hamblen was pastor. He remembered that the message was from the book of Acts, and somehow it puzzled him. At Pentecost,

Peter preached these words from an Old Testament prophet: "And it shall come to pass in the last days, saith God, I will pour out my Spirit upon all flesh: and your sons and daughters shall prophesy, and your young men shall see visions, and your old men shall dream dreams." Well, here in 1948 he is dreaming powerful dreams. And his soul is a student. He has caught the light which illumines his family, his friends, and his neighbors.

There was one more trip he had to take. He had to make a visit to the Cadiz area, to the slope, to see Anna. Most of his life he'd dreaded stepping on the train—for one thing the cinders, soot, and grime dirtied his spats, soiled his shoes. But he took the train. Somewhere near to Cadiz, he slumped over in a passenger car. His youngest sister, Pearl, who lived nearby in the hamlet named Hopedale, was called and took him to her home. This was, except for returning to Elyria for burial, his last trip on earth. Yet he was happy.

Cadiz, Ohio . . . 1959 . . . Eleven years after W.W.'s burial in Elyria:

Twice my driver has entered Aunt Anna's cottage to remind me of my flight out of Pittsburgh. The driver's second entrance was even more anxious. I had to leave Aunt Anna without delay!

She still had pep. However, during my visits these three days, she, like now, sometimes dozed off. I touch this ancient lady's shoulder to awaken her. "Aunt Anna!" There was one other thing I wanted to ask her about.

"Lord, ha' mercy! You still here? I s'pected you left. F'give me, son."

"Aunt Anna, I think W.W.—uh 'Willie'—wanted to see you on his last trip here." (Fact was, W.W. had mentioned this to a couple of his Elyria kinfolk.)

"Oh . . . I know he did! I was there with him, too. Jus' like thuh other one, his soul fought thuh good fight . . . an' won. I've know'd 'em since we all be young. I regard them as thuh 'young lions.' From Psalm 34, I b'lieve. I also know my Bible." Then she smiled and seemed to doze off.

She was a strange, mysterious, yet beautiful old lady. I'll always be enchanted by this memory of her—not so much as "Aunt," but as Anna.

CPSIA information can be obtained at www.ICGtesting.com
Printed in the USA
LVOW12*1416110813

347314LV00005B/65/P